WHEN Swans DANCE

KATIE EAGAN SCHENCK

Faery Whisper Press
Pasadena, MD

ISBN-9798988480334

Cover design by: Teresa at BookBrush

Printed in the United States of America.

For Mommom,
I promise the pope will approve.

Contents

Chapter One

SHAKESPEARE ONCE WROTE, "THE course of true love ne'er did run smooth." Steven McAllister shook his head with a smirk. No offense to the old bard, but he couldn't have been more wrong. Maybe wedding planning hadn't been going as well as Steven had hoped, but things were coming along, although slower than Rose might prefer. *What's that other saying? Slow and steady something or other?* Whatever it was, it worked for him.

He leaned back in his office chair and rubbed his eyes. A divorce petition glowed on his screen as if mocking him for working late. When had it gotten so dark? Early June usually meant daylight lasted well into the evening, but the sun seemed to have disappeared. He glanced at the clock and groaned. Rose was going to kill him.

As if on cue, his phone buzzed. Stifling another groan, he clicked the message.

Where are you?

To his surprise, it was from his sister. He smiled as he settled deeper into the seat cushion. Lanie was helping Rose with final alterations on her dress before the meeting with the caterer, which put her in the perfect position to stall. He would have to tread carefully, or else he'd press his luck.

Finishing up at work. Be there in 15.

More like a half hour, but Lanie wouldn't mind. The three of them were meeting with the caterer to make final selections on what would be served at the wedding. He could hardly believe that in just over three months, he would be a married man.

But he was ready. He'd never had one doubt about Rose. She'd come into his life just when he needed her the most, stayed through his mother's awful illness, and even helped Lanie through the turbulence of settling the estate. After the past year, they deserved some happiness.

With a sigh, he reread the last stipulation his client had insisted be added. Opposing counsel would never agree to it, with good reason. His client wanted to sell the house, but it was the soon-to-be-ex-wife's childhood home, which she had inherited long before they were married. Steven had tried explaining that, but it had fallen on deaf ears, much like the other legal advice he had given that particular client.

Oh well. He'd promised the client he would try, though it was a waste of everyone's time. As soon as that divorce was over, he hoped to never hear the name Willoughby again. But he knew better. A small-town attorney didn't have a lot of say in who hired him, and Cedar Haven definitely qualified as a small town.

Situated in southern Maryland and about an hour outside of DC, it was barely a pinprick on the state map. But it was Steven's hometown, where he'd been born and raised. And he was proud to have opened his law practice there, despite the lack of choice when it came to his clientele.

Steven raised his arms over his head and stretched, working the kinks out of his back. After saving the latest draft and forwarding it to his client for approval, he closed his laptop and stood. Work had kept him from his beloved long enough.

Just as he reached the office door, his desk phone rang. He stood in the doorway, debating whether to let it go to voicemail or answer it. His staff was long gone, as he should have been. The shrill ring called to him, and he hurried over to answer it.

"It's not enough," a gruff voice said in lieu of a greeting.

Steven stared at the ceiling as he sank into his chair. "What's not enough, Mr. Willoughby?"

"The house. Why should she get to keep part of my retirement while I have to split the cost of a building that's falling apart and not worth much?"

Pinching the bridge of his nose, Steven took a calming breath. As much as he wanted to point out that Mr. Willoughby had specifically insisted on selling the house and splitting the profit, it wouldn't help. He was by far the most difficult client Steven had ever had. Still, Mr. Willoughby's bill would pay Steven's mortgage for the next two months.

"All right," Steven said as he texted his sister that something had come up. "Let's talk numbers."

Better hurry. Rose is on the warpath.

If only it were that easy. But Rose would understand. She wouldn't be happy, but she knew how much pressure he was under to make his law practice a success. He'd spent the last six months building it from the ground up.

Mr. Willoughby droned on in Steven's ear, and though he took notes, his mind was elsewhere. He made the usual sympathetic sounds to ensure his client felt heard, but sometimes, he struggled not to feel like an overpaid therapist. Divorce clients were the worst. If he hadn't found Rose, he might have decided never to get married. The petty things people fought over made the whole institution of marriage sound like a lot of wasted effort.

Rose and I will be different. They'd had a nice long engagement, and he was anxious to have the wedding part over and done with. Who knew that planning what essentially amounted to an extravagant party would take up so much time and cost so much money? Rose and Lanie had done their best to find deals or do whatever they could themselves, but it was still an expensive endeavor.

"Mr. Willoughby." Steven interrupted his client midrant. "We've been over this. I've requested the sale of the house in the paperwork I'm sending opposing counsel, but we've had to offer something in exchange."

"She's going after my retirement, though! I earned that."

As did she. Rubbing his temples, Steven fought the urge to tell his client to shove off. Mrs. Willoughby actually hadn't requested the retirement, despite it being her legal right to do so. She'd been a stay-at-home mom for most of their marriage, which impacted her earning power and ability to save for her future. Steven had suggested offering the retirement as an enticement to sell her childhood home, even though by law, it wasn't marital property. Good luck getting any of that through to Mr. Willoughby, however.

"And as I've said, we are offering it in an attempt to entice your wife to sell the house. You'll more than make up for the loss of retirement in the sale of the home."

His client harrumphed. "I doubt that, and I don't see why I have to give up anything."

Steven had had enough of the circular argument. "Sir, with all due respect, you're lucky she didn't go after your retirement to begin with, and you'll be even luckier if she accepts this offer. Now if you'll excuse me, I must go."

Without waiting for a response, Steven hung up. He would likely pay for that later, but hopefully, Sandra, his paralegal, could smooth things over for him in the morning. She had a knack for knowing exactly how to deal with their more uncooperative clients.

Before Mr. Willoughby could call back, Steven grabbed his things and rushed to the door then locked up. Rose had texted several times while he was on the phone, and he was going to be in more trouble if he didn't get over there soon.

As he pulled out of the parking lot behind the building, he called her and put her on speaker.

"Where are you?"

"Just leaving the office."

The silence on the other end of the line was more deafening than if she had started yelling at him. He cleared his throat.

"I'm sorry, but Mr. Willoughby called and—"

"You stood me up for that philanderer?"

Living in a small town had many perks, but the gossip mill wasn't one of them. "Those accusations are unfounded and—"

Lanie snorted, alerting him to the fact that he, too, was on speaker. "Unfounded my butt. That man has more mistresses than there are blades of grass. I'm amazed he keeps them all straight."

She had a point, though Steven would never tell *her* that. "At any rate, I'm on my way now and should be there in a few."

"You owe me," Rose replied, and though she tried to sound stern, Steven could hear the smile in her voice. Once again, Lanie had saved the day and kept his fiancée distracted. *What would I have done if she had returned to the West Coast?*

"I'll make it up to you, I promise." He hit the end call button and focused on the drive ahead.

As he drove down the darkening street, he pondered how much had changed since Lanie arrived back in town six months ago. Despite her initial determination to leave small-town life behind in favor of the hustle and bustle of Los Angeles and a lucrative position at a prestigious school, she'd decided to stay. He sent up a quick prayer of thanks for her fiancé, Nate. Between telling Lanie about a local teaching job and winning her heart a second time, Nate had done what neither Steven nor his father could do. And his sister was currently engaged and planning a wedding of her own.

If only their mother could see them both, on the verge of walking down the aisle. The smile on Steven's face faded. With the estate finalized and the house sold, he and Lanie had been able to focus on happier things. But the anniversary of their mother's death was fast approaching. Lanie hadn't mentioned it, but she was struggling with it as much as he was. After all, she'd taken a semester off from grad school to care for their mother during those final months, something for which he would be eternally grateful.

Pulling into the parking lot of The Muddy Oar, Steven shut off the engine and pushed the depressing thoughts from his mind. Their mother would want them both to be happy and move on. *What better way to do that than to plan two spectacular weddings?*

He headed into the steak house and to the back of the small dining area. The restaurant doubled as the only caterer in town that could handle large events like weddings, and Steven supposed it could be considered upscale by Cedar Haven standards. Lanie, Rose, and Carissa, their wedding planner, were seated at a round table with more food than he had ever seen before piled around them. His sister's blond head was easy to spot among the crowd. They smiled when they caught sight of him, and Rose stood before running into his arms, her dark-brown hair flying behind her.

"Yay! You're finally here."

"I told you I was on my way." He pulled her close, inhaling her intoxicating scent of jasmine and vanilla.

"You also told your sister you'd be here in fifteen, which was well over a half hour ago," Rose retorted, taking a step back and putting her hands on her hips.

"Fair." Sliding a hand to her cheek, he brushed his lips against hers. "But it's okay if I lie to my sister."

"Sitting right here," Lanie grumbled.

Steven glanced over Rose's head at his very unhappy sister and grinned. "Love ya, lil sis."

"Stop calling me that!" she whined and stuck her tongue out at him, which only further proved he'd chosen the perfect nickname.

Rose led him to the table and sat down. She had a steak and some green bean concoction on her plate. His sister was sampling cake flavors. He hid a smile.

Carissa set a plate in front of him. "Our time is almost up, so you should try what you can before they clear all of this away."

"Thanks," he said before turning to Rose. "So, what do you think so far?"

"I like the steak." Rose took another bite and chewed thoughtfully. "But I'm not as sold on the sides. And we need a vegetarian dish as well."

"The green beans are a definite no from me." Lanie made a face at them.

"I thought the broccoli salad was interesting," Carissa said.

"That's one word for it." Rose sighed and rested her chin on her hand, surveying the table. "I liked the glazed carrots, but Carissa says we have to offer something green."

"What about this?" Steven pointed at a medley of green leaves in a bowl. Leaning forward with his fork, he speared one and brought it to his nose, sniffing it, a move he immediately regretted as the sour scent of vinegar burned his nostrils. "What *is* this?"

"They call it spinach surprise." Rose wrinkled her nose. "None of us are brave enough to try it." Her face morphed into a sweet smile, but he wasn't fooled. "You should do the honors."

I suppose I do owe her. Grimacing, he spooned some onto his plate. He sniffed it again, and the strange combination of vinegar and spice irritated his sinuses. *Here goes nothing.* After taking a tentative bite, he assessed the flavor. The vinegar came through pretty strong, but overall, it wasn't bad. He detected garlic and some sort of creamy substance.

When he looked up, Rose and Lanie were leaning forward as if waiting to see whether he would keep the strange food down. Carissa had a hand over her mouth, probably hiding a smile. With a shrug, he took another bite. "It's not bad, but I'm not sure I'd want to serve it at a wedding."

Rose groaned. "Why is this so difficult? If we'd gotten married in Baltimore, we'd have more options for catering."

Carissa put a hand on her arm. "But you'd pay far more for the experience. I know you want everything to be perfect, but remember, people are coming to see you and Steven get married. As long as you feed them something, they'll be happy."

With a pout, Rose pulled a salad toward her. "This is Caesar salad. It's boring, I'll admit, but at least it's something most people enjoy."

"Maybe you could have a small salad bar where people could make their own," Lanie suggested.

"That's a good idea," Steven agreed. "And then they can put whatever color of vegetable they want on their plates."

Rose smiled, her eyes lighting up. "I love salad bars at restaurants. I'm sure it'll be a big hit."

"That's settled." Carissa tapped away on her phone. "What were you thinking for the entrée? You said steak, but what else?"

Several different dishes sat before him—chicken, shrimp, crab cake, and pork chops—and he sampled each. The savory chicken was a tad on the dry side, and he could only imagine how much worse that would be after sitting over a chafing dish. Crab cakes made sense for a summer wedding in Maryland, but not everyone was a fan of seafood.

"How many entrees are we paying for again?"

Rose rolled her eyes at Lanie. "Typical male. Doesn't pay attention to the details."

"Hey!" Steven protested. "I've got a lot on my plate."

"You sure do." Lanie pointed at his literal plate and laughed.

"The package you picked includes three entrees," Carissa said. "One of which needs to be vegetarian."

Next, he tried the shrimp. The sweet-and-spicy marinade appealed to him but not as much as the crab. After all, the brackish water of the Chesapeake ran through his veins, and blue crabs were practically the state mascot. He reviewed the vegetarian options: wild mushroom risotto, three-cheese ravioli, and meatless lasagna. No matter what they chose, it would be some sort of pasta.

After a moment of contemplation, he tried the mushroom risotto. Good but not quite what he wanted. He sampled the rest of the vegetarian options. The cheese ravioli was better, but the lasagna somehow managed to taste just like it would with meat.

"My vote is for steak, crab cake, and the meatless lasagna."

Rose frowned. "I was partial to the three-cheese ravioli myself."

"The lasagna tasted just like the real thing to me." Steven shrugged. "But I'm not a vegetarian, so I'm not sure that's the goal."

Carissa laughed. "Unfortunately, we don't have time to bring in a vegetarian for their opinion, so why don't we look at it from a price perspective?" After a quick glance at her phone, she continued, "According to the PDF they sent us, the ravioli is cheaper than the lasagna."

"Then let's go with that." Between starting a business and trying to pay off his student loans, Steven hoped to curb the growing wedding costs as much as possible to avoid adding to their already strained finances.

Carissa finished tapping into her phone then stood. "Lanie, would you mind coming with me to talk to the caterer? While we're gone, you two should try the cakes."

Once they were alone, Steven leaned closer to Rose. "I know I complained about the expense of a wedding planner, but she sure is making this easier."

Rose pressed her hand to her chest. "You have no idea. I can't imagine what I would do without her. She's managed to keep everything on schedule, which has stopped me from losing my mind." She shook her head. "Why is wedding planning so hard?"

He rubbed her back. "I'm sorry I haven't been around as much as I promised I would. But now that it's summer, I'm hoping things at the firm will slow down."

Leaning back in her chair, she raised a thin black eyebrow. "I'm not holding my breath."

"I know I keep saying that, but between Sandra and Leslie, I feel like I'm starting to get a handle on things."

She pointed her fork at him. "You need a partner."

"It's too soon."

"Is it?" Her brown eyes darkened. "You've been running yourself ragged for months now, and you're not hurting for profit." He opened his mouth to speak, but she waved a hand. "I know that you've got student loans and bills to pay, but come on, Steven. You can't keep this pace up. You'll work yourself into an early grave."

With a sigh, he sliced off another piece of cake with his fork. Red velvet, if his limited knowledge of cakes didn't deceive him. He took a bite, more to avoid responding to her than because he wanted it. Their conversation had caused him to lose his appetite.

"New businesses always have a hard time getting off the ground. I just want to make sure things are stable before I bring someone else in."

"I understand that." Rose laid a hand on his arm. "But speaking as both your loving fiancée and as a nurse, I'm concerned. I've seen what happens to people who don't take care of themselves, who work too hard. You need to find ways to ease the burden, give yourself some breathing room."

After setting his fork down, he covered her hand with his own. "I promise I'll consider it."

Her forehead creased, but she nodded. "I suppose that's better than a flat-out no."

Just then, Lanie and Carissa returned, and the former grabbed another piece of cake. "Everything's worked out with the caterer. Did you choose a cake?"

"I'm partial to red velvet," he said, even though that was literally the only flavor he'd tried.

"Me too." Rose squeezed his arm.

He breathed a sigh of relief. *Crisis averted.* They were on the same page once more.

Chapter Two

ROSE WALKED QUICKLY THROUGH the hospital ward. Rounds were starting soon, and she wanted to check in on her favorite patient before they got underway. Mrs. Winslow was propped up in her bed with the sheet tucked around her legs. Her watery blue eyes struggled to focus as Rose came in, but her smile brightened the room.

"Good morning, Mrs. Winslow," Rose said as she moved to her bedside. "How are you feeling today?"

"Same as yesterday." Mrs. Winslow waved a hand over her face. "My eyesight is still poor, but the doctor said tomorrow's surgery will help."

"I've no doubt about that." After checking her vitals, Rose pulled up a chair. "Any new gossip since I last saw you?"

"I think Dr. Bryant has the hots for Nurse Claire," Mrs. Winslow whispered conspiratorially. "They were canoodling just outside my door late last evening."

Rose laughed. "Oh, that's old news. They've been dating for some time now, though they think they're being discreet."

"Well, they need to find a better dark corner because I could see them plain as day from here." Running a hand through her thinning blond hair, Mrs. Winslow raised an eyebrow. "And what of you and your fiancé? How are the wedding plans coming?"

"Oh, we met with the caterer and made our final choices for the menu," Rose said, forcing a smile. Her conversation with Steven had done little to assuage her constant worrying about him. Since the estate had finalized, she'd hoped he would have an easier time juggling his work and the wedding, but instead, his caseload had only gotten worse. The circles under his eyes grew darker every time she saw him.

"You don't seem as excited as I expected you to," Mrs. Winslow said with a frown.

"I'm excited!" But it sounded fake even to Rose's ears. "Steven has been a bit preoccupied with work lately. I'm afraid he's neglecting his health."

"He's lucky to have you to care for him."

Rose bristled, and she worked to keep her temper in check. Nursing was her job, one she preferred to leave at the end of her shift. Of course she would care for Steven if he needed her, but she would prefer him to take preventative measures *before* he worked himself into an illness.

Stifling a sigh, she stood. "I best get to my rounds." She patted Mrs. Winslow's hand. "I'll check with the doc on whether there's anything I need to do to prep you for surgery, but hopefully, we'll have you seeing clearly in no time."

Mrs. Winslow gave her a grateful smile before leaning back on her pillow and closing her eyes. Rose envied her calm nature. If she was facing complicated eye surgery, she wasn't sure she would be able to appear so serene.

Rose left the room to begin her rounds, mentally counting down the days until she had some time off for the wedding and honeymoon. The last winter had been rough, and she desperately needed a vacation.

As she picked up the clipboard outside the next patient's room, she wondered how much different her life would be once she and Steven tied the knot. They'd discussed children, but with their schedules, she didn't know when they might find the time. And the last thing she wanted to do was add to his stress load by bringing it up.

But she wanted children, at least two and close together. She hoped to start trying for them right away. An only child herself, she had come to the US from South Korea with her parents and had stayed on to finish her nursing degree when her parents returned to take care of her grandparents. Her family was planning to come to the wedding, but part of her worried the travel would prove too expensive. The price of flights had risen substantially in the last year, and she was glad she had locked in their honeymoon tickets when she did.

As much as she loved the McAllisters, relying on them just wasn't the same as having her own family there. While she had no plan to return to her homeland on a permanent basis, she wanted her children to understand their heritage and culture. Maybe once they were more settled, she and Steven could travel to South Korea for a visit—assuming Steven's business ever settled. She sighed and entered Mr. Patrones's room.

He sat up in his bed, staring out the window. The sight of him tugged at her heartstrings. He'd had a mild heart attack a week ago, but no one had been in to visit him. She'd asked about family, but his answers were vague, and she didn't want to make him uncomfortable.

"Good morning, Mr. Patrones. How are we doing today?"

He shifted in his bed, and his sad brown eyes met hers. "Same as yesterday."

Grimacing, she glanced over his chart. He had improved significantly in the last several days, and they would probably release him soon, not that she expected him to take that as good news.

"Your vitals are looking better." She tried to keep her tone cheerful. "I don't think you'll be with us much longer."

His eyebrows drew together, and she realized a moment too late how her words could be misconstrued. She moved to his side.

"I meant that you would be discharged soon."

"Either way, at least I'll be out of your hair."

What a very Eeyore thing to say. She checked his fluids and made a few notes on his chart. All the while, she racked her brain for some encouraging words but came up short.

"Any special requests for lunch?" she asked, wishing she could find a way to reach him. Her patients usually raved about her bedside manner, but with Mr. Patrones, she just couldn't break through the shroud of sadness that engulfed him.

"Does it matter what I request? The diet the doctor has me on hardly allows much wiggle room."

Rose bit her tongue to avoid saying something she might regret. Most heart attack patients struggled with the recommended dietary restrictions, but the ones who refused to follow the diet were at a higher risk of another attack. That probably wasn't the best thing to tell Mr. Patrones.

"All right. Well, push the button if you need anything," she replied, turning on her heel and moving quickly to the hallway.

"Mr. Patrones still as depressing as ever?" a quiet voice asked, making Rose jump.

Rebecca Masters leaned against the wall beside her, clutching a clipboard to her chest. Rose released a breath and nodded.

"He's doing better physically, but I wonder if we shouldn't keep him under a seventy-two-hour psych hold."

Rebecca rolled her eyes. "Dr. Myers will never go for that, especially since Mr. Patrones has never vocalized any suicide ideations. But we should add some recommendations for counseling to his discharge instructions." She glanced behind Rose. "I don't suppose we've found any family members?"

Rose shook her head. "Not that I'm aware of. It's sad. I can't imagine how he's lived alone all this time."

"Ah, well," Rebecca said. "I'll talk to Dr. Myers, but I'm afraid there's not much else we can do."

With a dejected nod, Rose went to complete the rest of her rounds. Other than checking on Mr. Patrones a few more times, she continued her shift uneventfully. At her break, she decided to call Steven to take her mind off things.

"Hey, honey, how's it going?"

"Not bad," Rose said, choosing not to mention her concerns about Mr. Patrones. "I just wanted to confirm we were still on for dinner tonight."

When he didn't immediately respond, her heartbeat quickened. *Not again.* His late arrival to the caterer had been bad enough, but he knew how important their weekly dates were to her. Her parents had maintained date night throughout their entire marriage, which she believed was the secret to their success. While she would never say it, sometimes she wondered whether Steven's parents might not have divorced if they had done something similar.

"Listen," he began.

She squeezed her eyes shut. "You've got to be kidding me."

"I've got a lot of work to finish up tonight." His voice was defensive, and a part of her wished she hadn't pushed the issue. After a beat, he sighed. "But we can go out this weekend instead."

"I work this weekend," she replied, her tone flat.

"Oh."

She rubbed her forehead, resisting the urge to roll her eyes. It was the beginning of June, and their wedding was set for the end of August. They should be spending more time together, not less. But of course, he had a lot on his plate. Sometimes she wished he had kept his job in the city rather than striking out on his own. Then again, some big-city law firms required eighty hours a week. Such a demanding schedule would likely have contributed to his workaholic nature even more.

"When is your next day off?" he asked, a pleading note in his voice. "Maybe I can leave the office early and take you out for a night on the town."

What would a night "on the town" in Cedar Haven entail? Karaoke at Seabreeze followed by a plate of pancakes at Bea's? Not quite on par with the images that phrase brought up. Sometimes she really missed Baltimore.

"I'm off on Tuesday." She braced herself for what she knew he was going to say.

"Ah... I have court Tuesday."

Of course he did. Tuesday was child support day at the courthouse, and he always had at least one client on the docket every week. She clenched her fist at her side.

"Can't you just come out with me for an hour tonight?" She hated begging for his time. Was this what their marriage was going to be like? "The work will still be there tomorrow."

"I'm sorry, babe, but I need to finish this brief. I promise I'll make it up to you."

Empty words. They'd already established that their schedules were both full for the next several days. Oh well, maybe she would have better luck next week, though maintaining their weekly date was becoming increasingly more difficult.

"It's fine," she lied, not wanting him to feel worse than he already did. He'd promised things would let up soon, and he'd said he would consider getting a partner. She needed to be patient. "We can just plan for next week."

"Thanks for understanding, Rose. I really am sorry."

"Promise me you won't stay too late at the office. You need to take care of yourself."

She could almost see him shaking his head, a rueful smile on his lips. Sometimes, despite her best efforts, the line between nurse and fiancée blurred for her, but she couldn't help it. She'd seen too many patients cause themselves avoidable health issues by working too much.

"I love you," he said, clearly trying to avoid the same old argument.

"I love you too."

She disconnected and leaned back against the wall, her head in her hands. How had they gotten there? Even when they'd had opposing schedules of law school and nursing school, they'd managed to find time for each other every week.

"Rose?" Rebecca called from behind her, pulling her from her thoughts.

She turned around and smiled. "Hey, I was headed to finish my rounds. What's up?"

Rebecca's forehead creased. "About that. Any chance you could stay on? Lisa called out with a sick child again, and I need someone to cover her shift."

Ordinarily, Rose would have said no. She rarely worked doubles because she tried to maintain boundaries between her work time and her personal life. But aside from Steven canceling on her, she had other reasons to consider accepting an extra shift. There weren't many opportunities for advancement at the small rural hospital, but she had her eye on the head nurse position that had just opened. What she lacked in tenure, she hoped to make up for with a strong work ethic.

"Sure, I can stay on."

"Thanks! I owe you one." Rebecca turned on her heel and headed down the hall.

Taking a deep breath, Rose shook her head. *At least I'll get overtime.*

A few hours later, Rose was standing at the nurses' station, reviewing a patient's chart, when Rebecca appeared beside her. Her coworker's face was pale, and she breathed heavily as she braced a hand against the desk.

"Have you heard?"

Rose raised an eyebrow. "Heard what?"

"There's been an accident. You need to go to the ICU."

"What? Why?" Rose shook her head. "Nobody told me I was being pulled."

"You're not," Rebecca said, leading Rose toward the elevators. "But you need to get up there. They'll explain when you arrive." She gave Rose's hand a squeeze before hurrying away.

Bewildered, Rose pressed the button, and the elevator doors opened. She stepped inside, chose the ICU floor, and waited, working to swallow her irritation. *What the heck is going on? And why wouldn't Rebecca just tell me?* Worry gnawed at her during the ride up.

The ICU ward was complete chaos as she stepped into the hall. She double-checked that she hadn't accidentally gone to the ER. *Nope, this is the right floor.* Rushing to the nurses' station, she halted when a familiar head of dirty-blond hair rounded the corner on a gurney.

"Steven?" She ran after him only to have someone grab her arm and spin her around.

"Rose, I—"

"Let go of me." She tried to shake free as she met the gaze of whoever had had the audacity to stop her. But Dr. Myers held firm, his blue eyes filled with concern and his expression grim.

"Come with me," he said and half dragged her to an empty office.

Once they were inside, he released her, and she staggered across the room to the desk. She whirled around, ready to march right back out that door, but Dr. Myers blocked her path.

"There's nothing you can do for him right now," he said. "They're in the process of determining the damage and hooking up his IV to start administering medication. I only have a moment."

Her legs gave out, and she sank into the nearest chair. "Oh God. What happened?"

"He was in a car accident, but we think he had a medical emergency that led to the crash." Dr. Myers glanced at her as if assessing how much to say. "Possibly a heart attack, but I'll know more once I get in there and run some tests. You stay here, and I'll get someone to sit with you."

Like hell. "Need I remind you, Doctor, I'm an RN? I'm coming with you."

"And need I remind *you*, Rose, we have a strict policy that prohibits hospital staff from treating family members?" Her five-foot-four stature was no match for Dr. Myers's six-foot frame when he put a firm hand on her shoulder and pushed her back into the chair. "I'll send word as soon as I can."

Without waiting for her response, he spun on his heel and was gone. Rose put her head in her hands. *A heart attack? How? Why?* Steven was twenty-nine years old and one of the healthiest people she knew. She'd joked he was going to work himself into an early grave, but she'd never expected *that*.

The door opened, and Marie, the head RN for the ICU, came in. "So he's told you, then." She handed Rose a cup of coffee.

Rose took a sip, more out of habit than because she actually wanted or needed the beverage. Marie perched in the chair beside her, taking her free hand. The room was dimly lit with a desk lamp, and Rose found comfort in the darkness.

"It'll be all right."

If only she could believe her. But Steven sounded like he was in a bad way. The other half of Dr. Myers's message finally resonated.

"What did he hit?" she asked.

"What's that?"

"Dr. Myers said St—" Her throat closed around his name. "Dr. Myers said he was in a car accident. What did he hit?"

"I don't know the full story," Marie said. "But I gathered from the little the paramedics shared that he lost control of the car and hit a tree."

At least no one else was injured. Small favors. She tried to focus on the good news. Steven was in the best hands in the area. She'd seen Dr. Myers work magic on patients in worse shape. And Steven was young. He had a better chance than most.

Still, she couldn't just sit there and wait. She needed to *do* something.

"I have to make a call." Not wanting an audience, she stood and raced out of the room. After glancing up and down the hallway, she ducked into a storage closet across from the office. Her fingers shook as she scrolled to Lanie's name in her phone.

"Hey, Rose, what's up?"

"You need to come to the hospital," Rose said in a rush. "It's your brother."

"Steven? What's wrong? What happened?"

"He was in a car accident." Rose couldn't bring herself to tell her the rest, not yet. It still didn't feel real. Besides, Dr. Myers had said a heart attack was possible but not confirmed. There was no sense in getting her future sister-in-law worked up over the phone.

"Oh no! Let me call my dad, and then I'll head on over. What floor are you on?"

"The ICU."

Lanie gasped and promised she would be there as soon as she could, but Rose barely heard her. She disconnected the call and went back to the office. Marie was still there, her eyebrows pulled together in a frown.

"Lanie is on her way, and she's calling her dad." Rose slid into her chair. Her coffee sat on the desk behind it, but she couldn't bring herself to drink it. Instead, she allowed her eyes to take in the details of the room in hopes it would ground her in the moment. A large leather rolling chair was turned to face the dual monitors set up above a docking station on the desk. Mahogany bookshelves towered in the back corner, casting ominous shadows in the soft light of the lamp.

"I'll stay with you until they arrive." Marie grasped Rose's hand again and gave it a squeeze.

Part of Rose wanted to protest, as she imagined Marie had a million other things to do, but she didn't want to be alone. Her stomach was already in knots, and she feared she would fall to pieces by the time Lanie arrived.

The sounds of machines beeping, muffled footsteps, and whispered prayers wafted into the room as they sat in silence. Rose was literally on the edge of her seat. Her feet ached to move, but her head was spinning, and she feared she would pass out if she tried to stand. With her free hand, she gripped the arm of the chair and stared at the office door, willing it to open with Lanie or Dr. Myers. Though if the latter came right then, it wouldn't mean good news. Not enough time had passed for Dr. Myers to have completed his assessment of Steven. He would run an EKG and assess for internal bleeding as well as broken bones. It was going to be a long night.

Time stood still, and Rose silently prayed for Steven to be spared. If—no, *when*—he survived, he would have to take better care of himself. She wouldn't give him a choice in the matter. Not after that.

Of course, that would all take time, and she hoped she could enlist Lanie and Steven's staff in determining what needed to be taken care of immediately at the law firm. She wouldn't allow him to stress over it, not while his health hung in the balance. They would figure things out. After all, they had the rest of their lives to do so. She refused to give in to despair. Steven *would* live, and they *would* have a life together. She had to have faith.

A knock sounded at the door, and Rose braced herself, but it was only one of the other nurses leading Lanie and Max into the room. When Rose jumped up to embrace them, Marie slipped quietly from the room.

"You made good time," Rose said, fighting back tears that threatened to spill over her cheeks.

"We broke several laws getting here, but we didn't get caught." Lanie cupped Rose's cheek. "How are you?"

Rose blinked. The fact that Lanie's first question had been about her and not Steven caught her off guard. Her face likely betrayed how she felt, but she forced herself to respond.

"Trying to stay positive." She gestured to the door. "There's no news, but I didn't expect there to be."

"He'll pull through," Max said, though it sounded as if he were trying to convince himself. "He's made of stern stuff."

"And he's in good hands." Lanie smiled, but the fear in her eyes was unmistakable.

The same nurse who had brought them to the office returned with two chairs, which she set up in front of the bookshelves. With Marie gone, the chairs weren't necessary, but Rose appreciated her thoughtfulness. When they were alone again, Max collapsed into one of them. Lanie took the seat closest to Rose.

"Do you have any more details about the accident?" Lanie asked.

"They think he had a medical emergency before he lost control of the car."

Lanie frowned. "What kind of medical emergency?"

After taking a deep breath, Rose told them everything she knew, which admittedly wasn't much. And when she mentioned the possible heart attack, their reactions matched her own.

"But he's not even thirty!" Max leaned forward, disbelief blazing from his eyes.

"Stress can cause a lot of health issues, Dad," Lanie said, her tone gentle.

But Max just scowled and faced the wall. Rose opened her mouth to respond, but Lanie shook her head, her message clear. Berating him with medical knowledge would be of little use, especially at that moment.

"What are they doing to him?" Lanie asked.

Rose shrugged. "Dr. Myers is a cardiologist. He's running tests to determine what happened and what damage was done."

Max stood suddenly and walked toward the door. When he reached it, he turned back, his expression blank.

"I can't stand all this waiting. I'm going to grab a coffee. Anyone want anything?"

"Sure, I'll take one," Lanie said, her eyes wide. Rose assumed she was puzzled by her father's erratic behavior. "Rose?"

Instead of responding, Rose gestured to the coffee Marie had brought, not trusting herself to speak. Max closed the door behind him, and she couldn't help the relief that coursed through her at his absence. While he had always been kind to her, something about him intimidated her. She suspected his perpetual bad mood was the cause of her unease.

"He never could handle hospitals," Lanie murmured, her eyes on the door. When she glanced at Rose, she forced a smile. "But he'll be fine, I'm sure."

"I'm sorry to have dragged you both here. Maybe I should have waited until I knew more."

"Nonsense." Lanie shook her head. "We want to be here. Besides, you shouldn't have to go through this alone, not when you've got family to help you through it."

Family. Sometimes Rose forgot what that was like. It had been lonely since her parents moved back to South Korea. But the promise of a future family with Steven had eased the pang. And that was currently in jeopardy. *Oh God, what if he doesn't make it? What will I do without him?*

"He wasn't even supposed to be on the road," she blurted out.

Lanie blinked. "What do you mean?"

"We had plans for dinner, which he canceled." Rose put her head in her hands. "If I'd been with him, maybe I could have prevented this. Or at least been there when it happened."

"Don't think like that." Lanie slid an arm around Rose's shoulders. "He's been working himself sick these last few months. I'd hoped things would calm down for him once the estate was finalized, but instead, he's working harder than ever. He needs to take it easy, especially with all the stress you both must be under from the wedding."

The wedding. Will it even happen now? Depending on his injuries, it could take weeks or even months to recover. There would be rehabilitation, physical therapy, and who knew what else ahead of him. Rose had no idea how that might impact their immediate future, let alone their wedding.

It felt silly to even think about that when his life hung in the balance, but somehow, it was all her mind could handle. Canceling the wedding wasn't the worst thing in the world, but it would be heartbreaking nonetheless. They'd been planning it for well over a year, and she would hate for their hard work to go to waste.

Not to mention that she was ready to marry him. She'd known he was the one for her since that first day they'd met in the library, when she'd accidentally knocked over a stack of books and heard a yelp of pain. She closed her eyes as the memory washed over her.

They had unknowingly chosen to sit at the same table to study. She hadn't been able to see him over the books in her arms. When she'd heard his cry, she'd rushed over to apologize and met the most interesting pair of eyes she'd ever seen—a delicate mixture of green and brown that she wanted to lose herself in. His frown of discomfort quickly morphed into a smile, and he'd brushed off her concern. He'd introduced himself, and the moment their hands touched, a spark shot through her like nothing she'd ever felt before.

A rueful smile pulled at her lips. Even with such a promising first meeting, it had still taken him months to work up the courage to ask her out. They'd met at the library several times and enjoyed each other's company while studying quietly. Her smile fell. With their busy schedules, their relationship had never been easy, but once they'd set a date for the wedding, she'd thought things were looking up for them.

"Hey." Lanie gently shook her arm. "What's going on in that head of yours?"

"Whether or not we're going to need to cancel the wedding." Rose raised her head and met Lanie's eyes. "I know it's the least of my worries right now, but I can't help it."

"I get it. Sometimes it's easier to focus on what you can control. But I can't imagine we would need to. Dad and I can pitch in more to help fill the gap if Steven needs to back off the planning."

"Assuming he survives this." Rose bit her lip. She hadn't meant to voice her deepest fears.

"He will survive it. McAllisters are made of stern stuff," Lanie said, echoing what her father had said earlier.

Rose nodded mutely. She wanted to believe her future sister-in-law, but she couldn't quite bring herself to do so. And if something happened to Steven... If he didn't make it, she didn't know what that would do to her.

Chapter Three

STEVEN WOKE GROGGY AND in pain. The room around him was unfamiliar with its fluorescent lighting and antiseptic smell. A repetitive beeping sounded near his head, and he swatted at the alarm with his right hand only to groan as something pulled at his skin. His veins seemed to burn with the movement. Raising his arm took effort, and he frowned at the IV sticking out of it.

What on earth? Am I in the hospital? He remembered getting into his car to drive to Rose's apartment, hoping to surprise her. He recalled the road was slick with rain, then an awful pain had bloomed in his chest. There had been a flash of bright light, but the memory was cut short, as if he'd fallen asleep in the middle of it.

He tried to move his head to search for a call button, but something prevented him from turning it. Breathing became more difficult as he coughed and sputtered. The steady beeping increased in rhythm, matching his heart rate.

A nurse he didn't recognize rushed in, and her eyes widened. "You're awake." She glanced behind him then stepped to his side. "It's okay. This is disorienting, but I'm going to need you to take deep breaths." She inhaled deeply through her nose and exhaled from her mouth in demonstration.

Forcing himself to focus, Steven imitated her, and soon the rapid beeping slowed to a steadier pulse. The panic subsided enough for him to take in more of his surroundings. Lifting his left hand, he attempted to touch his neck, but a brace prevented him from doing so. At least that explained why he couldn't turn his head.

"I'll go get the doctor," the nurse said with a smile before spinning on her heel and leaving the room.

He tried to open his mouth to stop her, to ask what had happened to him, but even his face hurt to move. Frustrated, he settled back against the uncomfortable hospital bed and took an assessment of himself.

His legs were numb with the pins-and-needles sensation he got if he sat on his foot too long. With careful movements, he lifted the blanket draped over him and noted a cast on his left leg. *Must have broken it.* But it didn't hurt. *Strange.* Perhaps they'd given him a great deal of pain medication. If he had to guess, he'd been in an accident. Maybe he'd totaled his car. *Ugh, that's the last thing I need.*

Just as he reached for the call button again, the doctor came in. Steven recognized him as one of the doctors Rose worked with, though he couldn't remember his name.

"Mr. McAllister, you gave us quite a scare. I'm Dr. Myers, though I believe we've met before." He moved a stool over to Steven's bedside and perched on it. "Can you hear me?"

"Yes," Steven croaked out.

"Good. And I assume you can understand me as well?"

Why was the doctor treating him like an invalid? He didn't have brain damage or anything. *Unless... How bad was the accident?*

"Did you understand what I asked you, Steven?" the doctor asked, prompting Steven to focus.

Steven gave a slight nod, as much as the brace would allow, then winced as the motion sent pain radiating through his head.

"Do you remember what happened?"

It took Steven a minute to respond. "I remember... getting in the car to drive to see Rose. My chest hurt..." As he spoke, his chest throbbed, and he rubbed a hand over it. His fingers probed the bandage over his heart. "Was I in an accident? How's my car?"

"Yes to your first question. Unfortunately, I don't know the answer to your second question." After making a few notes on his chart, Dr. Myers leaned forward. "So you remember the accident. Do you remember anything that happened before the accident? How you were feeling?"

Why does "before the accident" matter? His stomach twisted into one big knot, and he gritted his teeth. But to humor the doctor, Steven closed his eyes and tried to focus. Other than the chest pain, he didn't remember anything. Maybe if he said no, Dr. Myers would stop interrogating him and provide answers instead.

"Not really," Steven said, opening his eyes and meeting the doctor's gaze.

"It appears you had a mild myocardial infarction."

A what? Steven stared at Dr. Myers, hoping his expression demonstrated his confusion. When the doctor didn't elaborate, he risked more pain by shifting a fraction of an inch to look at the nurse.

"You had a heart attack," she translated helpfully.

Steven blinked rapidly, trying to digest the words. *Was that even possible?*

"Ah yes, sorry. I should have explained in simpler terms. You had a mild heart attack before you crashed into a tree." He stood and showed Steven a paper with a bunch of lines on it. "We've run an EKG and some other tests. There was a slight blockage in your artery, and I placed a stent."

But Steven barely heard him. *A heart attack?* Wasn't that something that only happened to the elderly? *I'm not even thirty!*

A million questions ran through his mind, but he couldn't articulate any of them. His breathing grew shallower as he tried to organize his thoughts, but they were flying too fast to make them coherent.

The nurse put a hand on his arm. "You need to calm down. You're going to hyperventilate."

It took effort, but Steven forced himself to take several deep breaths. While his heart rate and breathing slowed, the deep breathing did little to quell the panic growing in his belly.

"This is a lot to take in, but there is something else you should know."

"I broke my leg," Steven said, lifting the sheet again to reveal his cast.

"Well, yes, though I imagine it doesn't hurt."

Steven frowned. "I assume that's due to the pain medication."

With a shake of his head, Dr. Myers sat on the stool and moved closer to the bed. "Unfortunately, it's worse than that. You appear to have a spinal contusion, which is impacting your neurological transmitters." When Steven frowned, Dr. Myers pursed his lips. "A bruised spine, which has caused a temporary paralysis."

I'm paralyzed? Steven swallowed, trying to keep a brave face. The doctor had called the paralysis temporary, so perhaps there was some hope yet.

"We need to get you in for an MRI to assess the extent of the damage," Dr. Myers continued. "But I'm hoping there are no indications of tears or permanent damage to your spinal cord."

"What does that mean, though?" Steven tried to lift his good leg, but it wouldn't respond. "Will I be able to walk again?"

"Assuming it's just a bruise and not anything worse, then yes. In time," Dr. Myers assured him. "But it will be a long, hard road to recovery."

That brought up another question. "How long have I been here?"

The doctor stood and moved to the lone window in the room and pulled back the curtain. Steven winced as the bright morning light blinded him.

"Several hours. You were brought in last night, and you've been in and out of consciousness since the surgery." Dr. Myers shook his head. "You were lucky. Although it's rare for someone your age to suffer a heart attack." Moving to Steven's bedside, Dr. Myers folded his arms over his chest. "But Rose told me you've been under a lot of stress lately."

Rose. She must be out of her mind with worry. *Is she here? What about Lanie and Dad?* After what they'd just gone through with their mother, his sister had to be freaking out as well.

"Rose?" he croaked.

"She's here waiting to see you, but I'd like to get an X-ray and MRI of your back before I allow her to visit."

Steven wanted to protest, but there didn't seem to be much point. After all, he'd apparently been there for a while, so a few more hours couldn't hurt.

"I promise it won't take long."

Too tired to argue, Steven gave a quick nod, and the doctor and nurse left the room. Alone again, Steven stared at the ceiling and tried to process what he'd been told. While he would never have claimed to be in perfect health, there was no way he would have expected a heart attack. The stress at the office had been adding up over the last few months, and there were a few times his heart rate was higher than it should be, but he assumed that once he had things more under control, his health would improve as well. Besides, his practice hadn't even been open a year, so there were bound to be some growing pains. He just expected them to be financial, not physical.

The thought of his business made him shiver with cold dread. He looked at his legs again then tried to move one. He thought he saw a twitch, but it could have been his imagination. How long would it take for him to recover the use of his legs? The heart monitor began beeping erratically as realization sank in. *Will my life ever be the same again?*

The nurse came back with an orderly, and soon, he was taken to another area. Already, he was tired of the bed and itching to get up and move around, but he had no idea when that would happen. The fears about his future were enough to distract him from the multitudes of tests the doctor had ordered.

A little while later, he returned to his room, feeling like a human pin-cushion. Why did doctors always hurt people when they were supposedly trying to help them? What other profession could get away with such awful torture?

"Would you like to see Rose now?" the nurse asked after replacing a bag of fluids and making sure he was comfortable.

"Yes, please."

The nurse nodded before she hurried away. Steven tried to fix his face into a pleasant expression, but every small movement hurt. He could only imagine what he looked like.

When the door opened again, he swallowed his shock at Rose's appearance. Her dark eyes were bloodshot and puffy, with purple circles blemishing her skin. The blue scrubs she must have been wearing for her shift were wrinkled and stained.

And although she gave him a smile, the exhaustion behind it was evident, and a knife twisted in his gut. He'd done that to her—unintentionally, of course—but that offered little comfort. Whatever she'd been going through since the accident was his fault. The doctor had told him stress might have contributed to the heart attack, and Rose had been on his case for several months to take better care of himself. *I should have listened to her. Look where it got me.*

"How are you feeling?" She moved to his bedside and took his hand in both of hers. Her skin was soft, and he relished the warmth she provided to his cold skin.

"Not great." Even moving his mouth hurt, so he tried to keep his words to a minimum. "I'm sorry."

Her dark eyes filled with tears, and she squeezed his hand. "I'm just glad you're okay." She leaned forward and kissed his cheek. "I love you."

"I love you too." He shifted in the bed, trying in vain to find a comfortable position. "Did Dr. Myers tell you what happened?"

"Bits and pieces, but he's been busy." She searched Steven's face. "I know you were in a car accident and had a hea—" Her voice broke, and she covered her face with her hands. Each breathless sob that shook her body was like another knife to his heart.

"Hey," he whispered. "I'm okay." With careful movements, he lifted his left hand to touch her arm.

"I know." She took a deep breath and dashed away her tears. "But when I imagine what might have happened—"

"Shh." He gently pulled her head down to his level and brushed his lips against hers. The pain was worth it.

Too soon, she straightened up. "Lanie and your father are here. Would you like to see them?"

Before he could respond, Dr. Myers returned. "Actually, I think it would be good if we brought them in. You should all hear this together."

Rose left and reentered the room a few moments later with Lanie and Dad in tow. Lanie rushed to his side and gave him an awkward hug, careful to avoid the many wires and tubes that seemed to be coming out of him from every angle. His father's forehead was creased with worry, but he gave Steven a nod and patted his foot. Like Rose, they wore wrinkled clothes and appeared exhausted.

"So, we've run some tests and are waiting on the results, but it's important for you to understand what happened and start considering the next steps in Steven's recovery." Dr. Myers pressed his lips into a thin line before continuing. "The stent I put in Steven's heart should prevent another heart attack from occurring. However, we have another complication that we need to discuss."

Dr. Myers turned to the old-fashioned lighted board on the wall and placed the X-ray into it. "The MRI will tell us more, but I wanted to get an idea of whether anything was broken. It's difficult to get a clear image, likely due to fluid around the injury."

A small gasp sounded beside Steven. Rose squeezed his hand, clearly understanding something in the doctor's words that he'd missed.

When Dr. Myers turned back, his expression was grim. "I'm afraid Steven will need to undergo surgery to drain the fluid to ensure he has the best chance of healing."

"When will that happen?" Dad asked.

"Well, that's the thing." Dr. Myers scratched his head. "Normally, we prefer to wait to perform surgery on cardiac patients for at least seventy-two hours after the incident because of the increased chance of complications from anesthesia. And Steven has already been through one surgery to place the stent. However, studies have found that patients with spinal contusions have the best prognosis if the surgery is performed within twenty-four hours of the injury."

The room was silent as Steven's family digested the information. While he imagined everyone else was focused on the complications of the surgery, he wanted to know what his odds of recovery were if they waited seventy-two hours to perform it. He would do whatever it took to ensure he could recover and return to his life as quickly as possible.

"I don't want to wait on the surgery," he finally said, breaking the silence.

"It's too risky," Rose protested. "You could have another heart attack during surgery. You could—" Her voice broke.

"I know," he whispered.

"What happens if we delay the surgery?" Lanie asked, shifting her gaze between the doctor and Steven. "Will he recover?"

"I can't say for certain until the MRI results come in. Assuming his spine is severely bruised but otherwise intact, then yes, he should fully recover within six to twelve months."

Six to twelve months? "And how long will it take if we do the surgery now?" Steven asked.

Dr. Myers shook his head. "You're asking me for absolutes when I can't provide those. Every spinal injury is different. The recovery timeline is often shortened if the surgery is performed sooner, but it's impossible to determine at this stage how long recovery will take."

Once again, the room fell into silence. While Steven had made it clear what he wanted to do, he wasn't sure anyone in his family would support him. But at the end of the day, wasn't it his choice?

"Look," Dr. Myers said. "It's not even been twelve hours since the accident. The MRI results should be ready in about an hour, and then we'll know more. In the meantime, I'll leave you to discuss the options and visit with Steven. Once we have the results, we can decide which option is best."

After signaling to the nurse that it was time to go, Dr. Myers left them alone. Nobody spoke, but Steven's increasing heart rate filled the room with sound as the beeping behind him grew in intensity.

"Steven." Rose placed a hand on his shoulder. "Take a deep breath."

Instead of listening to her instruction, he pleaded with his eyes. "Only if you support my decision to go through with the surgery before the twenty-four-hour period is up."

"But—"

His sister stepped into his line of sight. "You heard what the doctor said. Let's wait until we know more before we have this discussion. For now, you should probably rest and relax." Her mouth turned down. "Well, as much as possible."

"I'll relax when you all agree to allow me to make this choice."

Rose and Lanie exchanged glances, but his father gave a quick nod. "I support you, son."

"Thanks, Dad."

Lanie sighed. "Of course it's ultimately up to you. I just wish you would wait until you have all the details so you can make an informed choice."

Though she had a point, Steven doubted there was much that could sway him. He needed to recover as soon as possible to get back to his life, his business.

A little over an hour later, Dr. Myers finally returned. Steven's anxiety had reached epic levels, and he was more than a little tired of Lanie and Rose constantly telling him to take deep breaths and calm down. As if they could be calm if they were in his position.

"So, I have good news." Dr. Myers rolled in a cart with a laptop perched on top of it. He turned the screen toward Steven and his family. "There are no tears or signs of permanent damage." Pointing at a shadow near the base of the image, he circled it with his finger. "This is where the injury is located, near the bottom of your spine. As you can see from this darker shadow, there is significant fluid building in the area. This is increasing the compression on your spinal cord, which is part of what is causing the numbness in your lower extremities." Dr. Myers glanced at the door. "Ah, Dr. Bhati, please come in."

A short man with black hair and dark eyes entered the room and nodded to Steven. He moved in front of the screen and studied it for a moment before stepping back.

"Dr. Bhati is a neurosurgeon." Dr. Myers placed a hand on Dr. Bhati's shoulder. "I've asked him to come in to review the MRI results and discuss the surgery option."

"I'm sorry to meet you all under such circumstances. I understand Dr. Myers has already explained the spinal decompression surgery option to you, and I'm sure you have questions. So why don't we start there?"

"What happens if we don't do the surgery within the first twenty-four hours?" Rose asked.

"There are two phases to spinal injuries, with the first phase occurring directly after injury and the second phase beginning a few days later. In the second phase, the body's immune system will sometimes attack the area, causing inflammation as well as a host of neurological problems." Dr. Bhati moved to Steven's side and touched his left leg. "Right now, Steven is only dealing with numbness in his lower body, caused both by the decompression and the shock to his nervous system. But in the second phase, he may start exhibiting more neurological symptoms including slow response time, increased risk of another heart attack, and a higher potential of developing multiple sclerosis."

Steven closed his eyes after hearing the grim future the neurologist had painted. To him, the decision was clear. Surgery, though risky, was worth it when put in such dire context.

"Why is surgery such a risk after a heart attack?" Lanie asked.

"It's not the surgery so much as putting a cardiac patient under anesthesia," Rose responded before either doctor had a chance to. "The heart is already weak from the recent incident, and extra precautions must be taken."

"This is a lot to take in," Dr. Bhati said. "But I assure you that I have performed this surgery several times before with a highly skilled anesthesiologist."

"I want to do it," Steven said. Rose stepped in front of him as if to stop him from speaking, but he wouldn't be deterred. "I understand the risks, but I'd rather avoid additional complications to my spine healing."

With a sigh, Rose moved to his side and patted his arm. His sister didn't look happy, but she held her tongue.

"All right," Dr. Bhati said. "We'll get you scheduled for surgery this afternoon." He glanced at the rest of Steven's family. "Until then, you should give him some time to rest."

Once the doctors were gone, Dad stepped to Steven's left side and gave him an awkward hug. "We'll be back to visit as soon as they let us."

His sister kissed his forehead. "You're either incredibly brave or incredibly stupid."

Steven chuckled. "Perhaps a bit of both?"

With a shake of her head, Lanie followed Dad out of the room. Rose held his hand tightly as if her life depended on it. When he shifted his head toward her, tears glistened in her eyes.

"It'll be okay," he said, though he wasn't sure how convincing he sounded. "I have faith in Dr. Bhati."

"He's a good doctor." But her words did nothing to erase the worry etched on her face. Leaning forward, she brushed a hand over his hair. "You must get through this. I have plans for you."

A small smile tugged at his lips. "Oh? And what plans might those be?"

She kissed his forehead. "Lifelong ones."

Chapter Four

A FEW HOURS LATER, Marie appeared and let them know that Steven was being prepped for surgery. As much as Rose wished she could assist, she had a new appreciation for the hospital's policy on treating family. If something went wrong, she wasn't sure she could handle being in the room and feeling completely helpless.

Still, sitting on the sidelines wasn't any easier. She was used to being part of the action. But at least she wasn't alone. Lanie sat beside her on the uncomfortable chairs while Max paced a trench in the carpet. Mercifully, they were the only ones in the small ICU waiting room. Despite working at the hospital for over a year, Rose had never spent time in that room. It seemed like it had been added as an afterthought. The pale-yellow walls were likely meant to be cheerful, though Rose couldn't imagine they brought much joy to anyone who had to sit there.

"Dad, you might want to take a seat," Lanie drawled. "It's going to be a while."

"I can't just sit here and do nothing." He checked his watch. "I'm going to check on what the cafeteria is serving for lunch. Do either of you want anything?"

"No, thank you," Lanie said.

Rose just shook her head. She couldn't imagine she would be able to keep food down at that point. Her stomach was a bundle of knots that she could only hope would untangle once Steven was safely out of surgery.

After Max left, Lanie turned to her. "What do you think the plan will be for his recovery? I mean, the doctors both said the surgery would speed it up, but they were rather vague on the details."

"Unfortunately, spinal injuries aren't like a broken leg. They're much more complicated and are harder to predict." Rose sighed. "It's more neurological, like a stroke."

"So it could still take six months to a year for him to be fully recovered?"

"It's possible." At Lanie's worried expression, Rose hurried on. "It might help to look at recovery as a progressive timeline rather than a deadline."

"What do you mean?"

Rose debated how to explain it. "Think of it like a baby's development. In their first few years of life, babies learn a lot of new skills. But we don't measure their development by the end goal of them turning eighteen and moving out, right? We measure it by milestones."

"Okay," Lanie said. "I understand what you're saying, but what will that look like?"

"Hmm... I would say Steven's first milestone is this surgery, which will hopefully prevent further complications and allow the healing process to begin. They'll probably put him in a back brace to keep his spine immobile until it heals." Tapping her chin, Rose channeled her training to predict what milestone he might meet next. "In a few weeks, maybe his back will have healed enough for them to remove the brace. Then he'll have some light physical therapy to maintain muscle density. Once the cast is off, he may start working toward walking again, first with crutches then maybe a cane."

"Do you think he'll be walking by the wedding?"

Rose swallowed. She'd pushed aside her concerns about the wedding to allow herself to focus on the details of Steven's diagnosis and recovery. "I guess we'll just have to wait and see."

Lanie nodded and grabbed a magazine, but Rose wasn't easily distracted. Part of her wished Lanie had never mentioned the wedding, as she didn't need to add one more worry to her already filled plate. At the same time, if Steven's recovery was expected to take longer than three months, decisions would need to be made, and the sooner the better.

"I'm going to run to the restroom," Rose said. "I'll be right back."

Once she was clear of the room, Rose bypassed the bathrooms and headed to the nurses' station on her regular floor. She was in luck. Nobody was around. Slipping into the chair, she toggled the computer on with the mouse. She'd saved their wedding contracts in the cloud so she could access them from anywhere. As she clicked through them, a growing sense of dread came over her. Each one included a deadline for canceling for a full or partial refund. Her heart sank as she realized those deadlines had long since passed.

After exiting out of the browser, she sat for a moment with her head in her hands. Perhaps she shouldn't worry yet. Dr. Bhati had said the surgery would speed up Steven's recovery, and it was early June. Maybe Steven would be much improved by the end of August.

With a heavy heart, she headed to the waiting room. Max had returned with an armful of snacks. She chose a bag of rainbow candy and tore open the corner. Maybe a little sugar would take the edge off of her anxiety.

About an hour later, Dr. Bhati finally appeared in the doorway of the waiting room. Rose rushed over to him with Lanie and Max on her heels.

"The surgery was a success," Dr. Bhati said with a weary smile. "We were able to drain the fluid, which should lower the possibility of further complications from the injury. Steven is resting comfortably now. You can see him, but I would prefer you to visit him one by one to avoid overwhelming him."

"Thank you, Doctor," Rose said, relief flooding through her.

"What happens now?" Lanie asked. "Will he be able to come home soon?"

Dr. Bhati pursed his lips. "That will depend a lot on his home environment. There are other options that we can discuss later with Steven when the anesthesia has completely worn off."

The doctor left them, and Rose resisted the urge to run to Steven's room. Although it pained her to do so, she deferred to Lanie and Max to go first. After all, she wasn't quite family.

"Why don't you go in first?" Lanie asked Rose, surprising her.

"But I thought—"

Max waved his hand. "You've been here the longest. Go see him and then go home and get some rest."

The idea of leaving the hospital while Steven was still in it didn't feel right, but Max had a point. She'd been there for well over twenty-four hours, and she was in desperate need of a shower and sleep.

With a grateful smile, she left them and headed to Steven's room. His eyes were closed when she entered, but he must have sensed her presence because he opened them a moment later.

"Rose," he croaked. "I'm still alive."

She glared at him. "Not funny." Her hands shook as she took his. "Are you feeling any better?"

"I honestly don't feel anything from my waist down."

"That'll improve over time."

Steven nodded, his eyes closing again. His breathing deepened as he fell asleep. Her need to stay with him warred with her growing exhaustion, and she squeezed his hand. When he didn't respond to her efforts to rouse him, she leaned forward and kissed his forehead. What he needed most at that moment was rest. The hospital would call her if there was any change.

"I'll come back tomorrow. I love you," she whispered.

⁓

When Rose arrived at her condo, she sat in her car and stared at the steering wheel. Though exhausted, she was also numb, like the last twenty-four hours had been a dream. The idea of going inside and having nothing but her own thoughts to comfort her was unappealing. Instead, she decided to take a walk around the grounds to enjoy the warm late-spring afternoon. As she headed to the pond near the other end of the property, a pair of swans glided gracefully into view. Their long white necks bent toward each other as if they were sharing some intimate secret.

Rose moved closer, leaning against the fence at the water's edge. The swans paid her no mind, as they were too wrapped up in each other. Their obvious love brought a pang to Rose's heart, and she wished Steven was with her to share in the moment.

"Quite the pair, aren't they?" a deep voice asked beside her.

Startled, she turned to find an older man standing knee-deep in the water. He held a fishing pole.

"They're beautiful," she said.

"At a distance, but don't get too close, or they can turn into some nasty little buggers." He smiled. "But they sure are a sight to behold when they dance."

"Dance?" Rose leaned forward, intrigued by the idea of birds dancing.

"It's a mating ritual." He cocked his head thoughtfully. "Sort of hard to explain. You'll just have to see it."

Rose nodded before returning her attention to the swans. They occasionally dipped their heads below the water before spraying it along their feathers.

A tear slipped down her cheek. *When will Steven and I be together again like the swans?* They had a long path ahead of them, and she had no idea how to traverse that road or where they would be when they reached the end. With worry weighing heavy on her mind, she headed to her condo.

The moment she entered, she sank into her favorite chair in her living room and put her head in her hands. Even with so much up in the air, Rose was clear on one thing. When Steven returned to work, he would have two new clients, including himself. The first thing they would do was draft their wills, especially a power of attorney, so the next time a situation like that occurred, they would be ready.

The next time. She shook her head. After Steven's mother passed, Rose had hoped for a reprieve for him and his family, but now *he* was in the hospital. She still couldn't wrap her head around the idea that Steven had had a heart attack. He was so young. It just didn't feel real.

Her stomach grumbled, and she reluctantly left the plush green cushions and headed to her small kitchen. It was more closet than kitchen, with just enough room for a fridge and oven on one side and a sink and dishwasher on the other. Her limited counter space was cluttered with a spice rack, a toaster, and yesterday's mail.

In no mood to cook, she removed some cheese, crackers, and a bottle of wine. Balancing them in her arms, she returned to her chair. Tears pricked behind her eyes, and she didn't even bother to fight them.

There was so much she didn't know. How long recovery would take. Where Steven would live in the meantime. Dr. Bhati had mentioned other options for when Steven was discharged, but he hadn't specified what they were. Steven's house wasn't exactly equipped for a wheelchair, and all of the beds were on the second floor.

Will he even consent to go somewhere else? While Steven was currently listening to his doctors, she knew her fiancé well enough to know he would be unhappy if anything kept him from the office for very long. In fact, she suspected that he had chosen the risky surgery because a speedy recovery would mean he could get back to work that much sooner.

After she finished her food, she settled back against the chair and sipped her wine. It had been a few days since she'd last FaceTimed with her parents. Part of her wanted to continue to put it off. They would pepper her with questions, first about the wedding, then she would have to inform them of the accident, which would bring a whole host of other concerns. She was in no mood to discuss either. Frankly, she was rather peopled out. But if she didn't call soon, then the worried texts would start.

With a sigh, she picked up her iPad and tapped the app. Plastering a smile on her face, she pressed Call.

A moment later, her mother's face filled the screen. "Rosie. It's been so long. How are you?"

"I'm good, Mom. How are things across the world?"

Her mother's eyes crinkled with her smile. "Oh, there's a lot going on here. And we're missing you, but we can get into that later. How is the wedding planning going? Are you excited for your big day?"

"Mm-hmm," Rose murmured, her lips pressed tight together. She swallowed her pain, not wanting to add to her mother's worry. Her parents had enough stress in their lives caring for her aging grandparents.

She racked her brain to recall the last wedding-related thing she and Steven had done. "We chose the menu for the reception and cake flavors. I'm meeting with the wedding coordinator in a few days to go over the details for the invitations, which should be sent soon."

"Ah, I wish we could be there," her mother said, a wistful note in her voice. "How's Steven? Is he helping with the preparations?"

Rose's thin hold on her emotions broke, and she burst into tears. Her hands flew to her face, but it was too late.

"What's wrong?" her mother asked. "Did something happen?"

"Steven is—" Her voice caught, and she cleared her throat. "He was in a car accident and is in the hospital." Saying the words out loud gave them power.

"Oh my goodness. Is he all right? Why aren't you with him?"

Rose shook her head. "He's... stable." She proceeded to explain what she knew of his condition. Focusing on the familiar medical terminology helped her regain control of her emotions. "I was with him earlier, but I had to come home. When I return tomorrow, they should know more about the next steps."

"When did this happen?"

"Late last night. I'm sorry I didn't have a chance to call you sooner. I've been at the hospital and—"

Her mother waved her hand. "It's fine. You were where you needed to be." She took a deep breath and frowned. "How will this impact the wedding?"

With a sigh, Rose shrugged. "I honestly don't know. Things have been too crazy here. I haven't had time to consider it."

"Is there anything we can do?"

"I doubt it." Rose rested her chin on her hand and studied her mother's face. Moments like that reminded her how much she missed her mother. "You're on the other side of the world."

Her mother raised an eyebrow. "We have friends in the States. They could bring you food, keep you company."

Spending time with virtual strangers wasn't much of a substitute for her parents, but she appreciated the sentiment.

"Lanie and Max were with me. And several of my coworkers brought me food."

"I'm glad you weren't alone." Her mother rubbed her chin. "And Steven is young. He'll heal quickly and be walking again before you know it. Everything is already arranged, right?"

"Yes. With the wedding only three months away, we're only paying the balances due at this point, but between Steven's hospital bills and the fact that he won't be bringing in any money while he's not working, I'm not sure how we'll afford it."

Mom's brow furrowed. "I wish we could send you money—"

"Nonsense. You've got enough on your plate with Grandma and Grandpa. How are they doing?"

"Not well." Her mother sighed. "Your father and I have been discussing finding a placement for them."

"Can you afford that?" From Rose's understanding, the long-term care insurance in South Korea covered more of the cost of a nursing home than insurance did in the US, but it was still expensive.

"I believe so, though it'll be tight." Mom bit her lip. "Actually, that was something I've been meaning to discuss with you."

Something about her mother's demeanor filled Rose with dread. "What's wrong?"

"I'm afraid we won't be able to come to your wedding. Between the nursing home costs and the rising prices for flights, I just don't see how we can swing it."

Could this day get any worse? Fresh tears welled in Rose's eyes, and she struggled to blink them back. Though she'd wondered how her parents would manage her grandparents' care if they were gone for the wedding, it never occurred to her they wouldn't be able to afford to come.

"I understand," Rose whispered.

"But maybe once things are settled, you and Steven can visit us."

"Yeah, maybe." The words sounded hollow. "I should go. I have an early shift tomorrow."

"Should you be working with everything going on?"

The idea of not working hadn't even crossed Rose's mind. With Lisa's daughter still sick, they were short-staffed. And she was going to the hospital anyway to check on Steven.

"I need to maintain some sense of normalcy," Rose said, hoping that sounded convincing enough.

"All right, then. Give our best to Steven and take care of yourself."

"I will. Love you, Mom."

She ended the call and leaned back in the chair, staring at the ceiling. In the span of thirty-six hours, her dream wedding had crumbled before her eyes. First Steven's accident then her mother's bombshell news that her parents weren't coming.

Maybe we should just postpone. She dismissed the thought as soon as it occurred. It was too late to cancel without risking losing all of their deposits and then some. Besides, it seemed selfish to postpone the wedding just because her parents couldn't make it when Steven had lost his mother only a year ago.

The financial aspect was a separate issue but one she and Steven could figure out. At least, that was what she kept telling herself.

Chapter Five

"I'VE CALLED YOU HERE today because we need to discuss next steps," Dr. Myers began.

Steven struggled to draw breath with all the bodies wedged in around his bed. His room in the ICU hadn't appeared so small until his family, Rose, and several members of the medical staff crowded in. He shifted uncomfortably in the tight quarters. At least his neck brace had been removed.

"We've been monitoring Steven since his surgery, and I'm pleased with the progress he's made. If things continue to look up, we plan to move him tomorrow." Dr. Myers gestured to Dr. Bhati, who stood beside him near the door.

"With Steven potentially transferring out of the ICU, it's time to start discussing next steps," Dr. Bhati said.

"What do you suggest?" Rose asked from Steven's right side.

Dr. Bhati frowned. "That will depend on what sort of living arrangement is available to Steven. His injuries will restrict his mobility, even once we're able to move him to a wheelchair. He'll need a lot of assistance, especially in the beginning as he's learning how to compensate for his limited abilities."

"He lives alone." Dad rested a hand on the left-hand bed rail. "In a two-story house where the beds are on the second floor."

"That presents a problem," Dr. Myers said. "Even if his mobility wasn't limited, I wouldn't want him climbing the stairs for a few weeks while his heart heals."

"Can a hospital bed be set up downstairs?" Dr. Bhati asked.

Steven scowled. The last thing he wanted was to continue sleeping in an uncomfortable bed once he was home.

"He could stay with me," Rose suggested. "I have a first-floor condo and a guest room with a twin bed." She glanced at Steven before continuing, "The doors are wide enough for the wheelchair, but the bathroom isn't ADA compliant."

"What about your house, Dad?" Lanie asked. "Could he stay in the den downstairs?"

"It'd be a tight fit for the wheelchair." Dad scratched the back of his head.

Dr. Bhati raised his hand. "These are all good suggestions, but I have another you might consider." After sharing a quick glance with Dr. Myers, Dr. Bhati cleared his throat. "There is a wonderful rehabilitation center just down the road. Dr. Myers and I can easily visit with Steven to keep up to date on his progress."

Rehab? Steven couldn't believe what he was hearing. While he understood his injuries required some drastic lifestyle changes, he hadn't imagined he would be forced to go to *another* medical facility after his discharge from the hospital.

"I can't go to rehab," he protested. "I want to go home."

Dr. Myers blew out an exasperated breath. "Steven, you have a broken leg and a bruised spine, which means you won't be walking for the foreseeable future." He gestured to Rose and Steven's family. "Based on what your family has said, there isn't anywhere you can stay that will meet your needs. If we can't get you the care you require, how do you expect to return home?"

Steven crossed his arms carefully, mindful of both the IV sticking out of his right arm and the bandage over his heart. Truthfully, he didn't have an answer to Dr. Myers's question, but he wasn't going to give the doctor the satisfaction of admitting that.

"Why don't we agree to two weeks?" Dr. Bhati suggested. "It will give you more time to heal and learn how to function with your temporary disabilities. Then we can reassess at that point."

"Are you able to give a better prognosis for how long the paralysis will last?" Rose asked.

Dr. Bhati shook his head. "Draining the fluid helped significantly, but it's difficult to tell the extent of the bruising. We'll run another MRI this afternoon to try to get a better idea. But regardless, he'll need extensive physical therapy, which he unfortunately can't start until his leg heals. The next six months are going to be critical for Steven's recovery."

"And you'll need to make some changes to your lifestyle," Dr. Myers added. "Consider this heart attack a warning. If you don't take care of yourself, it may be worse next time."

"Next time?" Lanie's voice sounded strangled.

"Having a heart attack can increase the likelihood of another one, but there are ways to avoid it."

"Don't worry, Doc," Dad said. "We'll make sure he does what needs doing to get back on his feet."

"If we're in agreement on the rehabilitation center"—Dr. Bhati gave a meaningful look to his patient—"then I can call over there this afternoon to request a bed for Steven. Assuming everything goes well, we may be able to transfer him by the end of this week."

Rose, Lanie, and Dad turned toward Steven. With a sigh of resignation, he nodded.

"I'll go to rehab for two weeks on one condition."

Lanie raised an eyebrow. "Which is?"

He pointed at her. "That you bring me work updates every day so my business doesn't go under."

Rose opened her mouth as if to protest, but Lanie put a hand on her arm to stop her. With pursed lips, Lanie appeared to mull over his request. For a moment, he worried she would say no, but she finally gave him a small smile and a quick nod.

"Fine, but only if you promise to follow the doctors' orders religiously."

"Deal." Steven breathed a little easier. If he could catch up on work while he was in rehab, perhaps he could save his business after all.

Dr. Myers frowned in disapproval before he and Dr. Bhati left. Lanie and Dad followed them out into the hallway, likely to get more information on the rehab facility.

Only Rose remained. At first, she stared at the floor, refusing to meet his gaze. But when she finally looked at him, he was taken aback by the warring anger and fear in her eyes. His stomach clenched as he worried what he might have just sacrificed to save his livelihood.

Steven slept fitfully that night. Despite his exhaustion, he couldn't turn his mind off. Thoughts raced through his head. *How long until I walk again? How am I going to keep my practice going while I'm stuck here? What will happen to my clients?* And the question he didn't dare speak aloud but that encompassed his greatest fear. *Will Rose change her mind about marrying me if I lose everything?*

That last one caused a pain in his chest that had nothing to do with the heart attack or his accident. He'd been looking forward to marrying her for so long. He wanted to start their lives together, and the accident had proved to him that they had no time to waste. Life was short, and he didn't want to lose another moment. They'd planned to start trying for a family soon after the honeymoon. The thought of losing all of that caused an ache that no amount of medication could ease.

Seeing the hurt in her eyes after the doctors left had almost broken through his resolve. He'd agreed to the two weeks in rehab in hopes of softening the blow, but it didn't appear to have had the desired effect. But she knew how important his business was to him—to both of them. Their future depended on its survival, and to ensure the firm survived, he needed those two weeks to fly by so he could return to his office.

Which was likely her other concern. She hadn't brought up him hiring help again, but he suspected it was on her mind. And if he were honest, he could admit bringing on someone to assist with his cases would help lighten his load during his recovery. But he adamantly refused to take on a partner.

Maybe he could hire a law clerk. They worked for dirt cheap, more for the experience than the money. Hiring one would alleviate some of his workload while not costing as much as a partner, which would ease Rose's concerns that he was working too hard without bankrupting his practice. It was a win-win.

The door opened, and a new nurse shuffled into the room. She murmured her apologies for waking him before tying a rubber band around his arm and waiting for a vein to appear. He stifled a sigh. Even if he hadn't been kept up by his own brain, a hospital wasn't the easiest place to rest. The nurses came in several times during the night, and at least one of those visits involved getting a blood sample. His arm was going to be awfully sore when he was finally released.

When the sun peeked through the blinds, he sighed in relief. *Survived another night.* With a shake of his head, he chastised himself for such morbid thoughts. As far as he could tell, he was much improved, and he hoped that meant he would be discharged soon.

The door to his room opened. He sat up, expecting Rose, but instead, his sister entered. She carried a bag over her shoulder and greeted him with a smile.

"Oh good, you're awake." After sliding the bag down her arm, she set it on the bed and removed stacks of paper. "I stopped by your office this morning and spoke to Sandra. She sends you get-well wishes."

He harrumphed, though it came out more as a groan. Lanie didn't seem to notice as she set up various piles on his bed.

"I asked her to help me pull together your most pressing cases so we can determine what needs to be done and how we can do it."

"Thank you," he said as he shifted to sit up in bed. Pain shot through his body from the incision in his back, and he winced.

Lanie put a hand on his shoulder and helped prop him up while she adjusted his pillows. It didn't help, as it was next to impossible to get comfortable after his surgery, but he appreciated the attempt.

"Have you given any more thought to taking on a partner?" she asked.

"No, but I considered hiring a law clerk."

"And that's going to be enough?"

He shrugged. "Maybe."

"What can I do in the meantime? The kids go on summer break next week, and I'll join them a week later. I can pitch in to help if you'll point me in the right direction."

His eyebrows shot up, and he gave an incredulous laugh. "You? What do you know about working in a law office?"

"Hey!" She put her hands on her hips. "I manage unruly children all day. How much harder could it be to corral your clients?"

He thought of Mr. Willoughby and shook his head. "You have no idea."

"Look." She leveled him with a fierce gaze. "You need to reduce your stress level, and I'm offering to do what I can to help with that. If you're not willing to cut back on your hours or hire an attorney with experience, then I suspect you'll be back in this very hospital in a month or less." Her hazel eyes darkened. "Or worse."

He wondered what he could trust her to handle. She'd just finished working through their mother's estate, and he had a couple of clients preparing for probate. Perhaps she could help there.

"Interested in dead people?"

Her eyes widened, and she faltered back a step. When she recovered from his strangely worded question, she stared at him. "You have more estate clients?"

He nodded. "Your experience with Mom's estate may come in handy. If nothing else, you can hold their hand and help them through probate." Lifting his left hand, he wagged a finger. "But no legal advice. You're not qualified."

Her teeth worried her lower lip as she appeared to consider his request. For a moment, he thought she would refuse, and he couldn't blame her if she did. She'd hated being the executor of their mother's estate. They'd once wondered why their mother chose her when Steven, the lawyer, was the obvious choice. Later, he'd suspected it was the only way their mother could guarantee Lanie would return to her hometown and Nate, her fiancé, would keep the promise he'd made to tell Lanie the truth about Mom's involvement in their breakup. It had all worked out in the end, but if Lanie wasn't in a hurry to get back into the world of trusts and estates, he completely understood.

As he opened his mouth to tell her to forget it, she squared her shoulders. "All right. I'll do it." She twirled a blond lock of hair around her finger. "I'll do my best."

"That's all I ask."

"Before we delve into this stack of papers, Sandra insisted I give you this note." Lanie handed him a piece of paper with a phone message scribbled on it.

Steven rolled his eyes because of course it was from his least-favorite client. Mr. Willoughby was demanding Steven contact him the moment he was back in the office. Sandra had added her own colorful language, detailing her conversation with Mr. Willoughby. She'd tried to offer her assistance, but the client had insisted he must speak to Steven.

"It's my most demanding client," Steven finally said, figuring that sounded more diplomatic than calling Mr. Willoughby a pain in his rear end. "He's still sore at me for hanging up on him the other day when I was on my way out the door."

"Doesn't he know you're in the hospital?"

"I have no idea what Sandra told him." Steven sighed. "But I doubt she would have informed him of my medical issues. She probably said I was out of the office for the foreseeable future."

"Well, I can call him if you'd like—"

Waving his hand, Steven shook his head. "No, that'll probably just rile him up more. I'll deal with him later." He gestured to the papers in her hand. "Let's see what you brought for me."

She gave him a dubious look, and he imagined she was wondering what Rose would say. But she nodded and began handing him documents.

For an hour, they went through the paperwork, with Steven dictating the next steps in each case. By the time Lanie left, Steven's confidence in the state of his law practice had increased, except for the matter of Mr. Willoughby. While nothing would replace going into the office to get work done, he was glad he could handle some of it remotely. He just hoped he could keep up with it all.

Chapter Six

"STEVEN IS BEING TRANSFERRED from ICU this afternoon," Dr. Myers said.

Rose looked up from her chart. "What time?"

He shrugged. "It depends on when they can find him a bed and get him moved, but I would imagine around lunchtime." When she didn't respond, he raised an eyebrow. "You can take your break then if you want."

As much as she knew she should visit him, part of her didn't want to. As if his reaction to being discharged to a rehab facility wasn't bad enough, he'd then had the audacity to ask his sister to bring work by on a daily basis—right after Dr. Myers had told him he needed to take it easy or risk another heart attack. Though she tried to see things from Steven's perspective, she couldn't help being frustrated. Was he in denial about the reality of his situation?

She understood his desire to go home. He was getting restless after being cooped up in the hospital. And the idea of continuing that existence probably sounded like a prison sentence to him. But throwing himself back into work when he was still healing wasn't going to get him out of a facility any faster. In fact, if he didn't give himself time to heal, his stay might just be extended.

With a forced smile, Rose nodded. "Thanks, Dr. Myers. I'll do that."

He leaned back, assessing her. "Trouble in the love nest?"

"Not at all," she said with feigned sweetness. "We all want him to get better so he can come home."

"It should only be a couple more days here, assuming everything goes well." His expression turned stern. "But I wouldn't expect him to be home anytime soon, and the recovery is likely to take months, if not longer."

"I know." Her tone hardened as her patience wore thin. *Who does this guy think he is?* Like she didn't understand how varied the recovery timeline could be for heart attack survivors, let alone the other injuries Steven had sustained.

"Oh, I have no doubt *you* understand, but does he?"

She glowered at the doctor. "I will ensure he follows all of your advice."

To her surprise, he laughed before turning to leave, calling over his shoulder, "Good luck with that."

"What's that supposed to mean?" she demanded, her hands on her hips.

Glancing at her with an impish grin, he said, "Just that I've seen his type before. Workaholics don't like to be kept away from the thing they love most."

"That shows how well you know him." She stomped away, heading to the nurses' station. His laughter followed her down the hall.

Her irritation rose when she realized Dr. Myers was right. Steven was a workaholic, and he'd already demonstrated that he would resist the changes his doctors had suggested he make. Rose sighed, leaning against the wall. Convincing him to take it easy would be a battle, but she was ready for it. At least, she hoped she was.

But she didn't need to worry about it yet. Steven would be in the hospital for a few more days. With that in mind, she started her rounds, all while mentally preparing herself for when she saw Steven again.

At lunchtime, Rose went up to the ICU and was surprised to find Steven already gone. The nurse at the station gave her his new room number, and she took the stairs to his floor.

Steven was propped up in his bed when she entered, watching something on the television on the opposite wall. His room already had several flower arrangements set up on the limited furniture, and the scent reminded her unnervingly of a funeral home. She knocked lightly on the door, and he turned toward her with a lopsided smile. His face still had angry scratches from where it'd been cut by glass, and a bruise bloomed on his forehead. But they'd removed the IV from his arm.

"How do you like the new digs?" he asked.

The tension in her shoulders eased as she took in his expression. No furrowed brow, no sense of frustration. Maybe moving out of the ICU was what he needed.

"Much less restrictive." She stepped over to his bedside and took his hand. "How do you feel?"

"Not as bad as yesterday." He gestured to his lunch tray. "Is the food served here different? It sure tastes better."

Rose laughed. "It all comes from the same place."

"Maybe it's just that I'm that much closer to freedom."

"You've got a few more days," she warned, trying to keep her tone light.

He waved a dismissive hand. "I'm hoping to be released early for good behavior."

"That's not really how it works." Panic swirled in her gut. "And even if that were true, you agreed to two weeks of inpatient rehab."

His face contorted. "Yeah, definitely not looking forward to that. But I'm not worried."

That made one of them. Swallowing her fears, Rose pulled a chair over and set her lunch box on her lap.

He peered at it. "What are you eating?"

"My usual ham sandwich."

His face clouded. "They won't let me have any meat. Can you believe that?"

"It's temporary," she assured him. "They'll start varying your diet more the better you do in recovery. But don't expect to have steak anytime soon. Red meat isn't good for your cholesterol."

"I *know*," he snapped.

Stop nagging him. He's been through enough. "I'm sorry."

He heaved a sigh. "No, I'm the one who should be sorry." He held out his hand, and she slid hers into it. "I know things are going to have to change, but sometimes, it's a lot to take in. One minute, I'm young and healthy, and the next, I almost die."

"We'll get through it, I promise."

"I don't know what I'd do without you," he said, and the warmth she'd seen earlier returned to his eyes.

"Same here," she said, her throat thick with emotion. The knowledge of how close she'd come to losing him weighed heavily on her heart. Clearing her throat, she tried a lighter tone. "But in order for me to not have to find out, I'm gonna need you to take it easy."

Closing his eyes, he nodded. "I'll do my best."

She squeezed his hand. "That's all I can ask for."

His breathing slowed as he fell asleep. She leaned forward and kissed his forehead before returning to work. At least while he was in the hospital, she found it easier to check on him. She also found comfort in the fact that he was limited in what he could get away with there. Things would be a little more relaxed in rehab, but once they discharged him home, she wouldn't be able to keep as close an eye on him. She suspected he would go right back to working himself into an early grave.

Rose drummed her fingers on the table as she stared at the door to Bea's Diner, willing Lanie to walk through it. The longer she sat there waiting, the more she feared she might lose her nerve. Usually, the restaurant was comforting, with its nostalgic 1950s theme and the familiar scent of fried food, but not even the swaying Elvis figure on the wall or the miniature jukebox on the table could distract her that day.

When a familiar blond head cleared the entryway and swiveled to look for her, Rose breathed a sigh of relief before waving her friend over. Lanie smiled and slid into the booth opposite Rose, setting her purse beside her.

"So, what's up?" Lanie asked as she opened a menu, though Rose couldn't imagine why. Her future sister-in-law had been coming to the place her entire life, and as far as she could tell, the options hadn't changed in that time. "More wedding details?"

"Actually, I wanted to discuss that with you." Rose hated how hesitant her voice sounded. She squared her shoulders. "I think we should postpone the wedding."

Lanie's eyes widened. "What? Why?"

"We don't know how long Steven's recovery will take, and it's smarter to start taking action now rather than move forward in the hopes he'll be recovered enough to go through with it." Rose removed her tablet from her bag and tapped the screen until she reached the document that contained their vendor contact information. "I figure between the two of us, we can call everyone this week and—"

Lanie raised her hand. "Wait. Have you talked to Steven about this?"

"Not yet," Rose admitted, dropping her gaze. "I didn't want to add to his stress level. But honestly, postponing the wedding will help alleviate his stress. Then he can focus on healing."

"Except that it may be more stressful for him if you postpone."

Rose frowned. "How do you figure that?"

"I know my brother," Lanie replied with a shrug.

"But he hasn't actually said that, has he?" Worry gnawed away at Rose's gut, but she worked to keep her expression neutral.

"Not in so many words, but he has seemed rather preoccupied with something lately. I thought it was the law firm, but I spent a good hour going over his cases with him yesterday." Lanie frowned. "While he was in better spirits by the time I left, I could tell something else was on his mind." Her hazel eyes narrowed. "You need to talk to him before you do anything."

The mood at the table shifted, and Rose struggled to regain control of the situation. "I'll discuss it with him, but don't you think it would be better if I could tell him I was taking care of it? Then he'd have less to—"

"No. Going behind his back isn't going to help. You need to have a frank discussion with him." Lanie's tone softened. "I know you didn't come to this decision lightly, and I'm sure Steven will understand that."

"You think he'll agree to postpone?" Rose was unable to keep the skepticism out of her voice.

Grinning, Lanie shook her head. "Of course not, but he might at least appreciate a well-reasoned argument." When Rose didn't respond, Lanie leaned forward. "Look, I agree with you that he has a lot of stress, and the wedding planning is unlikely to help, but before you go trying to convince him, I'd like to propose a counterpoint. It's early in Steven's recovery, and we don't know enough at this point to make such a decision. What would you say to monitoring the situation and deciding what to do in a couple of weeks? At the very least, we could talk to Carissa to get her opinion. She might have an idea of how to approach the vendors to give them a heads-up."

"I just hate to leave things up in the air. If it was only the heart attack *or* the spinal contusion alone, that would be one thing. But patient recovery is often unique to each individual. I'm not sure if we'll get a clear timeline, and the wedding is in almost three months."

Lanie pursed her lips. "Are you sure there aren't other reasons you might want to postpone?

That caught Rose off guard. "What other reasons would there be?"

Her future sister-in-law shrugged. "Maybe you're concerned about what Steven will be like once he's released from rehab. How it might place you in a caregiving role again."

Rose swallowed, reminded of the comment her patient had made about her being the perfect candidate to care for Steven. Although there was a trace of truth in Lanie's words, Rose shook her head.

"All I want is for Steven to focus on recovering, and I believe postponing the wedding will help him to do that."

For a moment, Lanie studied her, then she nodded, seeming to accept Rose's explanation. "I agree. But you should still talk to Steven before you do anything. I'll even try to help him see reason." She bit her lip. "Just as long as you remember, his whole world—both of your worlds—have been turned upside down. It's not a bad idea to take some time and let the dust settle before rushing to a decision."

Rose nodded. "I can agree with that."

Lanie turned her attention back to the menu. "Let's discuss our options with Carissa first. Once we have a clearer picture, we can go from there."

* * *

The next day, Rose walked into the hospital with her heart pounding in her chest. With Carissa's help, she and Lanie had contacted all of the vendors and had a better understanding of the situation with the wedding. Their responses, though not unexpected, were disappointing.

Most had pointed to the contract and the deadline for cancellation, which had already passed. If she canceled now, she would lose her deposits, which were too large to swallow. The one bright light was many of the vendors were willing to work with her on a postponement using what had already been paid to secure a new date. However, the vendors weren't willing to commit to altering the contract itself until the new date was determined. They all sympathized with her, but sympathy went only so far.

The only place that had extended her a month's grace period to decide was the church. She supposed they were doing Steven and her a favor since he'd been a member of the congregation since childhood.

Though Lanie had cautioned her against talking to Steven about a postponement while he was in the hospital, Rose had decided to go ahead with the conversation. It didn't seem appropriate to wait until he was discharged to the rehab facility. She hoped he would listen to reason. Her arguments were sound, and she'd even chosen a few potential dates for next summer.

But she wouldn't settle on one until they had a better sense of Steven's prognosis or until she spoke with her mother. She hadn't mentioned the possibility of buying her parents' plane tickets herself because she didn't want to risk upsetting anyone. It still felt selfish to postpone the wedding so her parents could attend, and she didn't want people to think her parents were her driving motivation to postpone. Because they weren't. Steven's recovery was her main focus. Yet the more she considered it, the more she hated the idea of her parents not being there for the wedding.

When she entered Steven's room, he was watching television. As he turned his head, his face lit up in such a way that it broke her heart, and she faltered in her resolve. But they needed to have that discussion, and with the wedding date rapidly approaching, the time to decide had arrived.

"I missed you yesterday," he said as she kissed his cheek in greeting. "I thought you'd stop by after work."

"I had a few things to take care of, but I wanted to see you before my shift this afternoon." She nervously pushed a lock of hair behind her ear. "We need to talk."

"The dreaded words," Steven joked, then his smile fell. "What's wrong?"

Steeling herself for his reaction, she took a deep breath and met his gaze. "I want to postpone the wedding."

Several emotions flitted across his bruised face. His eyebrows jumped up in surprise before furrowing with concern. As the reality of what she'd said sank in, his lips turned down, and his eyes widened. "No, Rose, I—"

"Let me finish!" She raised her hands to stop him before he could derail her carefully rehearsed speech. "We don't know what will happen with your recovery or how long it will take. And we're losing money every day you're in here." He opened his mouth as if to protest, but she hurried on, determined to show him she'd considered his counterarguments. "It's not just that you're not working right now." She waved a hand around the room. "The hospital bills are going to be high as well." *Thanks for nothing, US health care.* "We have enough on our plates right now without throwing the wedding into the mix. It makes sense to postpone until things are better. That way, you can focus on your recovery."

"But we've already put so much work and money into planning this wedding. At this point, we're just making final payments to the vendors, aren't we?"

"Yes, but with what? I can't afford to pay for it all myself on my salary, and since you don't have a partner, there's no one who can cover for you while you recover."

"We could ask our families for—"

"We agreed we would pay for this ourselves," Rose retorted. "And I don't need to remind you my parents are struggling to make ends meet as it is on the other side of the world. My mom told me they're putting my grandparents into a nursing home, and the last thing they should be worrying about is funding our wedding."

"I understand, but I'm sure my dad would be more than willing to contribute—er—loan us the money in the meantime."

Her facial expression must have caused him to change direction. But she shook her head. "We can't guarantee we'd be able to honor that loan. What if the law firm doesn't survive without you? That's not something I'm willing to risk or how I want to start our lives together." Without waiting for a response, she continued, "Now, Carissa and I have spoken to our vendors, and most of them are willing to honor the deposits we've made on a new date, provided they're available."

"So, that's it, then?" His voice was filled with pain. "You no longer want to marry me?"

Her heart sank, and she put her hand to her chest. "Of course I want to marry you!"

"Then why wait? If money's a concern, we can cancel some of the more extravagant aspects of the wedding and have a simpler affair." He grabbed her hand and pulled her toward him. "I just want to marry you. I don't want to wait another year to start our lives together."

"It's not that simple, Steven." After rummaging through her bag, she removed a folder filled with vendor contracts and shoved them into his hand. "You're a lawyer, so I know you understand contract law. If we cancel now, we forfeit what we've paid. And in some instances, we'd still have to fulfill our financial obligation regardless of whether we cancel or not."

His heartbroken face caused a chink in the armor of her resolve. Maybe Lanie was right. Maybe postponing the wedding would cause him more stress than forging ahead. But she couldn't see how that was possible when nobody knew what his recovery would look like.

She took a deep breath and pressed on. "Whereas, if we postpone, we might be able to salvage what we've already paid."

They were silent for a moment as she allowed her words to sink in. She hoped he would understand she wasn't backing out of their engagement or putting a pause on their relationship, just the wedding itself.

Finally, Steven sagged back against the bed and stared at the ceiling. "It's still early days. Why don't we wait to make any decisions about this until we know more?"

"I don't think—"

"You said the last day to cancel for a refund has passed, right?" He turned his head so he could look at her.

She nodded. "The only place that isn't holding us to that is the church."

"At least that's something." He sighed. "But if we're already beyond the cancellation date, what would it hurt to wait and see how things go? Maybe my recovery won't take as long as Dr. Myers expects it to."

"We can only hope." Her teeth worried her lower lip. Part of her wasn't ready to give up the fight. First, she wasn't sure the vendors would honor what they'd told her over the phone if she and Steven waited too long to make a decision. And second, she had been so sure he would concede to her arguments that she hadn't considered the very real possibility her wedding would go forward without any of her family there.

But all of her reasons to postpone evaporated as she took in the pleading expression on his face. He'd been through so much, and she couldn't bear to put him through any more pain, even if she believed it was for his own good.

"Please, Rose, just give it a bit more time."

No! She wanted to scream it, but instead, she nodded again, knowing that wasn't the answer he needed.

"And we're okay?"

Her heart panged at the doubt in his voice. "Of course. We're better than okay. Postponing had nothing to do with us and everything to do with aiding you in getting better." She cupped his cheek. "I love you."

"I love you too." He pulled her face down and brushed his lips against hers. "Promise me you'll talk to me first before you do anything."

She rubbed his nose with hers. "I promise." Straightening up, she smoothed her uniform. "I'll come back on my lunch break."

"I can't wait."

As she left the room, she prayed she wouldn't have to break that promise.

Chapter Seven

A KNOCK STARTLED STEVEN awake, and he opened his eyes to find an unfamiliar woman smiling at him. Her eyes were a bright green, and her dark hair was pulled back in a bun. It took him a moment to remember where he was, but when he did, he internally groaned.

He'd hoped the transfer from the ICU meant he would be discharged soon, but three days later and he was still stuck in the hospital. While he was sleeping better than when he'd been attached to a bunch of machines, he missed his comfortable bed at home.

"More tests?" he grumbled, not caring whether he was coherent.

"Worse," the woman said, rolling a cart forward. She typed on the laptop that sat precariously on top of the cart before shoving it to the side and moving beside him. "I'm Lacey Carter, your physical therapist."

Steven smiled, which apparently caught Lacey off guard. But he took a visit from a physical therapist as a good sign. He must be improving if they were going to start helping him regain his ability to move. And he would gladly take physical therapy over being poked and prodded with needles any day.

It took effort, but he shimmied into a more upright position, though his paralysis made it difficult. He hoped by the end of the session he would have a better idea of when he could expect to walk again.

"Where do we start?" he asked, eager to learn.

Her eyebrows pinched together as she studied him. "First, I like to learn what my client's goals are."

He appreciated that she hadn't called him a patient. "I want to be able to walk again. The sooner the better."

When she tilted her head, some of his enthusiasm deflated. *Is she going to tell me the odds are against me?* But she hadn't even examined him yet to determine what he was capable of. *Has Dr. Myers told her something? Or is my broken leg going to be a deterrent?*

"Yes, that's what most people focus on, but we need to start smaller. That can be an overall goal you can work toward over the next few months, but—"

There was that word again. *Months.* Sometimes he wondered if the surgery had even been worth it. While he understood the complications that might have arisen if they hadn't drained the fluid from his spine, the fact that he was still facing months of recovery left a bitter taste in his mouth.

Besides, it didn't make sense to him. Once his leg and back healed, he would regain feeling in both legs. He didn't understand why he couldn't just pick up and start walking like he had before. Surely his body couldn't really *forget* how to walk in such a short amount of time.

As if reading his mind, she sighed. "Relearning to walk as an adult isn't the same as learning to walk as a baby. The damage to your spine has blocked the neural pathways between the lower half of your body and your brain. So it will take time both for your spine to heal and for your body to reestablish that connection." She gestured to his cast. "And until this leg is out of the cast, you're going to be limited in what exercises you can do. I'm here to help you maintain the muscle and dexterity to walk on your good leg."

"Oh," he said. It was as if he'd watched a balloon filled with his hope get torpedoed to smithereens. He worried what that would mean for his business. But that wasn't the only concern that plagued the dark corners of his mind. Try as he might to ignore it, he couldn't help wondering how that would impact his relationship with Rose.

The fear was unfounded. Aside from her suggestion that they postpone the wedding, she'd shown no signs of having second thoughts about him or their impending marriage. Even when she'd brought up postponing, she'd insisted she was only concerned about his health and stress level. And yet... Ever since his parents had divorced, he'd believed their marriage fell apart because his father failed to pull his weight. While he'd brought in enough money, Dad hadn't contributed much to the housework until it was too late.

The last thing Steven wanted was to have a similar dynamic with Rose, even temporarily. And she'd already been through so much after helping Lanie with his mother during her final months. The idea of Rose becoming a caregiver again, especially for him, made his stomach turn. That wasn't at all how he'd envisioned them starting their lives together.

Lacey patted his arm, pulling him from his thoughts. "I know it's a lot to take in, but we've developed exercises to keep your muscles in good working order during recovery. It takes time."

Time. The one thing he didn't have a lot of if he had any hope of saving his business—or his relationship, for that matter.

"For now," she continued when he didn't respond, "I'm going to show you some exercises you can do to maintain function in your good leg. How does that sound?"

Steven inclined his head in his attempt at a nod, though all of his motivation had turned to dust. At the rate they were going, he would be lucky to be back at work by Christmas, let alone walking by then.

"I have good news for you today, Steven," Dr. Myers said as he waltzed into the room. "We're releasing you to the inpatient rehab facility. Your transport will arrive this afternoon."

Steven forced a smile. "Great!" And it was, sort of. Progress was progress, he supposed, but it felt like he was leaving one prison and heading to another. "When can I go home?"

That was the wrong question. Dr. Myers glared down his nose at Steven. "As I've told you several times, there is no way to predict your recovery." His expression softened. "But I'm happy to report a decrease in the amount of swelling around your spine. You need to be a little more patient."

I guess that's the most I'm going to get. Steven nodded and returned his attention to whatever mindless soap opera was playing on television. Ever since he'd woken up after his accident, he'd heard repeatedly how unpredictable spinal cord injuries could be. The nonanswer about what to expect during his recovery was getting old. *How hard is it to give a more definitive answer? Is this why they call it "practicing" medicine?* Because doctors were always learning.

He wasn't being fair, especially since most lawyers said they "practiced" law too. There was always some new law to learn, some new case that might provide nuance to a problem a client faced. So he could hardly blame doctors for their inability to predict the future, although that didn't make it any less frustrating.

But the doctor was right—he had made progress over the last week. They'd moved on from cold compresses to a back brace to keep his spine immobilized while it healed. There was still pain, but he managed it better with pain relievers than he could days ago when he'd first met the physical therapist. And he'd come to enjoy his physical therapy sessions, much to his surprise.

As if summoned by his thoughts, Lacey appeared in the doorway. "Ready for another session?"

He winked. "I'm ready for my daily torture appointment."

Lacey laughed as she lowered the rail on his bed and helped him sit on the edge of the mattress. "I know it's painful, but believe me, it'll be worth it."

Gritting his teeth, as any movement aggravated the healing incision on his chest, he worked through the motions of the physical therapy. Some of the feeling was returning to his legs, which was more muscle twitches and flutters. Still, it was more than he'd felt directly after the accident.

"I hear you're leaving us today," Lacey continued when he didn't respond. She lifted his right leg and bent it.

"They're discharging me to rehab."

She must have heard something in his voice because she looked up. "It's not as bad as it sounds. Think of it as similar to what we do here but with a team that's dedicated to your recovery, not just getting you stabilized." After she set down his leg, she held out her hands, and he grabbed them to gently pull himself up onto one leg. "Besides, I hear they have better food."

A laugh bubbled up in his throat, and she shot him a grin. As much as he hated being cooped up in the hospital, he had to admit he would miss her.

"I bet the PT there isn't as awesome as you are."

"Aw, you're my favorite too." She leaned forward and stage-whispered, "But don't tell anyone else."

When the session was over, he was surprised to find Lanie, Rose, and his father enter his room. Lanie and Rose came to either side of his bed and took his hands, but Dad stayed near the door, looking as uncomfortable as ever.

"The hospital has agreed to let us assist with the transport and get you settled in," Rose explained.

Steven nodded, but before he could respond, several attendants came in. One handed Lanie and Dad some paperwork, which he assumed was his discharge papers. Two others moved to his bed with a wheelchair. He resisted the urge to glare at it.

It took both attendants to lift and transfer him to the chair. Rose dutifully took her place behind him and began to push. He hadn't been out of his room except when more tests were needed, and Steven relished the cool air of the hallway. The elevator, on the other hand, jostled him more than he liked, and he cringed with each movement until they arrived on the main floor. When they reached the front of the hospital, a van was waiting for them. It had a wheelchair ramp and myriad belts to strap him in. Steven winced. *Is this really my life now?*

After he was all strapped in, Dad jumped behind the wheel and began the short drive to the rehab center. Steven appreciated the drive through the heart of Cedar Haven, passing Bea's Diner and the middle school where Lanie worked.

Once they arrived at his new home, Steven allowed his eyes to sweep over the building. It didn't look much different from the hospital, though it was noticeably smaller. Two stories tall, the facility had an array of windows on the second floor. He assumed that was where the patients' rooms were. As the attendants unbuckled his chair and took it down the ramp, he noted the circular driveway they had parked in was similar to those he'd seen at hotels.

Rose pushed him toward the doors, which whisked open upon their approach. The lobby area was pristine if a little dreary. The scent of chlorine wafted down a corridor, and Steven frowned. Maybe they had a pool.

"We've found water aerobics to be a great form of physical therapy, especially for those with joint pain," a voice said from beside him. He turned his head to find a man standing to his right in a red polo shirt with the name Chesapeake Rehabilitation on the left breast pocket. The man held out his hand to Steven, his gray eyes twinkling. "You must be Steven McAllister. I'm Marvin Anderson, the director of Chesapeake Rehab."

"Nice to meet you."

"Welcome." Marvin shook his hand before gesturing behind him. "Would you like a tour before we get you settled?"

At Steven's nod, Marvin led them through the facility. In addition to the pool, there was a gym and a cafeteria along with areas for speech therapy, massage, and other treatments that made the place feel more like a medical spa than a skilled-nursing facility.

Maybe this won't be so bad after all. He could certainly think of worse places to spend the next two weeks.

"And this," Marvin said as they came to a stop outside of a door, "is your room."

Rose pushed him through the wide doorway and into what looked like a presidential suite in a hotel. A wave of nausea came over Steven. How were they going to afford that? His insurance wasn't anywhere near as good as what he'd had at the law firm in Baltimore.

She leaned forward and whispered in his ear, "Your father is paying. He insisted."

That sounded like something his father would do. Guilt gnawed at Steven's gut. His father had retired years ago and lived on a fixed income. While Dad had a very comfortable lifestyle, he didn't have the means to throw money around. Steven opened his mouth to protest, but before he could say anything, Marvin began showing off the various features of the room.

"We have a lot of entertainment options to keep you from growing bored, though with the many hours of therapy before you, there's little chance of that." He laughed at his own joke, but no one else joined him. "The bathroom also has some amazing amenities, which you'll be able to enjoy more as you progress in your recovery."

Steven read between the lines. The bathroom amenities were meant for people who could walk. Based on what he'd learned while at the hospital, he doubted he would be able to enjoy any of them. Still, he could barely focus on that as he digested the reality that his father was footing the bill for his recovery. *How can I ever repay him for this?* Tears pricked Steven's eyes, and he wasn't sure if he wanted to thank his father for his generosity or berate him for wasting his money.

Either way, Steven planned to make darn sure he recovered as quickly as possible to avoid becoming a burden. Two weeks should be more than enough time for him to learn what he needed to function. Then he could return home.

"Why don't I let you get settled." Marvin signaled for Steven's father to follow him. "I'll be back to discuss your therapy schedule with you."

When he was alone with Rose and Lanie, Steven leaned back in his chair and sighed. "This is too much."

Lanie snorted. "You have no idea. It would have been cheaper for you to have a roommate, but Dad refused. I'm not sure what's gotten into him, but at least you're going to get the best care possible in Southern Maryland."

Steven smiled. While his sister was making a dig at their hometown, her words had some truth to them. It was no Johns Hopkins, but several doctors in the area had participated in a federal program that paid off their student loans in exchange for them opening medical practices in rural communities. That facility was one example of how well the program had worked out.

"I'm grateful for your father's generosity," Rose said as she wandered through the room. "Hopefully it'll reduce some of your financial stress, knowing this is taken care of."

"If anything, it makes it worse."

"Of course you'd say that. Paying for the wedding is fine, but assisting with your recovery is a deal-breaker," she muttered. With a sigh, she stepped beside him and kissed his forehead. "Unfortunately, I need to go run some errands before my shift. But I'll come by tomorrow. I love you."

When she was gone, Lanie sat on his bed. "And then there were two."

"Did Rose mention the wedding?" he asked.

"She did." His sister turned to the window. "You have a nice view. Would you like to see?"

"Nice try." He smirked. "But you're not getting off that easy."

Lanie glanced over her shoulder. "There's really not much to say. I convinced Rose to discuss the situation with the vendors. I assume she told you their response was less than ideal?"

"She did. But I told her we should determine areas where we could cut back on expenses."

"I'm sorry, but that's not realistic."

He narrowed his eyes at her, but she didn't even flinch.

"Steven, come on. You're in rehab, for goodness' sake! And no one can give a definitive answer for how long you'll be here or even what exactly happens next. Wouldn't it make more sense to postpone until you're recovered so you can actually enjoy your wedding?"

Shaking his head, he clenched his jaw. His sister would probably see his refusal to listen as stubbornness, but he'd chosen his hill, and he would die on it if he had to.

Dad and Marvin entered then, and Lanie breathed a sigh of relief. Steven hid a smile. If she thought the conversation was over, she had another thought coming. As soon as he got out of that place, he would do whatever was needed to get his life back on track.

—— *elle* ——

The first day of physical therapy at the rehab facility was probably the worst day Steven had had since his heart attack. While Lacey at the hospital had been willing to work at his pace, gently pushing him beyond his comfort zone, Adrian, his new physical therapist, was a drill sergeant. At the end of his physical therapy session, which lasted for two hours, Steven could literally feel every muscle in his body. Well, *almost* every muscle. His legs were still disconnected from the rest of his nervous system.

"You look like you could use a session in the massage room," Adrian said as he laid several bags of ice over Steven's arms and right leg.

Steven could only grunt, too tired to articulate a response. Resting his head against the bed's pillow, he closed his eyes. *Will I even be able to move the parts of my body that weren't broken tomorrow?* Everything felt like a dead weight.

"It'll get easier." Adrian patted his back. "I promise."

"Sure it will," Steven muttered.

Adrian's laugh drifted away as Steven dozed off. But he was abruptly awakened a moment later when Adrian shook him. He opened his eye to a slit, not at all happy to have his well-deserved nap interrupted.

"You can go back to sleep in your own bed," Adrian said, reading his mind. "I need to prepare for my next patient."

"More like your next victim," Steven scoffed, which earned him a grin. He had to admit that despite how much he'd hated every minute of their session, he liked Adrian. And if he wanted to stand next to Rose at the altar and walk with her down the aisle at the end of the summer, he needed to push himself. He just wished the exercises hadn't been so grueling on his first day.

Adrian helped Steven into the wheelchair, then an orderly came and took him away. Once he was settled into bed, his mind was too preoccupied for him to sleep. Lanie had promised an update on how things were going at the office, but he hadn't heard from her yet. It took some shifting and shimmying in the bed, but he managed to grab his phone from the nightstand. His email was filled with messages from Mr. Willoughby, which he ignored. The one nice thing about being stuck in rehab was his ability to avoid some of his more annoying clients, though he would have to deal with Mr. Willoughby eventually.

A knock on the door startled him, but he breathed a sigh of relief when he met his sister's gaze. She had a bag slung over her shoulder and gave him an apologetic smile.

"I'm sorry I couldn't come sooner, but I've been sorting things out at the office."

"How's it going?"

"Not bad, though I'm still getting my bearings." She bit her lip. "Sandra and I were discussing putting an ad in the paper for a law clerk."

He crossed his arms. "I want to be there for the interviews."

"But the work is piling up without you. Sandra can only handle so much. You need someone who knows what they're doing."

"Bring the work here. I can review it between my therapy sessions."

Her mouth dropped open. "You can't be serious. Rose would kill me if she knew! Besides, we don't even know how long you'll be—"

"I'm only staying here for two weeks," he insisted, interrupting her.

"That was the bare minimum," she retorted, throwing up her hands. "And how long do you think we can hold off your clients? Mr. Willoughby has been blowing up the phone. Poor Leslie looked about ready to quit when I was there."

"She won't," Steven said, though he sounded a lot surer than he felt. He nodded to her bag. "Do you have something for me to sign?"

He thought she would continue to press her case, but she sighed and removed a pile of folders. After setting them on his bed, she flipped the first one open.

"Just a few pleadings. And then Sandra drafted a will and trust she wanted you to review."

It took a few hours for him to review the work she and Sandra had done. But as Lanie slipped the folders into her bag, he had a sense of accomplishment.

"Thanks," he said.

"You're welcome." She checked her watch. "I better go. Visiting hours are almost over."

After a brief hug, she promised to file the pleadings he'd signed with the court the next day, then she was gone. He rested his head against his pillow and stared out the window. As much as he hated to admit it, Lanie was right. The situation wasn't sustainable, but he couldn't allow them to hire someone without his input.

He would have to make the most of the two weeks he was there then continue his recovery at home. It was as simple as that.

Chapter Eight

ROSE STARED AT DR. Myers with growing annoyance. For the second time in a week, he'd asked her to work a double shift. Despite knowing it was a possibility, she'd hoped to get out of it.

"But I have plans tonight," she protested. She couldn't believe his gall. He knew her fiancé was recovering after a stint in the hospital. *Why can't he find someone else?*

"I'm sorry, but Lisa's daughter is still sick, and Rebecca is out of town." He shrugged apologetically.

Steven wasn't the only one who needed to hire extra help. The hospital had been hemorrhaging staff for ages, and they struggled to replace the nurses who left.

"I promise I'll make it up to you," Dr. Myers continued.

Rose raised an eyebrow. "And how do you plan to do that?"

"You're being considered for head nurse," he said, leaning against the wall. "I can put in several good words for you."

While she appreciated the sentiment, she doubted it would help her in the long run. Dr. Myers had a lot of clout, but he wasn't even on the hiring board. The members might listen to his recommendations, but they didn't mean anything, especially when Rebecca and Lisa both had seniority.

Rather than say any of that aloud, she forced a smile and thanked him before returning to start her rounds... again. She texted Lanie that she wouldn't be able to see Steven before visiting hours ended after all. Maybe it was for the best. Every time she saw him, he and Lanie were discussing some new concern at his office. Rose hated seeing his stress mounting. But she kept quiet to avoid an argument, and quite frankly, she was tired of biting her tongue.

Mr. Patrones was her first stop, and she braced herself for his glum demeanor. She supposed she should be grateful Steven wasn't more like him. But Mr. Patrones had several years on Steven, and his health had been poor even before his heart attack.

Pasting a smile on her face, she knocked then opened the door. "Good afternoon, Mr. Patrones. How are we doing?"

"The same as I was the last time you were here." He blinked at her. "Shouldn't you be off duty?"

"I'm working a double," she said, keeping her voice cheery. Glancing over his chart, she was surprised by Dr. Myers's note at the bottom. *Discharge tomorrow.* "Good news! You're getting sprung tomorrow!"

His eyebrows pulled together. "So soon?"

I thought he couldn't wait to get out of here. "Aw, Mr. Patrones, I'm glad to hear you're going to miss me, but you've made so much progress. You should celebrate."

"With what?" he demanded, his tone acerbic. "I can't have red meat or alcohol, and I'm not much of a cake person."

Rose took a deep breath and released it slowly, counting down from ten. Only that man could make something wonderful like being released from the hospital seem like a chore.

"I'm sure your friends will be happy to see you."

He stared at her, his face expressionless. "I don't have any friends."

Can't imagine why. No, that was unfair. She didn't know anything about him other than what she'd learned from his medical record and the little he told her. If his heart attack hadn't happened in public, he wouldn't have survived it. When she thought of him returning to the condo where he lived alone, her heart went out to him. She wondered what had happened in his life to cause him to be so utterly alone.

"Now you have a chance to make some," she said, though she didn't know why she was bothering to pretend to be upbeat. Mr. Patrones's defeatist attitude drained the life from her whenever she was in the room with him.

He snorted but said nothing else. After she finished marking down his vitals on his chart, Rose attempted one last smile and hurried from the room.

She took a minute to reorganize her thoughts before moving on to the next patient. As much as she dreaded dealing with Mr. Patrones's depressing comments, she shouldn't judge him. After all, were it not for Steven, his family, and the few friends she'd made since moving to Cedar Haven, her life might not be that much different. Even with all of those people in her life, she struggled sometimes to open up and to let people help her. Her parents had raised her to be self-sufficient and to take care of those around her, which was why being a nurse came so naturally. But she wondered sometimes if she was *too* independent.

—————

The end of her shift neared, and Rose couldn't wait. She dragged herself through her rounds once more. Most of her patients were sleeping, which did nothing to help her pass the time.

"You should grab a quick nap," Dr. Myers said, startling her. She spun around to find him leaning against the doorframe of Mr. Patrones's room with a lopsided grin.

"I've only got an hour left." She shrugged. "Not much point to it now."

He stepped toward her, the grin dissolving into a frown of concern. "Yeah, but you still have to drive home. Take a nap. I can check on your remaining patients."

She quirked an eyebrow. "How are you not dead on your feet? You've been here as long as me, if not longer."

It was his turn to shrug. "I'm used to little sleep." Turning so his back pressed against the wall, he stared at the ceiling. "Before I came here, I was an on-call with the ER in Baltimore."

"Oof." Several of her nursing friends had gone on to work in ERs all over the nation. The last time she saw them, they'd told horror story after horror story. She couldn't imagine the chaos. It'd been hard enough when Steven had come through, and she wasn't even his nurse.

"Yeah," he said. "Oof."

"What made you decide to move to our little town?"

The lopsided grin returned. "Would you believe me if I said a girl?"

That got her attention. "Really?"

He raised his eyebrows. "Didn't you come here for Steven?"

"Well, yeah, but we'd been together awhile by that point." She cocked her head. "You just don't seem the type to go chasing after someone."

His laugh was hollow, bitter. Rose deduced he had quite the story to tell, but she shifted uncomfortably. It wasn't her business, and she wasn't sure she wanted to know the details. They weren't friendly outside of the office like she and Rebecca were. In fact, that conversation was the longest one she could ever remember them having.

He nodded at the chart in her hands. "How many more patients do you have?"

"Just one. Why?"

"If you're not going to take a nap, you should get some coffee in you." When she frowned, he gave a sad smile. "Meet me downstairs when you're done, and I'll tell you the whole sordid tale."

Despite her misgivings, curiosity bubbled up inside her. With a nod, she turned on her heel and headed off to check on her last patient. She didn't know why she cared. Based on some of his cocky behavior at the hospital, she could only imagine what he had done to cause the end of his relationship. But learning that someone else had moved to their tiny town for love intrigued her.

About ten minutes later, Rose entered the cafeteria and allowed her eyes to sweep the room. Though technically the place was closed, a couple of coffee and vending machines were available. A few residents sat around a table by the door, but they paid her no mind. Finally, she spotted Dr. Myers seated at a table on the far side of the room with two coffees set before him.

"Two sugars and a splash of cream, right?" He slid her drink over.

She sank into a seat, dumbstruck by his thoughtfulness. "How'd you know?"

"I pay attention."

Just the scent of the roasted beans was enough to rouse her, but she took a sip anyway. He was right—she needed something to stay awake. Though she lived only fifteen to twenty minutes from the hospital, she always struggled to keep her eyes open after working a double.

"So, tell me," she said. "Who broke your heart?"

His eyes widened. "How do you know she did the breaking?"

"Lucky guess?"

He shifted, his fingers fiddling with the flap on the lid of his cup. "I'd say we broke each other."

When he didn't continue, she leaned back in her chair and sipped her coffee. "We don't have to talk about it if you don't want to."

"No, I want to. I'm trying to think of where to begin." Wrapping his hands around the cup, he stared at the table. "Melissa and I met at Johns Hopkins. I had been accepted into their cardiology fellowship, and she was pursuing her MFA in creative writing." He shook his head, a faint smile on his face. "We came from such different worlds—it was a wonder ours connected at all. In some ways, it felt like fate."

Rose leaned forward, growing more interested in his tale with each word due to the similarities with her own story. She and Steven had also met in college, and though they'd both gone to the University of Maryland, their programs had almost nothing in common.

"So, how did you meet?" she asked.

He shrugged. "At a party. We had a few mutual friends. Actually, her best friend and my best friend were both 1L's in law school at the time." He coughed a harsh laugh before he continued. "They dated casually. Their schedules made it impossible to make it anything more. But after I saw Melissa, I knew I'd find a way to make it work. And I did." Pausing and draining his cup, he cleared his throat then gestured to Rose. "Did you want another one?"

She blinked then shook her cup. The coffee sloshed around inside, confirming she'd barely drunk any of it. When she declined, he got himself another cup from the machine.

While she waited for him to return, she sipped the now lukewarm liquid, contemplating what he'd told her so far. What had happened between them to cause him to say they broke each other? He sounded like he still cared a great deal for her, if the wistfulness in his voice was any indication.

When he returned, he slid into his chair and grimaced. "So, Melissa and I dated throughout my fellowship and her master's. After we'd completed our programs, we discussed where to live. At first, we got a place in Baltimore, and she got a job at a small publisher while I did a residency at Mercy Hospital.

"But she wasn't happy, and one day, she asked if I would consider leaving the city life for something quieter." He raised an eyebrow at Rose. "I didn't realize how quiet she meant until she brought me down to meet her parents."

"So she lives here?" Rose asked. *Have I ever met her before?* She racked her brain, but she couldn't remember any Melissa from the people she'd met since moving to town.

He shook his head. "A few towns over, but this was the closest hospital."

"Did her parents not like you?"

"Oh no, that wasn't the problem. And my parents loved her." His eyes grew sad, and he sighed. "I guess you could say I took a long time to adjust to small-town life."

"It can be a big change," Rose said, her heart going out to him. "I'm used to living in a city too. But I don't know, Cedar Haven has kind of grown on me."

"That's the thing. I asked her to move here." He brushed his dark hair off his forehead and gazed intently at Rose. "We had rented a little place near her parents, which was quite the hike to the hospital, especially in an emergency."

"She didn't want to?"

"Her father became ill, and she wanted to stay nearby so she could care for him and help her mother."

Rose rested her chin on her hand. "What did she do? Was she still working at the publisher?"

He shook his head. "No. She had decided to pursue writing full-time, so she was working on a novel, which was the other reason I was frustrated she didn't want to move. She had no commute, and I'd already made sacrifices in turning down a lucrative job in Baltimore to move here."

"So, did you move?"

Hunching his shoulders, he nodded. "Briefly. We found a place not far from the hospital." He gave another bitter laugh. "I actually still live there."

"Then what happened? Did she go back to her parents?"

At first, he didn't respond, and Rose wasn't sure whether she should say something comforting. But then he took a deep breath and pushed his coffee cup away.

"As her father got worse, she spent more and more time over there. It got to the point where we barely saw each other." His mouth pressed into a thin line. "Between caring for her dad and comforting her mom, she didn't have much time for me."

"Did you consider moving back closer to her parents?"

He leaned back and nodded. "But I also sat her down and had a long talk about the importance of taking care of her health. She'd become a ghost of her former self. She'd even stopped writing, devoting all her time to her father."

"I'm guessing he didn't make it?" His story was beginning to sound eerily familiar.

Shifting in his seat, he folded his arms on the table. "He did not. She was a wreck afterward. She moved back in with her mother and basically shut herself away."

Rose narrowed her eyes. "And what? You broke up with her?"

He sighed. "Of course not. I tried to talk to her, to pull her out of the depressive funk she was sinking into." Gulping down more coffee, he grimaced. "But she was angry with me for taking her away from her father in the first place, when we'd moved closer to the hospital. And then I couldn't bear to watch her wither away as she poured everything she had into a hopeless case." His eyes shot to Rose's face, and he bit his lip. "I'm sorry. I didn't mean that the way it came out."

She gave him a weak smile. "I know." Then she shook her head. "That's awful."

Leaning forward, he pushed her coffee into her hands and gave her a meaningful look. Dutifully, she raised it to her lips. The cool liquid did little to enliven her as it slid down her throat, but she hoped the caffeine would kick in soon.

"There's a reason I'm telling you this story," he said.

"What's that?"

He cleared his throat. "I'd only recently joined the hospital staff when Steven's mother took a turn for the worse." Rose dropped her gaze, but he continued, "And I saw how you rallied around her, helping Steven's sister and caring for her yourself. While you didn't fade as quickly as Melissa, I could see the toll it was taking on you."

"But Lanie did most of her care," Rose protested. "And they hired hospice nurses, so my contribution was minimal."

"I know." He took a deep breath. "I also know the situation won't be the same with Steven."

She stilled, her heart pounding in her chest. *What does he mean by that?*

"You're a caretaker, Rose. I've seen it here at the hospital with your patients." When she frowned, he hurried on. "That's a good thing. It makes you an amazing nurse. But here, it's easy to maintain boundaries with your patients."

"You think I can't do the same with Steven?" she asked coolly.

"Can you?" He raised an eyebrow. "He's your fiancé, the love of your life, I assume. And I imagine he isn't taking too kindly to staying in the rehab facility." She made a face, and he nodded as if she'd confirmed something. "I know his sister has been going there regularly since the school year ended, which is likely lessening your burden." His eyes narrowed. "But I don't expect that to last much longer."

"So what are you saying?"

He touched her hand, his mouth turning down. "Don't become the next Melissa."

Chapter Nine

AFTER TWO WEEKS IN the rehab facility, Steven was ready to leave, and he didn't care if it happened to be against medical advice. He'd seen through Lanie's lame attempts to hide how much his business was flailing without him, and the longer he remained in rehab, the more the firm would suffer.

Marvin and his medical team were sitting around the conference table opposite Steven, his father, Lanie, and Rose. Everyone's face was grim. Dad was the only one who supported his decision, though Steven suspected that had more to do with how much continuing rehab for another two weeks would hurt his father's bank account.

"You've made such amazing progress," Marvin protested. "Why leave now? Your cast comes off in three weeks, and in another four, we might have you standing again."

"Outpatient therapy can do that as well," Steven countered, keeping his voice cool and detached.

"But these first few months after a spinal cord injury are critical. You'd do better with more therapy than you can receive on an outpatient basis."

"And my firm will fail," Steven retorted. "I've heard the arguments, but they don't take into account the impact to my personal life." With a deep breath, he worked to remain calm. "I need to get back to work."

"Where will you live?" Rose asked quietly. Her brown eyes were filled with unshed tears. It wasn't the first time she'd asked him that question. "Your house isn't equipped for a wheelchair."

"I visited Steven's house yesterday. Despite the concerns expressed at the hospital, I found the door to the house and to the bathroom on the first floor are wide enough to accommodate his wheelchair. But even if they weren't, he'll need a two-person transfer assist to go to the bathroom or to move from the bed to the chair and vice versa," Adrian, his physical therapist, responded for him. "But that can be accomplished with home care aides."

Steven sat up a little straighter. While he hadn't expected his decision to receive much support from his medical team, he was grateful his progress was at least being acknowledged.

"So you support this decision?" Marvin demanded.

"I wouldn't go that far." Adrian sighed. "But determining what's best for Steven depends on all the facts, and quite frankly, the stress of being here, away from his work, isn't good for his spinal injury or his heart." He turned to Rose. "Some adjustments would need to be made, such as placing a hospital bed downstairs until he's able to climb stairs again. I believe, with some adjustments and Steven remaining mindful of his limitations, he could live there." His gaze met Steven's, and his face hardened. "However, there are other things to consider. How will you get to appointments?"

"While I understand being away from the office is stressing you out, how will you maintain a low stress level if you return to work?" Dr. Myers's voice came through the intercom in the middle of the table. He hadn't been able to get away to attend the meeting in person. "I don't need to remind you of the risk of a second heart attack."

Steven gestured to Lanie to speak. She shot him a withering look but nodded and leaned forward.

"We plan to hire a law clerk to help while Steven recovers. An experienced law student, even if they haven't passed the bar, could perform most of the tasks Steven does." Her hazel eyes flashed fire as she glared at him. "But Steven would still have to review the work and sign off on it."

"And the appointments?" Marvin asked.

"I'll drive him," Steven's father said. "I'm retired and have already rented an accessibility van."

The medical team exchanged glances, and Dr. Myers heaved a heavy sigh over the phone. Steven held his breath.

"Again, I state for the record, Mr. McAllister is choosing to leave of his own free will and against medical advice." Dr. Myers's voice was authoritative but resigned. "Marvin, fill out the discharge paperwork and let me know if Dr. Bhati or I need to sign off on anything."

"Thanks for calling in." Marvin pushed back from the table and stood. "We'll prepare everything for discharge."

Rose burst into tears beside him and ran out. Lanie chased her, leaving Steven with his father. Without a word, Dad grabbed the wheelchair handles and guided him back to his room for hopefully the last time.

***

"What's this?" Steven demanded as his father pulled up in front of his house. Several cars were parked along the street and in the driveway.

"Nate and Lanie wanted to welcome you home," Rose said a little too brightly. She'd barely spoken on the way back from the rehab facility, though he'd tried to engage her in conversation. While he understood her fears about his health, he wished she would trust him. After all, he was hiring a law clerk and finding ways to manage his workload. *Why isn't that enough for her?*

Dad cringed but said nothing as he parked and began the complicated process of removing Steven's chair from the van.

Steven raised an eyebrow at Rose. "What's going on?"

"It's just a small gathering of your favorite people to celebrate your release." But she wouldn't meet his eyes.

He leaned back in the seat and crossed his arms. "I'm not leaving this vehicle until you tell me what I'm walking into."

Dad snorted, and Steven flushed. Even he could hear how empty the threat was. Until he was out of that blasted chair, he didn't have a lot of say about where he could and couldn't go. He'd learned to maneuver around in it, but it was easier to be pushed by someone else. They'd recommended a power wheelchair instead of a manual one, but he'd refused. No sense in spending the money if he planned to walk again as soon as possible.

With a sigh, Rose turned in her seat and faced him. "We're holding a family meeting."

His brow furrowed. "Why?"

"Because you're a stubborn workaholic who won't listen to reason," Dad said.

"What he means"—Rose cut in with a glare— "is that we need to discuss how things are going to be now that you're home."

Steven's lips pressed into a thin line. "And if I don't agree?"

Rose opened her mouth, but his father beat her to it. "Then I'll turn this van around and take you right back to the rehab facility."

"You wouldn't dare."

Dad stopped fiddling with the belts strapping Steven in and stepped out as if ready to slam the door. "Try me."

Steven scowled. "Fine. I'll at least listen, but don't think for one minute that I'm going to change my mind."

"Of course not," Rose muttered as she slipped out of the car and headed into the house.

"Let's get this over with," he grumbled as his father pushed him up the sidewalk. His family had had a ramp installed over the stairs. As Adrian had promised, his chair fit easily through the front door.

The scene that greeted him didn't alleviate any of his frustrations. His sister and her fiancé, Nate, sat on the black love seat on one side of the living room. Rose had claimed a matching recliner near the kitchen. Nobody spoke as Steven came in.

"Well, let's hear it," he said, gesturing to Rose. Somehow, he suspected she was the mastermind behind the whole charade.

Dad smirked, raising an eyebrow at Lanie, who simply nodded. Without waiting for an invitation, he sank onto Steven's black leather couch and made himself comfortable.

Nate had moved closer to Lanie, almost protectively, as if he expected Steven to lash out at her at any moment. It took all of Steven's willpower not to throw them out of his house. He'd promised Rose he would listen to what they had to say, even if every instinct told him not to.

"I'm sorry to have ambushed you like this," Rose began, catching him by surprise. "But your decision to leave the rehab center against medical advice left me little choice."

He struggled to keep his emotions in check. "What's wrong with my choice?"

She fiddled with her engagement ring, and he half expected someone else to swoop in and take control of the situation. But no one did, and she seemed to steel herself.

"You aren't taking this seriously," she said. Her tone was firm, but her beautiful brown eyes swam with tears.

His anger faltered, but he tried not to let it show. Perhaps he was being unreasonable, but he couldn't help feeling an intervention was over the top and unnecessary.

"You can't go back to the way things were," she said. "We have to make some changes to not only allow you time to heal but to reduce the likelihood of another heart attack."

"But I'm continuing therapy on an outpatient basis." *Quite reluctantly,* he wanted to add. With his schedule, those appointments would take up a huge chunk of time. "And I'm adhering to the strict diet the nutritionist put me on."

"I'm referring to overall lifestyle changes."

Somehow, he knew the conversation was about his job, and he clenched his jaw to keep from lashing out. Didn't she understand he needed to work, or he'd lose everything? His business? Their future? Everything was all tied together.

"I've already offered to assist with your business over the summer," Lanie piped up. She glanced at Nate. "And we're happy to help Rose with the wedding planning, as it's a good chance to learn the business before we plan our own."

"But you're going to need to figure something else out soon," Nate said. He took Lanie's hand and fixed Steven with a steely gaze. "Lanie starts teaching on her own in August, so you can't lean on her for too long."

Steven pressed his fingers into his temples. "I already promised I would cut back."

"I'm afraid that's not enough," Rose said, her tone gentle. "And that's what we're here to discuss. How we can pitch in and help you to alleviate as much of your stress as possible."

"Lanie and Sandra are helping me hire a law clerk." He met his sister's gaze. "I'm truly grateful for your help, both while I was in rehab and now. While my staff can handle daily tasks, there's benefit in having someone who knows me and is aware of my..." He couldn't say the words. "Condition."

Rose looked like she wanted to say more, but he held up his hand. "Before you ask me about a partner again, let me explain why that's not possible. The fact is, I can't afford to bring on a full-time attorney right now. There's not enough profit to support something like that at this point." He sighed. "At the same time, there's too much tied into this firm to go belly-up so soon."

"Then what can we do to make sure that doesn't happen?" Dad asked.

"Finding a law clerk is the first step." Steven glanced at Rose. "Though it would be easier if I could go into the office."

"Absolutely not." She crossed her arms. "Dr. Myers said you aren't cleared to return to work yet."

He released a frustrated sigh. "I appreciate everything. And I *am* aware of the risk of another..." He choked on the words again. "Incident." Clearing his throat, he pressed on. "But you also have to understand I have a lot at stake, and there are certain things I'm not willing to compromise on."

Rose clenched her hands into fists. Steven's jaw ached from grinding his teeth. They appeared to be at an impasse, and he had no idea where to go from there.

"Why don't we continue with the arrangement we had while you were in the rehab facility?" Lanie asked in a clear attempt to break through the tension. "I can keep you up to date on the goings-on in the office and bring you things to sign."

Before she finished speaking, Steven was already shaking his head. "I need to start catching up with my clients." At Rose's glare, he added, "But I can do that through phone calls and video conferences."

His sister visibly relaxed and smiled. "That seems fair to me."

All eyes turned to Rose for her verdict. At first, he thought she was going to keep pushing him to stop working entirely, but then she nodded.

"I won't stop encouraging you to take it easy," Rose said, her voice much more tentative than it had been moments ago. "But I understand the need to save your firm." Her teeth worried her lower lip. "Just... promise me you won't overexert yourself."

"I promise." Steven put his hand over his heart, which felt more than a little overdramatic, but he wanted to assure her of his sincerity.

"But you better believe I'll be watching you like a hawk," Lanie said, her hazel eyes darkening.

"I'd expect nothing less," Steven replied drily. He forced himself not to grin. Against all odds, he'd won. Well, he'd won a battle, but if he knew his family, the war was far from over.

⁓ℯℓℯ⁓

As happy as he was to be out of the rehab facility, Steven had to admit being home wasn't much better. Despite his pleas, his family refused to allow him to return to the office, not even to visit his staff. And his attempts to convince his sister to bring him work beyond the occasional need for his signature had been met with her threatening to tell Rose. The last thing he needed was another dressing-down from his fiancée. But as the days wore on, his restlessness grew.

To her credit, Lanie was surprisingly lenient with him. She was happy to just sit and talk to him, watch TV together, or play board games. If Rose had stayed, he probably wouldn't get off so easily. She would play nursemaid and insist he follow every recommendation from the doctor. But as long as he didn't overexert himself, Lanie didn't fuss.

"Are you enjoying your summer vacation?" he asked one afternoon while they played Uno.

Lanie shrugged. "I'm not hating it, but since I only got to work a few months before the school year ended, I don't feel like I've earned the break."

He raised an eyebrow as he considered his next move. "I disagree. After everything you've been through this last year, you deserve to relax."

"What about you? How are you feeling about the forced recovery period?"

For a moment, he didn't answer, pretending to concentrate on his cards. "It's nice to be home, but I do worry the work is piling up."

"I've been by the office every day this week to coordinate with Sandra. She said she's handling your cases just fine, though Mr. Willoughby continues to call daily."

Steven rolled his eyes. As much as he missed the office, he had to admit he was in no hurry to return to dealing with that particular client. But he kept that to himself.

"I'm glad Sandra is staying on top of things, but it may be too much for her."

"All the more reason for you to start looking for a law clerk," Lanie said, laying down a draw-four card.

He scowled, both at the insistence he needed help and the move she'd just played. He'd had only two cards left. But his mind wasn't on the game at all, and there were some advantages to letting Lanie win.

"How can I advertise for one if no one will let me work?"

"I've already discussed placing an ad with the newspaper, and I've researched how to advertise at law schools in DC and Baltimore." She glanced at him quickly before hitting him with another draw-four card. "Of course, we'll need your help with the wording."

"Doesn't that count as work?" He winced at how sullen he sounded. His predicament wasn't Lanie's fault, and if he had any hope of convincing her to let him go into the office, even if just for a few hours, biting her head off wasn't the way to do it. He tried a different tactic. "I appreciate your help."

She smiled. "Anytime."

Taking a deep breath, he pushed his shoulders back. "But I'd like to review my files." When she opened her mouth to respond, he rushed on. "It'll aid me in writing the ad if I know exactly what I'll need the law clerk to do."

Her brow furrowed. Whether that was because she was open to his request or debating her next move, he couldn't tell. He fidgeted with his cards while he waited for her response.

With a sigh, she shook her head. "You know Rose will never go for that."

"She's my fiancée, not my keeper," he retorted.

Lanie laughed. "Try telling her that."

"I have," he muttered. *Time to go with plan B.* "You know, I have a special calendar where I track my deadlines and upcoming court dates. I should review that as well."

"Does Sandra not have access to this calendar?"

With a triumphant smile, he shook his head. "It's locally saved on my computer."

"Don't you have a laptop?" Lanie frowned. "Couldn't I bring that home to you?"

Score! "Would you? That would be helpful."

"Sure. I'll swing by the office tomorrow and drop it off next time I stop by."

Steven smiled. Another battle won, and that one was huge. With his computer there, he would be able to work without anyone being the wiser, especially at night, when no one else was around. He was so excited by the turn of events, he didn't even react when Lanie yelled "Uno!"

Chapter Ten

THE NEXT DAY, ROSE pushed Steven's wheelchair along the sidewalk near her condo, taking in the late-June evening. It was the first chance they'd had to be truly alone since his accident, and she relished the time with him. For one night, she had committed to put aside all of the uncertainties they faced and just enjoy their time together.

Steven took a deep breath. "This is nice."

"I'm so glad it's summer," Rose said. The recent change in seasons had given her a renewed sense of hope. After all, summer was her favorite season with its long days, warm nights, and plenty of bright sunshine to banish the shadows from her mind.

"And soon, we'll be married."

Rose bit her lip. They hadn't discussed the wedding since that day in the hospital. With everything else going on, she'd tried not to think about it, promising herself they would discuss it later. But the wedding was two months away, and she still wasn't sure what their next steps should be.

"Rose?" Steven called, and she realized she'd stopped walking.

Forcing a smile, she resumed their stroll. "Sorry about that."

The air between them became thick with everything they weren't saying, but Rose didn't want to ruin their evening with an argument. Instead, she angled the wheelchair toward the pond.

"There's something I want to show you," she said.

"Are we going swimming?" Steven joked as they neared the water's edge.

Once they reached the fence, Rose locked the wheelchair's brakes before stepping around to kneel beside Steven. She searched the pond for her favorite birds.

"Look," she said when she spotted them. "Those are our resident swans."

Steven followed her finger and smiled. "They're quite beautiful."

"Aren't they, though?"

The swans glided through the water, seemingly without a care in the world. Rose couldn't help envying them. How simple their lives must be in comparison to hers. Find a mate, raise a brood of cygnets, and live in such a peaceful place.

"Did you know there's an ancient belief that swans sing before they die?" Steven asked.

Rose frowned. "Really? Why?"

He shrugged. "No idea, but that's where the term 'swan's song' comes from. The idea is they're mute most of their lives, but right before they die, they sing a sweet, mournful song."

That didn't sound right to her. "They aren't mute. I can hear them grunting from here."

"I'm sure it's just some old folklore," Steven said with a laugh.

Like Lanie's cardinal. A smile tugged at her lips. She liked having her own legend, especially since she could share it with Steven.

"Did you know swans have their own mating dance?" Rose asked, remembering the man she had seen fishing the last time she was at the pond.

"Most animals do." Steven winked at her. "But I'd rather not sit around waiting to see if they start going at it."

A laugh bubbled up in her throat. "Too true. We should get back anyway. I need to start dinner if we want to eat before midnight."

He took her hand and kissed her knuckles. "I wouldn't mind if it meant I got to spend more time with you."

Her heart melted. She missed moments like that. Sometimes she worried they got too caught up in the day-to-day of life and didn't take time to really enjoy each other's company. With the accident, there had been even less opportunity.

Impulsively, she leaned forward and cupped his cheek before pressing her lips softly against his. He wrapped his arms around her waist and tugged her into his lap, almost tipping over his chair in the process.

Her laughter echoed off the buildings, and she kissed him once more before standing and brushing off her clothes. "Come on. Let's go home."

As she pushed his wheelchair to her condo, the sweet scent of honeysuckle filled her nostrils. She closed her eyes and breathed it in, allowing her mind to be transported back to a special evening two summers ago.

Steven had made reservations at an upscale Irish restaurant overlooking the Inner Harbor. They'd been there plenty of times before, but something felt different about that evening. After a delicious meal of boxtys and fish and chips, Steven had ordered a couple of glasses of champagne.

"What are we celebrating?" Rose had asked as she accepted her glass from the server.

"This," Steven said before sliding off his chair and dropping to one knee in front of her.

Her heart had leapt into her throat as he produced a small black-velvet box and opened it to reveal the most beautiful ring she'd ever seen, a pear-shaped diamond bracketed by a ruby on one side and an amethyst on the other.

"Will you marry me?" His eyes had searched hers as if he didn't already know the answer.

"Of course!" she exclaimed.

He stood, and she jumped into his arms. The rest of the evening was a blur, as she'd spent more time than she cared to admit staring at the ring on her finger. She'd loved that he added their birthstones. It was the perfect representation of their love.

Rose blinked herself back to the present as they reached her door. After unlocking it, she maneuvered the wheelchair into the condo and parked it in the living room.

"Did you want to watch television while I get dinner started?"

He shook his head. "I'd rather sit in the kitchen and talk to you, if you don't mind."

While her kitchen was too small for the chair to fit, she moved it over to the doorway so they could talk without yelling. She grabbed ingredients for stir-fry, one of Steven's favorite meals.

"Any news on the head nurse position?" he asked as he watched her work.

"Not yet. I know they're going to open the application sometime this summer, but I doubt I'll get it. Rebecca has seniority."

"I heard she doesn't want it."

That caught her attention. She turned from the stove to look at him. "Where did you hear that?"

"In the hospital." He grinned. "You'd be surprised how much the nursing staff gossips."

"Actually, I wouldn't," she said with a laugh.

After setting a pot of water to boil and pouring oil into the wok to heat, she began chopping vegetables. But her mind wasn't on the task. Truthfully, she hadn't given a lot of thought to the head nurse position in the last few weeks, for good reason.

"Did Rebecca say why she didn't want it?"

"Just that she wasn't interested in the extra responsibility," Steven said. "I also got the impression she's not that ambitious. She seems happy where she is."

"Hmm." If Rebecca wasn't planning to put herself in the running, Rose might actually have a shot.

"I also heard Dr. Myers say he thought you would be the best fit for the job."

Rose stopped chopping and stared at Steven. "What?"

"You must have made quite the impression on him with all your double shifts."

"Not that I had much choice in the matter," Rose replied through gritted teeth.

"Sounds like I'm not the only one who needs to find a better work-life balance," he teased.

She glared at him. "Not funny." Returning her focus to the vegetables, she racked her brain for a change of subject. She didn't want to get within even a hair's breadth of an argument that evening. "How are things going with the home health aides?"

"Rather well. They're always on time and insanely efficient."

"That's good to hear." Though it did surprise her. While the hospital was understaffed, she'd heard the shortage of home health aides was becoming its own epidemic, particularly in rural areas. As the population aged, more people needed assistance in their homes. That had been one of her main concerns when Steven had insisted on leaving the rehab facility after only two weeks. Knowing he was being well cared for eased some of her worry.

"But I'm not sure I'll need them much longer."

Rose froze. *What could he possibly mean by that?* Clearing her throat, she focused on her chopping. "Why do you say that?"

"Dad and Lanie come by every day, and they help with food prep. The only thing I need the aides for is transitioning, and I'm hoping I'll be able to do more in PT once this blasted cast is removed."

The tightness in her chest eased a little, but she frowned as she dumped the chopped vegetables into the oil and stirred. Something about what he'd said didn't sit right with her.

"The cast isn't due off for at least another two weeks, right?"

"That's what Marvin said." Steven shrugged. "But that's not that far away now."

The pot of water was finally boiling, and Rose added rice to it. Then she removed chicken that had been marinating in teriyaki sauce and added it to the wok.

She glanced over at him and chose her next words carefully. "I would suggest tempering your expectations regarding your recovery. It might not be as swift as you would like."

"It's already slower than I want," Steven grumbled. "But I've been doing some research, and once the cast is off, I expect to make a lot more progress." He leaned his head back against his chair and stared at the ceiling. "And the sooner I do, the sooner things can return to normal."

Warning bells went off in Rose's head. He was so focused on his ability to walk, he seemed to conveniently forget his heart condition. Her desire to keep the peace between them clashed with her concerns about his health.

She'd bitten her tongue multiple times that evening, and she wouldn't be surprised if she'd put a hole in it.

Instead of responding, she busied herself with finishing dinner. She stirred the vegetables and chicken together in the wok and checked the rice. Everything was coming along nicely. If only she could say the same about her relationship.

She grabbed two plates and silverware before stepping around Steven and setting the dining room table. On her way back in, he grabbed her hand and gave it a squeeze. She hoped her smile looked more genuine than it felt.

"What would you like to drink?" she asked.

"I'd say a beer, but Dr. Myers would probably kill me."

"And I'd help him," Rose said with a sweet smile. "Water or iced tea?"

Steven sighed. "Water, please."

By the time she'd filled the glasses, dinner was ready. She drained the rice and put it into one bowl with the stir-fry in the other. After setting the food on the table, she unlocked Steven's chair and brought him over.

"This smells amazing," he said before lifting his glass. "To us."

She tapped his glass and took a sip. Then she served Steven and herself. Soon the only sound in the room was forks scraping against plates. She relished the break from cherry-picking her words and pretending everything was fine.

When they finished eating, Steven leaned forward and took her hand. "Thank you for tonight. It was fun being just us for an evening."

Rose's lips turned up in a genuine smile. "It really was. Hopefully, now that you're out of the hospital, it can happen more often."

"From your lips to God's ears."

"The night's not over yet. I made dessert."

Without giving him a chance to respond, she stood and cleared their plates. After dropping them off in the sink to clean later, she removed a pan of brownies from the fridge and plated up two.

She returned to the table and set Steven's plate in front of him. "Enjoy."

"Oh man, you make the best brownies." He took a bite and closed his eyes. "I can't wait to eat your food all the time."

"Hey, mister." She playfully shook a finger at him. "I'm no personal chef. You'll be helping me."

"Of that, I have no doubt." Once he finished his brownie, he brushed the crumbs from his fingers. "I meant it'll be nice to be together every evening. Well, I mean, the evenings you don't have a shift."

And the ones you aren't working late. But she kept that comment to herself. They'd managed to make it through dinner without devolving into an argument, and she was determined to keep it that way.

A knock sounded at the door, and his face fell. "That'll be my dad."

With a heavy heart, Rose stood to answer it. How had the evening passed so quickly? But sure enough, Max stood on the other side.

"Evening, Rose."

"Hi, Max." She stepped to the side to let him in. "He's in the dining room." As she turned to lead him there, Max stopped her.

"How's he doing?"

"Much better. He seems to be happy to be home."

Max searched her face. "And how are *you* doing?"

"I'm okay," she lied.

But her soon-to-be father-in-law wasn't fooled. "I know you worry about him. We all do. He's a hardheaded man."

Rose raised an eyebrow. "Wonder where he got that from."

His face broke into a wide grin, and he laughed. "Fair enough."

"Hey, you two," Steven called. "Stop whispering about me like I'm not here."

"Who said we're talking about you?" Max demanded as he walked into the dining room. "Maybe I was trying to convince your fiancée she's with the wrong McAllister."

"Very funny." Steven crossed his arms. "You're early."

"I'm sorry, son, but the home health care aides had to move your appointment time. They're coming to your house in a half hour."

With a sigh, he nodded. "All right. Well, can you at least turn around? I want to give Rose a proper goodbye."

Max rolled his eyes but did as Steven asked. Rose moved beside Steven and bent down to give him a quick kiss, but that was clearly not what he meant by a "proper goodbye." Instead, he pulled her into his lap and tangled his hands in her hair.

"Have I told you how much I love you lately?" he murmured between kisses.

"No," she whispered. "But now hardly seems the time."

"Then we'll just have to find another time." His final kiss was deep and passionate, almost like a promise.

"You can turn around now," he called to his dad.

Max came over and grasped the wheelchair handles. "You have a good evening, Rose."

"You, too, Max."

She followed them outside and waved as they headed down the sidewalk to the van. Once Steven was secure, Max drove away.

Rose went inside and leaned against the door. Her lips still burned from Steven's fervent kisses, but the fluttering in her stomach wasn't from butterflies. It was guilt. She couldn't keep up the charade of pretending everything was fine between them. Eventually, she and Steven needed to have a frank discussion about their present and their future.

Chapter Eleven

"HERE'S YOUR COMPUTER, AS promised," Lanie said the next day as she blew into Steven's house, loaded down with bags of groceries and his laptop.

"Thanks!" He grabbed the computer and eagerly opened it before he caught himself. *Not yet.* He needed to wait until he was alone. Then he could delve into his workload and make a dent. If he tried to do that right then, Lanie would likely rat him out to Rose, or worse, she might return the computer to his office.

With a resigned sigh, he set it on the kitchen table and lifted a few items from the grocery bag. He moved to the pantry and put them on the lower shelves. Although he hated being cooped up and treated like an invalid, he didn't miss grocery shopping. He could get used to having groceries delivered, especially when it didn't cost him any extra in fees.

"I bought stuff to make chicken piccata for dinner tonight." Lanie grabbed the package of chicken and stuck it in the fridge.

"You don't have to do that," he responded quickly. If she stayed for dinner, he wouldn't be able to get to work until late in the evening.

"I know, but I want to." She shot him a smile. "I suspect you miss red meat, but I think you'll love this anyway." Her smile turned wistful. "It tastes just like Mom's."

How can I turn that down? "That sounds great. I appreciate all you're doing for me."

"Rose may be joining us as well," she continued as she filled his pantry with different canned goods. "She wasn't sure whether she'd have to work a double tonight."

Ducking his head into his fridge, he put away some produce, glad for a moment to fix his expression. If Rose came over, he would never get a chance to work. She'd probably stay until the aides came to transfer him to his bed for the night, and then he'd have no way of accessing his computer. For a moment, he hoped she wouldn't be able to get off in time, then he chastised himself. He wasn't being fair.

"That's great," he finally said, hoping he'd added enough enthusiasm to his tone.

"Dad may stop by, although there's a game on tonight."

Sometimes Steven envied his father. Nobody forced him to do anything, mainly because he was stubborn enough to do the exact opposite of whatever anyone wanted him to do. But that might be part of the reason things hadn't worked out between Steven's parents. His father wouldn't bend or compromise, which had led his mother to a breaking point.

That thought sobered Steven up. He refused to fall into the same habits as his father. If Rose stopped by, he would deal with it as best he could. Perhaps he could use the excuse that he needed to compile the ad for the law clerk.

"It's not like Dad can't watch it here," Steven said, coming back to the present.

"Yeah, but you know how he is."

After the groceries were put away, Lanie moved over to where she'd laid his laptop on the counter and pushed it toward him. "So why don't we work on the law clerk ad? We've got some time before I need to start dinner."

He tried to hide his relief as he moved over to her and signed in to his computer. The machine booted up quickly, and he opened his email, skimming through the growing number of unread messages staring back at him. He itched to start reading them in greater detail, but he didn't want to test his sister's patience. The fact that she'd brought him his laptop and was willing to allow him to do some work was more than he could have hoped for.

Instead, he clicked into his files and opened his special calendar, noting with growing alarm that some of the deadlines he'd set were fast approaching. As he surveyed the dates, he debated what cases he would feel comfortable passing on to a law student.

"I need someone who's already graduated," he murmured half to himself. "A 3L might be acceptable, but anyone lower than that is too wet behind the ears."

Lanie gave him a puzzled look. "What does that mean?"

"Ah, sorry." He chuckled. "Basically, a third-year law student, someone who's preparing to graduate."

She nodded and grabbed a pen and paper from the drawer by the fridge. "Do they need to specialize in any area of law?"

"Not really. But their research skills need to be impressive, especially if they aren't familiar with a certain area like estate planning or family law."

After jotting that down, she peered over his shoulder. "That looks like a lot of work. How do you keep up with it?"

"Sandra helps," he said, trying to ignore the growing panic in his belly. "But it's why I work such long hours."

She raised an eyebrow. "Do you expect a law clerk to do that?"

Cocking his head, he considered her question. *Do I expect a law clerk to keep my crazy schedule?* From what he knew of the larger law firms, associates were often expected to work long hours, especially if they hoped to get on the partner track. But he wasn't a large law firm, and he wasn't hiring an associate.

"No, though I do hope they'll be open to working after hours sometimes."

"We'll discuss that in the interview," she said.

He turned to her. "You're planning on joining the interviews?"

"Of course." Her eyes widened. "Why wouldn't I?"

He frowned and glanced at his computer. *What does Lanie know about hiring anyone, let alone for a law practice?* He figured she would assist with the day-to-day, performing more secretarial tasks like editing pleadings or mailing correspondence. But it appeared she had bigger plans for her time with him.

"I didn't expect you to. I mean, no offense, sis, but do you even know what to look for in a law clerk?"

She glared at him. "I know what to look for in an *employee*, regardless of their job title."

After searching her face for a moment, he nodded, though he wasn't convinced. Still, it might be helpful to have another person evaluating the candidates. She might have a different perspective than him, and he wanted to be sure he made the right choice.

"All right. First things first, let's decide what to put in this advertisement to attract quality candidates." He leaned back and crossed his arms. "In addition to research skills, I need someone who's a good writer. Sandra helps draft a lot of my pleadings, but I don't want to rely solely on her. And if I have to spend all my time editing something poorly written, I'd be better off writing it myself."

With a nod, Lanie jotted that down. "But I assume you'll have to review everything since they won't be licensed to practice yet, right?"

"Of course." He waved a hand. "I'd review it even if they were licensed to practice since it's my name on the letterhead." Drumming his fingers on the table, he tried to think of what else might be useful. "Excellent customer service skills."

She frowned. "Won't most of the clients be handled by Sandra or your receptionist?"

"Not necessarily. If I'm not around, they may need to speak to the law clerk if they need something more technical explained. While the clerk can't give them legal advice, they can at least explain the contents of a contract, for example. And they'll likely be in regular contact with the court. I want to make sure they can manage." He ran his fingers through his hair. "Besides, what if Sandra or Leslie are busy? At the very least, the clerk will need to know how to handle clients well enough to take detailed messages."

"Duly noted."

Nothing else immediately came to mind. He glanced at his sister's notes. "Do you think you can draft an ad with what I've given you?'

She nodded, her face breaking into a smile. "I'll go over it with Sandra tomorrow and bring it by when we're done."

"That's great!" The tension in his shoulders eased. He hadn't realized how much it would help to have a plan. "I appreciate your help."

"Anytime." After a quick glance at her watch, she moved toward the kitchen. "I'd better get started on dinner before Rose and Dad arrive."

"If they're still coming," Steven said, crossing his fingers under the table in hopes that they wouldn't. The fewer people there, the greater his chance of getting to work after Lanie left.

———

"Thanks for dinner." Steven patted his stomach and gave his sister a warm smile.

Rose had been pulled into a double shift, and his father had preferred a night in with pizza and beer to Lanie's cooking. Everything had turned out as he'd hoped. He just needed to see Lanie headed home, and he could get to work.

She shook her head and grimaced. "There's so much food left over. I should have saved some of the chicken for another night."

"Nonsense. I'll have leftovers for lunch and dinner tomorrow."

"True, though I had planned to stop by to make you dinner."

He waved his hand over the table. "Look at all of this. There's really no need."

Her lips pursed as if she wanted to argue with him. He stacked plates and silverware before setting them on his lap and wheeling himself to the sink. His sister jumped up to help him. Between the two of them, they should be able to make quick work of it.

"Did you want to play a game tonight?" Lanie filled the sink while he stuffed the leftovers into the fridge.

Shaking his head, he moved to the table and leaned against it, trying to look tired. "I'm pretty beat. When the home care aides arrive, I plan to have them help me into bed and call it a night."

For a moment, he feared she would see right through him, but instead, she gave a quick nod. "That's wise. You don't look like you're getting enough rest."

"What's that supposed to mean?"

She raised an eyebrow. "Don't get defensive. I'm only saying I'm concerned." Wiping her hands on a towel, she leaned forward and scrutinized his face. "You've got dark circles under your eyes."

"I've got a lot on my mind." He shrugged. "It's hard to turn my brain off, especially with everything I need to do."

"I can understand that, but you've got to try." Her teeth worried her lower lip. "Have you taken any of the sleeping medication the doctor prescribed?"

"You know I hate feeling like I'm drugged. I can't even stand Benadryl."

"But if it'll help—"

"It won't. Trust me."

She shot him a dubious look. "How do you know if you won't try?"

"Look, I appreciate your concern, but I'm fine." When she opened her mouth, he held up his hand. "Or at least, I will be once we find a law clerk and relieve my work burden a bit."

She turned to the sink and grabbed another dish. "It's just, Rose has been talking my ear off every chance she gets about how worried she is. I promised her I would try to intervene."

"Let me handle Rose."

Lanie snorted. "Good luck with that."

I'm gonna need it.

After she put away the last dish, Lanie grabbed her purse, and he followed her to the front door. She leaned down and gave him a quick hug.

"I know you keep telling us not to worry, but we can't help it." She pinched his cheek. "You're the only big brother I've got."

Shaking her off, he smiled. "I'll take care of myself, I promise."

As soon as she was gone, Steven returned to the kitchen and grabbed his laptop. What he'd told Lanie was partially true. When the home care aides arrived, he did plan to have them set him up in bed, but what he didn't tell her was he intended to take his laptop with him.

But it wouldn't help much. Reviewing his emails only confirmed his fears. Due to the amount of work he'd missed, deadlines were pressing in from every direction. With a sigh, he began reading and responding to emails. And he vowed to himself that one way or another, he would find his way back into his office—and soon.

———

The next morning, Steven woke with a crick in his neck. He'd slumped over while working, and his laptop hung haphazardly off his good leg. He rubbed his eyes and stretched, wincing at the stiffness in his shoulders.

After he righted his laptop, a low groan rumbled in his throat. His emails appeared to have multiplied overnight.

A knock on the door alerted him to the arrival of the home care aides. Two men in scrubs entered the house and helped him to his chair. Neither was very talkative, which was fine with Steven. Their assistance with his morning routine was awkward enough, especially in the bathroom. Once he was showered, dressed, and sitting at the kitchen table, they left, promising to return that evening.

He longed for a cup of coffee, but since his heart attack, Rose had insisted he switch to decaf. That wasn't going to do it this morning. He went to the kitchen to see if Lanie had taken pity on him and stashed real coffee away somewhere.

After searching the cabinets to no avail, he grabbed the decaf canister, grumbling the whole time. But, he reasoned, it was better than nothing, and perhaps the scent of fresh coffee would trigger his brain.

He checked his phone as he waited for the coffee to brew. Lanie had sent him a draft of the advertisement for a law clerk. As he read it, he had to give his sister credit. She'd managed to sum up everything he needed in very few characters. He gave her the go-ahead to post the ad and poured himself a mug of coffee before heading to the living room.

A few hours later, another knock on the front door startled him. When the person didn't immediately enter, he scrambled to hide his computer under a couch cushion before rushing to open the door.

"Hey, big bro." Lanie stepped around him and into the house. Her arms were laden with packages.

"I thought I told you that you didn't need to cook for me tonight," he replied, struggling and failing to keep the annoyance out of his voice.

"I'm not here to cook for you, but I did note you were low on a few things. I took the liberty of picking them up." She side-eyed him. "Don't worry. I'm not staying, so you can return to working on the sly without my interference."

His mouth fell open, but before he could respond, she moved by him and carried her bags into the kitchen. After he recovered from his shock, Steven followed her down the hall.

"Did you tell Rose?" he demanded from the doorway.

She rolled her eyes. "No, I'm not your warden. But *you* should tell her."

Once she put the groceries away, she turned and leaned against the counter, folding her arms.

"I thought you weren't staying," he said, shifting uncomfortably.

"I'm not, but I did want to let you know we already got our first applicant."

His eyebrows shot up. "That was fast." He leaned forward. "Did you have a chance to look over the application?"

She nodded. "I'm no expert, but he sounds perfect. And I'm taking his quick response as a good sign we'll be able to find someone to assist you real soon." She pushed off the counter and stepped toward him. A wave of relief washed over him, and he moved out of her way. When she reached the front door at the end of the hallway, she glanced over her shoulder. "But if you want to interview him in person, you'll have to get the okay from your actual warden."

He waved a dismissive hand. "If it's to help me reduce stress, she won't mind."

His sister's doubtful look made him second-guess himself, but he kept his face neutral as she left. Once she was gone, he retrieved his computer from the couch.

As he reviewed the application, he was buoyed by the credentials of the applicant, a recent Georgetown University graduate looking to gain experience while he studied for the bar exam. Based on the address, he lived in the suburbs, which were about forty-five minutes away from Cedar Haven. Steven hoped that meant the applicant wasn't also applying to the big law firms in DC because there was no way his tiny firm could compete with their salary offers.

After making a few notes on the application, he debated how to approach Rose about his returning to the office to conduct interviews. Lanie had made it sound like Rose wouldn't be amenable, but he couldn't imagine why. After all, the only reason he was hiring a law clerk was to appease her. He couldn't very well hire someone without an interview. And although he could hold a virtual meeting, he was old-fashioned enough to want to meet candidates face-to-face. There was only so much he could discover about a person over a computer screen.

With any luck, Lanie could schedule the interviews to occur on the same day, which would limit the time he needed to be in the office. Whether that would be enough to appease his fiancée, he didn't know, but if nothing else, it might at least postpone an argument. After crossing his fingers, he sent a text message to Lanie to start setting up interviews.

Chapter Twelve

Rose tapped the steering wheel as she drove to Steven's house. They'd planned to get together to discuss the wedding budget. Since she'd had the morning off, she spent it going over the figures, and things weren't looking good. Although she had made some decent overtime with all of her double shifts, she couldn't say the same for Steven. She planned to ask him about his business's finances, but she didn't expect to hear good news. Their current financial situation had renewed her desire to discuss postponing the wedding again.

She'd spoken to Carissa that morning regarding their upcoming payments. Though Carissa had sympathized with their situation, she told Rose they needed to decide what they were going to do and soon. The vendors were willing to negotiate a new date for the wedding but only if they got paid by the deadline, which was the next day.

When she reached the door, it swung open before she could knock. Steven greeted her with a smile.

"How are you feeling?" she asked as she followed him into the house.

"Better." He maneuvered to the table, where he had set out a pitcher of iced tea and two glasses. "How was work? Is Lisa's daughter better?"

Rose nodded. "Yes, thank goodness. I couldn't handle another double shift this week." After pouring the tea, she squared her shoulders and removed the binder she'd used to track the wedding details and expenses. "So, about the wedding budget."

His body tensed, and he fidgeted beside her. *This is not a good sign.* But she focused on the figures because she needed him to understand what they owed before they discussed his share.

"We've got several items coming due in the next few weeks. Invitations should have been sent this month, but with everything that happened, I ordered them late. I'm hoping to get them out before the Fourth of July." She pushed the binder closer to him. "The next payment to the caterer is due next week, which is fifty percent of the total charge. Our last payment will be due once we have a final head count in August." Then she flipped the calendar page. "The final payments will be due two weeks before August twenty-sixth."

Steven's eyes widened as he took in all of the four-figure amounts. "And how much does this total?"

After flipping back to the previous page, Rose pointed at the equations she'd added yesterday. "It comes down to about fifteen thousand dollars still to pay."

His throat moved as he swallowed thickly, and Rose braced herself for what she expected him to say. But he surprised her when he pushed away from the table and went to the couch. A moment later, he returned with his laptop.

"I'm going to be a little short for my share," he admitted as he opened the computer and signed in.

She pressed her lips together and fought back frustration. She'd known that, expected it, but it didn't make it any less aggravating. While her main focus had been on his recovery, she'd known their finances would take a hit after his accident.

"How short?" She kept her tone even.

He didn't answer immediately. Instead, he seemed to be doing some calculations of his own. His eyebrows knitted together, and he bit his lip.

"Steven?"

With a sigh, he turned the screen toward her. "About seventy-five hundred short."

Her stomach dropped. It was worse than she'd thought. They'd been splitting the wedding costs equally and had opened a joint account to pay for them, with the plan to use that account for joint expenses once they were married. Steven hadn't deposited anything into it since April.

"All of it?"

He gave a grim nod. "And it gets worse."

"How could it possibly be worse?"

"Mr. Willoughby is threatening to find a new lawyer if I can't work on his case."

Though Mr. Willoughby was Steven's biggest client, she couldn't deny she would be thrilled to see the back of him. He was the absolute worst kind of person.

"I'm sure you can find someone to replace him."

He shook his head. "I know he's a pain, but between the drama of his divorce and his real estate business, he's been a very lucrative client, and I'd be underwater without him."

"So what are you going to do?"

When he didn't answer, she decided to try her next strategy. "Can we discuss postponing the wedding now?"

His mouth set in a thin line. "Not this again. We'll lose more money if we cancel now."

"I spoke to Carissa this morning, and the vendors are still willing to work with us on finding a new date next summer." Rose left out the part about needing to pay them by the original deadline. Her share of the cost would cover the payments due in July, and once they had a new date, she hoped to renegotiate a payment plan for the remaining balance.

He searched her face, and she tried to keep her expression neutral while her heart hammered in her chest. She prayed he would see reason.

"I'm doing what you asked, Rose. Lanie and I are setting up interviews to hire a law clerk. And who knows, maybe they'll do well enough to work toward becoming a partner someday. In the meantime, I'm trying to keep my business afloat so we can afford to start our lives together." His chest expanded as he took a deep breath, and she held hers as she waited for whatever he would say next. "I want to marry you. I want a life with you, and I'm doing everything I can to make that happen. So why don't you tell me what's really going on?"

What the—What was that supposed to mean? They were financially strapped and could no longer afford the wedding they'd planned. *What other possible motive could I have? Does he think I want to keep having this conversation? Does he think I enjoy pushing him on this?*

A cold wave of dread washed down her spine. He couldn't possibly know about her parents' deciding not to attend, could he? Rose hadn't told anyone else about that, and she highly doubted Steven had spoken to her parents since he'd left the hospital. But his insistence that she had some ulterior motive in postponing the wedding was making her paranoid.

Pushing those thoughts away, she glared at him. "What's really going on is that we can't afford to get married the way we planned. And unless you've got seven thousand dollars stashed away somewhere, I don't know how you suggest we pay for the commitments we've already made." When he opened his mouth to protest, she rushed on. "Besides, wouldn't you rather hold the wedding of our dreams when you're fully recovered and able to enjoy it?"

He dropped his gaze to the table as if the fight had gone out of him. Tears pricked behind her eyes because she didn't want to postpone the wedding, but she didn't see any other option.

"I'm not saying forever, Steven. Just a year. One year where you can focus on healing and we can get our lives, and our finances, back on track. Then we can have the wedding of our dreams without bankrupting ourselves." *A year for me to save up for my parents' flights.*

A tear slipped down his cheek. "It's not fair." He raised his head and looked at her. "I don't want to wait anymore. We already put it off for a year because of my mother and opening the law firm. I don't want this to be like Scrooge in *A Christmas Carol* where we keep postponing the wedding until the 'right time.'" He put air quotes around those last words. Sliding his hand across the table, he grasped hers. "It may never be the right time for us to get married, but I don't want to risk losing the right person for me."

Her heart melted. But she looked at Steven, really looked at him, and she could see the toll the situation was taking on him. Dark circles bloomed like purple bruises under his eyes, and his skin was paler than usual. When he'd led her into the house, she could hear his labored breathing as he pushed his wheelchair. It wouldn't take much for him to be right back in the hospital, and who knew whether he would survive another heart attack.

"I want to marry you too," she said in earnest before pulling her hand away. She stared at the table as she spoke the words she'd avoided even thinking let alone saying out loud. "But I don't want to be a widow so soon after becoming your wife."

His jaw dropped open. "Is that what you think is going to happen?" He maneuvered his chair around to her side of the table. His arm slid around her shoulders. "I promise you, I *am* taking better care of myself. Lanie has been buying me healthy food, and I've been getting plenty of rest."

"But some things haven't changed, have they?" She gestured to his computer. "You're still working way more than you should considering you haven't been cleared to return to work. You were already stressed about the law firm's finances, and now the wedding expenses are stressing you out."

"I'm not—"

"I saw the panic in your eyes when I showed you what we owed."

He scratched the back of his head. "We could ask my dad for a loan—"

"You can't be serious." Without another word, she grabbed her purse.

"Where are you going?"

"Home. This conversation is over."

"Come on. Be reasonable." He tried to grasp her arm, but she backed away.

"I *am* being reasonable. Do you really believe it's appropriate to ask your father for money after he just paid for your two-week stay in the rehab facility? He's retired and on a fixed income. He can't afford to throw more money at *our* financial problems."

With that, she turned and fled the house. She jumped into her car and took off, wanting to put as much distance between her and Steven as possible.

Instead of going to her condo, Rose parked by the pond nearby. She breathed in the thick summer air and walked down to the water's edge. Ducks swam near the shoreline, and a lone swan circled near the center. A commotion on the other side of the pond caught her attention, and she hurried over, worried something had happened to half of her favorite bird couple.

Two men were trying to wrangle the swan into a cage but were having quite the time of it. As she approached, the swan was clearly fighting, though it favored one leg over the other.

"What's going on?" she asked.

One of the men coaxed the swan into the cage while the other shut the door. The swan settled into the corner, hissing at its captors.

"This one broke its leg," the man who had shut the door said. He lifted his baseball cap, revealing a bald head, and wiped it with a handkerchief. "We're taking it to a wildlife rehabilitation center where they can set the leg and allow it to heal."

"But we had a time getting it away from its mate," the other man said, wiping his face on his shirt sleeve. He nodded at the remaining swan. It looked lonesome out there on its own.

"Will it be okay without its mate?" Rose asked. She couldn't help comparing their situation to her own.

"Should be," the bald man said. "But swans are one of the few bird species that mate for life. She may grieve as if he's died. We'll keep an eye on her, though, and make sure she takes care of herself for when he returns."

"And when will that be?" Rose asked, unable to hide her interest.

The men exchanged a look, then the bald one shrugged. "Hard to say." He inclined his head toward the cluster of buildings where her condo was. "You live around here?"

She nodded, hoping she wouldn't regret revealing that information to strangers.

"We'll let you know how the male gets on," he promised with a smile. "And you'll definitely want to be here when they're reunited."

Cocking her head, she frowned. "Why's that?"

The other man just laughed. "You'll have to see for yourself."

They loaded the swan's cage into the truck bed and secured it before climbing in and driving away. Rose watched until the truck had driven out of sight before closing her eyes and sending up a short prayer for the swans.

Her earlier anger had dissipated, and she felt hollow. With a heavy heart, she turned and walked to her condo.

⁓ℓℓ⁓

When Rose finally checked her phone later that evening, she was surprised to find only two texts and one voicemail. Steven's messages were full of apologies and his insistence that he would be fine. But she'd meant what she'd said about not wanting to be a widow before she'd even had a chance to be a wife. And Steven could wax poetic all he wanted about his dietary changes; the real crux of the issue was the stress load on his heart.

This isn't how I imagined my life when Steven asked me to move to Cedar Haven. It always seemed like something new came up just as she thought they were finally moving forward.

Did I make a mistake? After working for a few years in Baltimore, she'd received a job offer at a prestigious hospital in Boston. But when Steven had learned of his mother's cancer diagnosis, he decided to open a practice in his hometown to be closer to her.

So Rose gave up her dream of Boston and found a position at the small hospital in the middle of nowhere. Of course, there were many things she loved about the town. The hospital's size allowed her to have closer relationships with her patients. She'd become more active in the community, and she had found a best friend in her future sister-in-law. Most importantly, she had Steven.

But sometimes, she wished she'd worked harder to convince him to move to Boston. Several law firms in the city would have snapped someone like him up in a heartbeat. Perhaps he could have found a better work-life balance. At the very least, he would have less stress about finances. Those firms were known to pay very well.

After his mother passed, Rose thought Steven might consider going back, but he had his heart set on opening his own firm. In the end, it hadn't taken much to convince her to stay in Cedar Haven. She was already in town, and the thought of packing up everything to move again sounded exhausting. So they'd stayed.

But he'd never told her how much capital he had sunk into the venture until it was too late. On top of that, he still had to pay off his student loans from law school. The sixty-five thousand dollars he'd inherited from his mother after paying off the estate helped, but it wasn't enough to make a substantial dent in what he owed.

To say they were financially strapped was an understatement. If only they hadn't moved to Cedar Haven so quickly. Maybe if they'd stayed in the city, they could have saved a nest egg to help him build his business.

She checked her phone again but had no new messages. Perhaps he'd decided to give her some time. She grimaced. Or maybe he was doing something he wasn't supposed to be doing, like working. It would be like Steven to take advantage of her absence to dive into his caseload and make some headway. After all, he probably reasoned that if she was mad at him, she would be less likely to stop by and catch him in the act. She hated how well he knew her sometimes.

She'd stewed long enough. She needed to have it out with him, and if she caught him working, it would add fuel to her already simmering fire.

After grabbing her purse and keys, she headed out the door and drove to the house. They hadn't been able to afford much of a mortgage, even that far from the city. But it was enough for them—two bedrooms and one and a half baths in less than sixteen hundred square feet. One of the bedrooms hardly qualified as a full room, but it allowed for a home office. Part of her wondered if she should have insisted Steven use that until they could afford to buy commercial space, but he'd fallen in love with the location of his firm, and his father had helped him secure the loan. It hadn't seemed worth it to fight at the time.

Her hand hovered over the doorknob. Shaking her head, she turned the knob. He always said it was her house too. So she supposed she shouldn't feel weird walking in.

"Steven?" she called. The late-summer-evening sun poured into the room from behind her, basking the hallway in an orangey hue.

No response came, but the distinct sound of keys clacking on a keyboard drifted down the hall. *Unbelievable.* She prepared to catch him in the act.

Sure enough, Steven scrambled to shut his laptop as she entered the living room. He was in his chair beside the couch. His hazel eyes widened, and he bit his lower lip in quite possibly the guiltiest expression she'd ever seen. If she wasn't so angry, she might have laughed.

"What do you think you're doing?" She crossed her arms.

"Nothing," he said a little too quickly. "I mean, it's not what it looks like."

"It looks like you're working." She raised an eyebrow.

"Not really. I mean, I'm trying to catch up on email, I swear." He raised his hands as if in surrender. "I'm not working on any briefs or pleadings, nothing that would cause me undue stress."

She scoffed. "Knowing some of your clients, I find that hard to believe."

With a wry smile, he slid the laptop onto the coffee table. He moved over to her cautiously. When he grabbed her hand and began pulling her into his lap, she stiffened, and he released her with a frown.

"What are you doing here?" He searched her face.

"I came to finish our argument," she said coolly, narrowing her eyes. "But it appears we're about to have another one."

He sighed. "I told you Lanie brought the laptop here so I could catch up on work."

"No." She jabbed him in the chest. "Lanie brought the laptop home to write the advertisement for a law clerk, which you've done. She should have taken it back to the office where it belongs."

"Be reasonable, Rose," he whined. "I can't just sit here day in and day out doing nothing while my business goes to hell." He leaned closer to her, both eyebrows raised in a challenge. "Do you want me to fail?"

That caught her off guard, and she staggered back. "Of course not, but I don't want your heart to either."

Taking her hand, he placed it on his chest. His pulse pounded beneath her palm. "It's still ticking."

A faint smile pulled at her lips before she could stop it. She tried to rearrange her features into a sterner expression. "For now."

But Steven took advantage of her faltering anger and brushed his hand over her cheek. She started to pull away, but he slid his other hand around her waist, pulling her into his lap and kissing her.

"Not fair," she murmured against his lips.

He chuckled and released her. "But the best part of fighting is the making up."

"You assume we're done fighting," she retorted as she stood and put her hands on her hips.

"I took a nap earlier, and I've taken multiple breaks. I promise you, even though I'm working, I *am* heeding Dr. Myers's advice."

Rose was losing the battle, but she held on to the last shreds of her aggravation at finding him typing away like he hadn't just suffered a heart attack. "How long a nap?"

His gaze went to the ceiling. "I didn't time it." After a quick glance over his shoulder, he turned back to her. "But I'd guess maybe forty-five minutes?"

She pursed her lips and nodded. "I suppose that's better than nothing."

"And I have an idea for how to pay off the remaining balance for the wedding, though it might not be easy."

Despite her apprehension about the direction of the conversation, she laughed. "What do you propose?"

"Mr. Willoughby," he said. Her face must have betrayed her shock and misgivings because he hurried on. "I spoke to him this afternoon. While he's still not happy with me for not taking his calls, he was much more focused on the latest response from his wife. She was open to the settlement I had sent her before my accident, but she had some minor adjustments, which he is, of course, blowing out of proportion." Steven let out an exasperated sigh. "He's bound and determined to take this to court, and that means if I can keep him happy, he'll owe me an even larger retainer fee than what he's already paid." His teasing grin melted her heart. "The irony is he may single-handedly ensure our marriage through his divorce."

She giggled, then her face fell. "But he's your most demanding client."

"And the law clerk will help alleviate some of that demand."

"It's a start," she admitted.

Slipping his arms around her waist again, he pulled her close. "Can we make up now?"

It would be easy to give in, but she needed to clear the air on one more thing. "First, there's something I need to tell you."

"Oh?"

She took a deep breath. "You were right. I did have an ulterior motive for wanting to postpone the wedding." At his alarmed expression, she cupped her hand over his cheek. "It's not what you think. I promise."

"Then... what is it?"

"My mom told me she and my dad can't make the wedding." Tears pricked behind her eyes, and she tried to blink them back. "They can't afford the plane tickets."

"Oh, Rose," Steven murmured, tightening his arms around her.

"It feels stupid saying this to you." She sniffled.

"Why? I can only imagine how devastating that news was for you. Heck, I'm disappointed, and they aren't even my parents."

"Yes, but you just lost your mom." Rose pulled back to search his face. "It's selfish to want to postpone the wedding so they can be here, especially with the anniversary of your mom's death coming up soon."

His eyes got a little misty. "I'd forgotten that." He took a moment to compose himself. "But my feelings don't trump yours. I wish you had told me."

"Would it have changed your mind about postponing?"

He averted his eyes. "If I'm honest, probably not, but that's because I don't want to wait any longer to marry you. Maybe we can go visit them in South Korea when we're in a better place both physically and financially. How would you like to have a small ceremony there?"

Instead of answering, she knelt beside his chair and wrapped her arms around his neck before peppering him with light, grateful kisses.

Chapter Thirteen

A FEW DAYS LATER, Steven entered his office for the first time since his accident. It felt good to be back, like coming home. Despite Rose's protests, he'd managed to catch up on much of what he'd missed from the comfort of his home, but there was something about being physically present that made him feel more productive.

The reception desk sat to the left of the door, though Leslie wasn't in yet. To the right was the waiting room, which he'd furnished with four straight-backed chairs surrounding a small table covered with magazines. A few bookshelves graced the back wall, but the majority of his law books were tucked in his office and the conference room.

"Welcome back, boss," Sandra said as she came in behind him and handed him a coffee cup.

"Thanks, Sandra, but I can't—"

"Chill, dude. It's decaf."

"In that case..." He lifted the cup to his lips and sipped the warm beverage while missing the taste of real coffee. One day, he hoped to get Rose—and for that matter, Dr. Myers—to relent on the dietary restrictions, but... baby steps.

"Lanie texted me to say she was running late but she'd be here in time for the first interview," Sandra continued, moving farther into the reception area and flipping on a light. "Did you want me to sit in as well, or do you think the two of you can handle it?"

"Don't you want to have a say?" He frowned. "You'll be working directly with whomever we hire."

She shrugged. "I can get along with pretty much anyone. Besides, I've got a lot on my plate. I'd prefer to have the time to get through that."

He ran a hand through his hair. "Well, okay, but if we find someone we like, can we bring them to meet you?"

"That works for me." She lifted her cup in salute. "If you need me, I'll be drowning in pleadings."

After checking the mail bin at the receptionist's desk, Steven continued on into his office. A low groan rumbled in his throat as he stared at the mountains of paperwork on his desk. He might have kept up with things electronically well enough from home, but *that* was why he needed to be in the office.

At least he had a couple of hours before the first interview. Maneuvering around was a challenge, but someone had removed the rolling chair behind his desk, and his wheelchair fit well enough in its place. He set his coffee cup on the only clear space he could find and began sorting through the piles, determining what needed his immediate attention and what could wait.

Just as he had finally gotten into a groove, someone knocked at his door. A quick glance at the time confirmed it was almost ten.

"Come in," he called.

Lanie entered the room and carried two coffee cups.

"Ah, thanks, sis, but I've had about all the decaf I can handle for today."

She leaned down and plopped the cup in front of him with a conspiratorial wink. "It's not decaf."

His head snapped up, and he raised an eyebrow. "Real coffee? You're playing with fire."

"I figure you deserved a treat for good behavior."

Chuckling, he sipped and sighed with pleasure. "I'm not sure if Rose would agree with you on that."

"Eh, she worries too much." Lanie slipped into one of the chairs on the other side of his desk and raised an eyebrow. "So, you ready for this?"

"I don't have much choice, do I?" He pulled the pile of applications in front of him. "I just hope there's a true diamond among the rough you found."

She snorted. "Sorry I couldn't find anyone from Yale or Harvard, but somehow, I doubt they would be interested in sleepy little Cedar Haven."

"But you did find a few from decent local schools. I guess I can forgive you."

"There's even a Georgetown in there," she said, separating the pile and pushing a file toward him.

"Yeah, but what are the odds they'll leave DC to come here? I can't compete with the salary, let alone the prestige." He sighed, laying his head back on his chair and staring at the ceiling. "I need someone who can share my vision and is willing to do the work."

A warm hand covered his own, and he glanced at his sister.

"We'll find someone." He must not have looked convinced, because she hurried on. "Maybe not today, but the ad is running for another week."

Leslie appeared in his doorway, her dark-brown hair pulled back in a bun. "Your first interview has arrived."

With a quick nod, Steven focused on Lanie. "I guess it's now or never."

"That's the spirit!" she deadpanned.

He gathered the application for the first interview and motioned for Lanie to head into the conference room, where Leslie had already set them up. The moment they entered the room, the applicant, Jason Gilherst, pushed his chair back and jumped to his feet. His pleasant smile faltered as he took in Steven's wheelchair, and he ran a hand through his disheveled hair. But his eyes widened when they landed on Lanie, and his smile morphed into a leer.

Steven tensed, bracing himself for some inappropriate comment toward his sister. To her credit, she caught on to the man's sudden interest and lifted her left hand to brush her hair away from her face, putting her shiny diamond ring on display.

Well played. Steven bit the inside of his cheek to keep from laughing.

"Mr. Gilherst, this is Steven McAllister," Leslie said. "And this is Lanie McAllister, his sister."

"Do you work here as well?" Mr. Gilherst asked Lanie, clearly undeterred by the prominence of the diamond on her finger.

"I'm just filling in."

"You'd mostly be working with Leslie, our receptionist, and Sandra, our paralegal, until I'm able to return to the office full-time," Steven broke in, hoping to ease the tension and direct Mr. Gilherst's focus elsewhere.

Mr. Gilherst's face fell, and Steven shot a look at Leslie before she closed the door. If her grim expression was any indication, they were in agreement. Their first candidate was a bust.

Still, the interview must go on. He and Lanie went through the motions, which only further confirmed that Mr. Gilherst wasn't a good fit for the firm. He had high expectations of salary with no experience to back up the demand and talked as if he would be running the place in Steven's absence.

When the interview ended, Steven stifled a sigh of relief. *Thank goodness that's over.* His chest tightened. If all of their candidates were like that one, he would be even worse off than if he'd just returned to the office full-time himself.

By the time they reached the last interviewee of the day, Steven was ready to throw in the towel. He'd seen one or two applicants he could tolerate, but nobody appeared up to the task. Maybe he was asking too much.

Lanie didn't seem encouraged either. With a sigh, she dragged the last application in front of her and flipped through it.

"Ah, it's the Georgetown applicant," she said with more enthusiasm than Steven could muster.

"He'll probably want a bigger salary than the first interviewee," Steven moaned. The situation was hopeless.

"He can't be any worse than Mr. Gilherst," Lanie said with a wry smile.

A moment later, Leslie knocked on the door and led a young man into the room. He had wavy dark-brown hair and light-brown eyes. His suit was neatly pressed, and he walked right up to Steven and shook his hand. If he noticed Steven didn't stand to greet him, or the wheelchair, he didn't let on.

"I'm Michael Ellerson," he told Lanie as he extended his hand.

"Lanie McAllister, Steven's sister." She gestured for him to sit, and Steven was relieved Mr. Ellerson didn't seem as infatuated with his sister as Mr. Gilherst had been.

Steven and Lanie took turns explaining the job and what was expected. Mr. Ellerson didn't flinch when they informed him of the accident and Steven's limitations, though he did ask some thoughtful questions.

"Will there be a lot of overtime?" Mr. Ellerson asked.

After a quick glance at Steven, Lanie shook her head. "Not necessarily. We do have a substantial workload at present, but we don't anticipate needing someone to work beyond office hours."

"And we likely won't be taking on new clients until I'm fully or at least mostly recovered," Steven added.

"I only ask because I'm still living near DC, and it can be a bit of a challenge to travel if I miss the train."

Steven couldn't help but laugh. "Metro closes at midnight. I can't imagine we would ever need you to stay that late."

Mr. Ellerson nodded, relief apparent in his eyes. "That's good. Some of the law firms I've interviewed at in the city implied I'd be on call around the clock."

"While we can't compete with their salaries, we can offer a better work-life balance," Lanie assured him.

"Honestly, that's more important to me right now. I've heard too many horror stories of first-year associates having nervous breakdowns in the bigger firms." Mr. Ellerson shook his head. "I'd like a bit of a break now school is over." His eyes widened as if he realized he'd implied something negative. "I mean, not that this job isn't hard or that it wouldn't be challenging... I just, er, I only meant—"

Steven raised a hand and smiled. "I worked for a year at a large law firm in Baltimore. Believe me, I understand what you mean, and I can promise you will have that work-life balance you seek here."

His sister raised an eyebrow at him, and he made a face. Just because he didn't have a good work-life balance, that didn't mean he couldn't guarantee his employees had one.

"Would you consider moving here if the job lasted beyond the summer?" Lanie asked, surprising Steven.

Mr. Ellerson glanced from one to the other and cleared his throat. "I wasn't aware that was a possibility, but I'm definitely open to it if the position was extended."

What's she playing at? Steven managed to keep his suspicions off his face. "Of course, there is always room for growth, and that's something we could explore with the right candidate." He wanted to remind everyone no decision had been made yet.

Lanie rolled her eyes at him. It seemed she had made up her mind about Mr. Ellerson and was ready to offer him the job on the spot. While Steven didn't disagree with her, he wanted more time to ensure they made the right decision.

After they finished the interview, Lanie introduced Mr. Ellerson to Sandra before showing him out. When she returned, she leaned against the doorway and crossed her arms.

"Say whatever you're thinking," Steven said, knowing she would anyway.

"He's perfect. You should have offered him the job."

"That's not how I do things." He gathered his notes and the applications before stacking them neatly in a pile. After placing it on his lap, he left the conference room.

"What if someone else snaps him up?" Lanie demanded, following him into his office. "He's the best candidate we've seen."

"So far." As he dropped the paperwork on his desk, he had to admit Mr. Ellerson was probably the best candidate they would see. But in some ways, that made him almost too good to be true.

"You're assuming we'll get more responses to our ad."

He cocked his head. "Weren't you the one who said the ad was still running and we might have more applicants?"

"That was before we interviewed the perfect fit," she scoffed.

"Look, I'll review my notes from today and sleep on it. If we don't have any additional applications tomorrow, then I'll make the decision."

"And hope no one else gets to him first."

In the end, Lanie was right. After letting the ad run for a few more days, no one else applied, and none of the other interviewees could hold a candle to Mr. Ellerson. When Steven called him later that week, he enthusiastically accepted the position. To Steven's surprise, Mr. Ellerson was even willing to start immediately, and they planned his first day for the following week.

Despite not being medically cleared to do so, Steven went into the office that day. He wanted to be there to show the new guy around and make sure everything got off to a great start. Lanie, Sandra, and Leslie had promised they could handle it, but Steven wasn't leaving anything to chance.

Michael Ellerson arrived promptly at nine o'clock that morning. His suit was freshly pressed, and his brown eyes were filled with excitement as Steven greeted him at the door. Steven showed him around the small office, reintroducing him to everyone before taking Michael to where he would be working.

"Wow, my own office," Michael said, turning in the small space with a wide grin. "I figured I'd get a cubicle."

It wasn't much larger than a storage closet, though at least it had a window. Steven wished he had a better space to offer, but the only larger space available was being used as a conference room. If Steven hired a partner, that would likely change.

"We don't have any of those," Steven replied with a wry smile. "But I hope you can make yourself at home here." He headed to the door. "I'll leave you to get settled. We can meet in my office at ten to go over the cases I want to get you started on. How does that sound?"

"Perfect." Michael set his bag down and pulled out his chair. "Do I need to do anything special to log in?"

"I'll send Leslie in with instructions. Welcome to McAllister at Law."

After stopping by Leslie's desk, Steven entered his office, where his sister was waiting, perched on his desk with a coffee cup in hand. He accepted the cup and took a tentative sip. His lips quirked up as he tasted the robust flavor of real coffee.

"Rose is going to murder you," he said, shaking his head.

"What she doesn't know won't hurt her." Lanie angled her head toward the wall Steven's office shared with Michael's. "So, do you think this is going to work?"

He nodded. "I do." Then he sighed. "Well, I hope so. Do you mind sticking around this morning when I meet with him? You and Sandra need to be aware of his workload so you can keep on top of things when I'm not here."

"Sure thing," Lanie said. "I'll be in Sandra's office. Come get me when you're ready to meet with your new employee."

In the meantime, Steven braced himself for a conversation he'd been dreading. While he had briefly spoken to Mr. Willoughby the other day after Rose had stormed out of his house, he'd promised his client a more in-depth conversation when he was back in the office.

The phone rang once before a gruff voice answered, "Hello?"

"Good morning, Mr. Willoughby. It's Steven McAllister. Is now a good time to talk?"

"It's about time. When do I get my day in court?"

Steven stifled a sigh. "I've drafted a response to your wife's last proposal of settlement, and I'm working on a motion for a pretrial hearing. The judge may order mediation."

"I don't want to go to mediation," Mr. Willoughby growled. "If you can't get me my trial, I'll have to go find someone who will."

Same threat, different day. But since Steven couldn't be sure Mr. Willoughby hadn't already started shopping for a new attorney, he had to play the game.

"Unfortunately, this is how the court system works, sir. In contested divorces, the court would prefer the parties resolve things on their own. Trial is considered a last resort." Steven cleared his throat. "But if you'd like to start over with someone new, potentially delay your divorce another year, and give your wife an upper hand in the proceedings, I have several attorneys I can recommend."

The silence on the other end of the line was deafening, and Steven smiled. The only thing his client would hate more than a further delay of his divorce was giving his wife a win.

"I know my rights," Mr. Willoughby finally said. "And I have a right to a speedy trial."

Steven rolled his eyes to the ceiling. "That's for *criminal* prosecution." Sometimes he wished his fellow citizens had been required to take basic civic and government classes as adults. "A divorce is a *civil* matter."

"Oh," Mr. Willoughby said. "I don't see how it's fair she's been able to drag this out for so long."

Pinching the bridge of his nose, Steven took a deep breath. The fact was, Mr. Willoughby, *not* his wife, had caused the delay. But mentioning that would only aggravate his client.

"I promise, Mr. Willoughby, I'll file the motion for the pretrial hearing tomorrow, and we'll work to get your divorce on the court's docket as soon as possible."

"All right. But I expect you to keep me updated on the process."

Translation: He expects a daily phone call. That wouldn't be easy with Steven coming into the office only sporadically, but he would make it happen. After his discussion with Rose about the law firm's finances, he couldn't afford to lose Mr. Willoughby.

"That shouldn't be a problem," Steven promised.

"And I want to schedule a meeting to go over a real estate dispute I'm having with my neighbor."

"I'll have Leslie set up a time."

"Good," Mr. Willoughby said with a grunt. "Glad you're finally earning your keep again."

"Yes, sir. I'll talk to you soon."

After he hung up the phone, he put his head in his hands. His accident couldn't have happened at a worse time. But he'd managed to salvage his relationship with his client.

He glanced at the clock and groaned. It was almost ten. With a resigned sigh, Steven gathered Lanie, Sandra, and Michael and led them into the conference room. Michael and Lanie sat on one side of the table with Steven and Sandra on the other.

"How are you settling in?" Steven asked as he laid out several folders in front of Michael.

"So far, so good. Leslie got my computer booted up, and I'm logged in. I took a look at your electronic filing system, and it looks similar to what I used last summer during my clerkship."

"That's great!" Steven tapped the folders. "While we've mostly set up everything electronically, we do maintain paper files as well. These are some of the cases I was working on before my accident." He slid them across the table. "I'd like you to review these today. We can meet either this afternoon or tomorrow morning to discuss any questions you have. There are several deadlines coming in fast, and I'd like to get you up to speed so you can draft the necessary motions."

"Sounds good," Michael said as he flipped open the first folder.

"Sandra is familiar with the cases and has old drafts you can look at to get a feel for how we word things here. But if you have any questions, I'll be in and out of the office this week and available by phone."

"Are you anticipating any court dates in the near future?"

Steven shook his head. "I've filed continuances on all of my court hearings for this month, and I'm not sure if they'll be rescheduled before the summer is up."

Michael's face fell. "Oh, okay, then."

"But if anything does come up, I'll of course be taking you with me."

That perked the law clerk up, and he smiled. "I appreciate that. I haven't had much of a chance to be in a courtroom."

Steven pressed his lips together. How he wished he could say the same. "Don't worry. That'll change soon enough, I'm sure." As he maneuvered out of the room, exhaustion began to take its toll. "Sandra will give you a quick summary of where we are in each case before you start your review, but I'm afraid I need to rest for a minute."

Lanie immediately jumped up and came to his aid, pushing him to his office. Unable to find the energy to protest, he sagged against the back of his chair. Once he was behind his desk, he leaned forward and rested his head on the wooden surface.

"You really shouldn't be overdoing it." Lanie slipped into the chair on the opposite side of his desk. "Maybe I should take you home."

"Stop mother-henning me." He closed his eyes and took several deep breaths as the pain in his chest subsided. "I'll be okay. I just need a minute."

"Are you sure—"

Opening one eye, he glared at her. "Not another word. And don't you dare tell Rose."

She stuck her tongue out at him but didn't argue. After a few more minutes of deep breathing, the pain passed, and he sat up with a groan.

"Do you think he's up for it?" Steven grabbed the water bottle from his desk and took several large gulps.

"He seemed to be. If nothing else, he's eager to learn." Lanie shrugged. "But even if he turns out to be a terrible writer, it's easier to edit a first draft than a blank page."

"True," Steven agreed, albeit reluctantly. "And at least it'll get Rose off my case for a while."

"You hope." Lanie grinned.

He gave a grim nod. "I do."

***

Around five in the evening, Steven packed up his things. How he had managed to work a whole day, he couldn't say, but he was already paying for it. Lanie had arranged for their dad to pick him up, and Steven glanced out the window to confirm Dad had arrived. His spirits lifted at the sight of the van parked outside the building, waiting for him.

Before he left, he popped his head into Michael's office, thrilled to see the law clerk still hard at work. He knocked softly, and Michael glanced up, a proud grin on his face.

"How'd it go?" Steven asked.

"Great so far! I've already finished a rough draft for one of the motions, and I'm hoping to have two more ready for you by tomorrow."

Steven blinked, though he wasn't sure why he was surprised. One of the reasons he had chosen Michael was his can-do attitude and the ambition in his eyes, an ambition Steven had once shared. He hoped it would return once he was fully recovered, but he would be happy if he could find enough motivation to keep his head above water. Drowning in a financial crisis was not something he wished to contend with, especially with his wedding looming.

"Good work." He gave a thumbs-up. "But you should head home and start celebrating the Fourth of July early."

"Sure thing, boss. Just let me save my work, and I'll walk out with you."

While he waited, Steven headed to Sandra's office. She was packing up as well. When she noticed him lurking in the doorway, she motioned him closer.

"You picked a real winner with that one," she whispered, peeking behind Steven as if to make sure Michael wasn't in earshot. "He's been sending me emails left and right with intelligent questions and additional case law he intends to include in his motions. He's going to do nicely here."

"Yeah, I wouldn't mind offering to extend his clerkship into the fall, but I imagine once the bar results from July post, he'll receive more lucrative offers from DC law firms," Steven responded, voicing the thought that had gnawed at him since making the offer.

"Well, Rose wants you to take on a partner. He wouldn't be a bad bet."

Steven bristled. "That's a bit premature, don't you think? I'd like to work with him for more than a few months to make sure he could handle something like that."

"Then it'll be your loss." Sandra shrugged. She straightened as Michael came into view. "Great job today!"

"Thanks for your help," Michael responded with a grin. He turned to Steven. "Mind if I pick your brain on the way out? I had some ideas I'd love to run by you."

"Sounds good." Steven gestured for him to go first. "Lead the way."

"So, what made you decide to set up shop in this town?" Michael asked as they reached the door to the law office.

"I grew up here." Steven lifted his face toward the sky, relishing the late-afternoon sun on his skin. The best part about summer was that it didn't matter how late he worked, the sun was still high in the sky when he left.

"And you decided to come back?" Michael's eyes widened, and a knot formed in Steven's stomach. "There's not much to tempt you here, is there?"

Steven shrugged. "More than you'd expect. I lived in Baltimore for a time, but I'm not cut out for city life. Besides, I prefer the ability to make my own schedule, something I couldn't do at big law firms."

"Ain't that the truth," Michael agreed. "I do love Georgetown, though. Plenty to do nearby or just a short trip downtown." His gaze swept over Main Street. "It's much quieter here."

"You get used to it, and who knows? You may even come to prefer it."

Michael snorted. "I doubt it." Then he seemed to realize how he sounded. "Not that I don't appreciate the opportunity."

"It's fine." Steven chuckled. "A young guy like you needs something more than small-town living. I get it."

"And you have your fiancée," Michael said, shaking his head. "If I had someone to settle down with, I might feel differently."

"None of the women in your class caught your eye?"

"Nah. I didn't have time for dating while in school, and the last few months, I've been studying for the bar." He raised an eyebrow. "Does Cedar Haven have any nightlife?"

"There's Seabreeze." Steven grimaced. "Though it's kind of a dive bar."

"Better than nothing, I suppose."

An idea formed in Steven's head. "If you're looking for a slightly younger crowd, my sister is going out with some of her friends tonight, and several of them are single. If you don't have any plans this evening, maybe you could join them."

"I wouldn't want to impose." Michael frowned.

"Doesn't hurt to ask her." Steven texted Lanie. If anyone could show him what Cedar Haven had to offer, it was her.

A moment later, he received a response. "Is it all right if I give her your number? Then she can add you to the group chat."

"Sure. Why not?" Michael grinned. "Can't hurt, right?"

Chapter Fourteen

"COME ON, ROSE," LANIE pleaded as she leaned against Rose's kitchen counter. "Come with us tonight. Steven's probably going to bed early. There's no sense going over there to play nursemaid."

Rose bristled at the implication she was *playing* at caring for her fiancé. Her skills were worth more than babysitting or handling his medications, no matter what her future sister-in-law might have thought. Lanie had stopped by to go over some wedding details, but her true purpose appeared to be convincing Rose to go out that night. Crossing her arms, she leveled Lanie with a glare.

"Oh, don't give me that look," Lanie said. "I didn't mean anything negative by that. I'm just saying Steven is doing better. Besides, he's got the home care aides coming by to help him as well." She flipped her blond hair over her shoulder. "Stop searching for an excuse to hide, and allow yourself to have a little fun."

"I have fun," Rose protested. Though she couldn't help finding the situation a little ironic. Just a few months ago, she had been the one trying to convince Lanie to go out. How the tides had turned.

Lanie raised an eyebrow, seeming to read her mind. "Yeah? And when was the last time you went out on the town?"

"Probably for the Memorial Day parade," Rose admitted as she rinsed off the last plate and put it in the drying rack.

"Exactly." Lanie smirked. "So, find something hot to wear and be ready in twenty." Without waiting for a response, Lanie spun on her heel and rushed out the front door.

Rose considered bolting it, but she suspected Lanie wouldn't give up that easily. In truth, Rose probably deserved that treatment since she'd done the same thing when Lanie had wanted to wallow. *What's that saying? Turnabout's fair play or... something?* With a resigned sigh, she flung open her closet to find something to wear.

Flipping through her clothes, she settled on a yellow sundress. The humidity had been ramping up in the last several days, and she could only hope for a thunderstorm to bring them some relief.

Once dressed, she applied her makeup, keeping it light. No sense in going overboard when she was likely to sweat it all off anyway. She brushed her hair back and twisted it against her head before securing it with two sticks.

A moment later, Lanie banged on the front door, and Rose rolled her eyes at her reflection. But she hurried to answer the door before Lanie broke it down. Her neighbors wouldn't appreciate that, not to mention her landlord. As much as she loved her condo, there were advantages to going forward with the wedding and moving in with Steven. The single-family home provided more space and privacy than her current accommodations. And it had plenty of room for a growing family.

When Rose wrenched open the door, Lanie's eyes drifted down her body. Playing along, Rose struck a pose. Though she wasn't in the mood to go out, she could fake it with the best of them.

"You look perfect." Lanie grabbed her hand. "Now, let's go!"

Rose allowed herself to be led to Lanie's car. Well, really, the car she'd inherited from her mother. Nate sat in the passenger seat, and he gave Rose a big smile as she approached.

"You got roped into this too?" Rose asked as she slid into the backseat.

"Lanie's very persuasive," Nate replied.

"Hey, now." Lanie climbed into the driver's seat and glared at Rose in the rearview mirror. "Don't act like I'm some awful bully. I'm just making sure everyone I love has a good time."

"And we appreciate you for it." Nate rested his hand on her knee and gave it a squeeze.

"All right, you two lovebirds. Stop canoodling and let's go," Rose said, though her heart panged a little at the sight. Steven should have been with them, and in another world, he would be. But it would be a while before he was well enough to go out like that again.

When they arrived at Bea's, Trudy and Toccara were waiting for them. Both wore light-colored sundresses that contrasted nicely with their ebony skin. Rose greeted them each with a hug before turning to the newest member of the group, Steven's law clerk, Michael.

"Hi." She stuck out her hand. "I'm Rose, Steven's fiancée."

"I recognized you from your photos," Michael said, bypassing her hand and pulling her into a hug. "I feel like I already know you."

Her body stiffened, not used to such close contact with a complete stranger, and he quickly released her with an apologetic smile.

"Sorry, that was a bit forward."

She waved her hand. "It's fine. Just caught me by surprise is all."

Discreetly, she tried to assess him. He was younger than she'd expected, closer to Lanie's age than her own. But he seemed friendly, and Lanie had told her how impressed she was with his credentials. Perhaps he was the answer to Rose's prayers. At the very least, he might relieve some of the burden on Steven, allowing him more time to heal.

"So, how do you like the office so far?" she asked.

"It's great! Everyone has been nice, and I'm excited to dive in to the cases Steven's assigned me."

Rose smiled, and the tension in her shoulders ebbed away. While she wished Steven would have taken on a real partner, she could be grateful for the assistance Michael provided in the short term. And maybe he would stick around beyond the summer.

Lanie grabbed her arm and pulled her toward the door. "I'm starving. Let's eat!"

The diner was packed, and it took a minute to find a place for them all to sit. As they made their way to the back, Rose caught the owner's eye. Bea's white hair was in a hairnet, and she flashed a grin, signaling that she would stop by their table later.

As they settled into their seats, Lanie immediately started flipping through the jukebox beside her. Everyone else picked up their menus. Rose followed suit, though she wasn't hungry. Lately, she hadn't had much of an appetite, between her worries about the wedding and her concern for Steven.

After the server took their orders, Lanie began laying out the plan for the evening. Once they finished dinner, they would head over to Seabreeze for karaoke and drinks.

Rose couldn't help smiling at the way the tables had turned. The last time she and Lanie had gone to Seabreeze, she was trying to cheer up Lanie, who had spent most of the evening making eyes at Nate.

"Are you going to sing this time?" Lanie asked, giving Rose a pointed look.

"I'm not much of a singer."

"Is anyone at karaoke?" Michael joked.

Rose opened her mouth to respond when she caught sight of a familiar face. Her stomach churned, and she swallowed the bile rising in her throat. Carissa, her wedding planner, was heading their way. Rose should have known she couldn't avoid her forever.

"Rose!" Carissa's gaze swept over the table before settling on Rose. "I've been trying to get ahold of you."

"I'm sorry. I've, uh, had to work a few double shifts lately."

Carissa clicked her tongue. "We have a lot of work still to do for the wedding, you know." She pulled out her phone and tapped the screen. "Since I have you here, why don't we set up an appointment?"

Sweat gathered on Rose's upper lip, and she shot Lanie a pleading look, hoping she would intervene. She was Rose's maid of honor, after all. Lanie took the hint and turned to Carissa.

"Hey, Carissa, I'm glad we ran into you. I've been meaning to ask if you would be available to handle my wedding."

Nate blinked. "You have? I thought we were going to—ouch!" He reached under the table, presumably to rub the shin Lanie had just kicked. Rose bit her lip to hide her smile.

Lanie patted his hand in apology. "We haven't decided on a date yet, but we were thinking late fall, early winter."

"Let me check my schedule," Carissa said, and she seemed to forget Rose was there. "Is tomorrow too soon?"

"Tomorrow's great!" Lanie cleared her throat. "And Rose has her hands full taking care of Steven. But as her maid of honor, I'm happy to go over anything pertinent with you at our meeting."

"Is that okay with you, Rose?" Carissa tucked a lock of graying hair behind her ear.

"Yup, that works for me. Lanie knows my vision better than I do."

"Then that's settled." Carissa gave Rose one last assessing look. "But I do want to chat with you at some point. Give me a call when things slow down."

"You bet!" Rose promised, though it sounded hollow, even to her. She had no idea when anything in her life would slow down.

When Carissa was gone, Nate frowned at Lanie. "What was that all about? I thought we were going to do everything ourselves."

"Rose needed a save." She shrugged. "And besides, it can't hurt to pick the brain of a wedding planner. It's not like we know much about weddings." She gestured to Rose. "What I've learned so far has been through trial and error while helping Rose and my brother."

"Fair," Nate agreed. "But you didn't have to kick me."

She leaned forward and gave him a kiss. "I'll make it up to you. I promise."

Envy needled in Rose's belly at the ease of their interaction. It used to be that way for her and Steven, but lately, everything was a struggle. The accident had exacerbated the problem. She couldn't help wondering if they would ever find their way back to that level of contentedness again.

The rest of the dinner passed without incident. Rose barely touched her salad, her stomach too tied up in knots. She'd planned to go on a diet anyway to look her best for the wedding. At least her growing anxiety was good for something.

When they filed out of the restaurant, she followed Lanie and Nate to the car. Part of her wanted nothing more than to spend the rest of the evening at home, but she didn't want to disappoint Lanie. So she did her best to pretend she was having fun.

Unfortunately, Lanie saw right through it. "Jeez, Rose. We're going to a bar, not a funeral. Would it kill you to smile?"

Rose bared her teeth before sliding into the back seat, which caused both Lanie and Nate to laugh.

"If that's her smile, maybe we'd be better served by her pout," Nate said as he climbed into the passenger seat. "It's way less scary."

Even Rose had to laugh. She'd never considered herself someone who could intimidate people, though sometimes she could make Steven apprehensive, especially if she said words like *we need to talk*.

"I'm sorry," she said, and she meant it. "I don't want to bring down the mood of the evening."

"The point of tonight"—Lanie fixed her eyes on Rose's in the rearview—"was to raise your spirits. If I'm failing at that, I need to either try harder or change tactics." She glanced at Nate before returning her gaze to Rose. "Look, if you don't want to go to Seabreeze, I'm not going to force you. But I'm also not taking you back to your condo. And I'm definitely not dropping you off with my brother." Rose opened her mouth to protest, but Lanie cut her off. "We both know you need a break."

That shut her up, and she nodded. "I can't promise I'll be much company, but you're right." Pushing as much enthusiasm into her voice as she could muster, she continued, "Let's go to Seabreeze!"

"That's the spirit." Nate turned around in his seat and gave her a smile.

The packed bar did little to build her enthusiasm. They found a booth near the back of the bar, far enough from the stage that they could tune out the singers if they wanted to. The outlandish tropical décor was gaudy but somehow fitting. Lanie and Nate went to grab a round of drinks, leaving the rest of them to make small talk.

"How's your baby?" Rose asked Trudy.

"Crawling all over everything," Trudy said with a tired smile, but the pride in her voice was unmistakable. "He's also pulling up on tables. I expect it won't be long before he takes his first step."

"That's exciting!"

"Exciting is one word for it," Trudy quipped. "But it also means we need to double-check our babyproofing." She waved a hand. "Anyway, I came out tonight to escape the baby brain. Tell me all about your wedding planning."

Ugh—the one topic Rose had hoped to avoid. "Everything's booked, but we're struggling a bit financially."

Why did I say that? The last thing she needed was for word of their money troubles to spread throughout Cedar Haven.

"I imagine it's been tight with the opening of the firm." Toccara placed a hand on Rose's arm. "Start-up costs are a nightmare."

Rose blinked, then she remembered Toccara had her own business as well. It made sense that she understood what most people didn't. And her friend was right—the start-up costs had been a huge drain on their finances.

"We'll make do," Rose said brightly, trying to brush away the cloud that hung over her whenever the question of finances came up.

"He's certainly got a robust clientele," Michael piped up. "I'm impressed he was handling the caseload by himself before he hired me. It's a lot for one person to take on, even with his capable paralegal."

A brick settled in the pit of Rose's stomach. She'd known Steven was working with a lot of clients. It helped that he was the only law firm in the tiny town. The last attorney had retired several years ago, and most folks had been forced to venture several towns over to find someone reputable. As much as she wondered if moving there had been a mistake, she recognized the lucrative business opportunity it offered Steven. If only it hadn't been at the cost of his health.

"I've tried to convince him to take on a partner, but he said he can't afford it." She felt disloyal saying the words out loud, especially in front of his new employee, but maybe it would sway Michael to decide to stay.

"Even if that person could buy their way in?" Michael's face held a strange expression, one she couldn't quite interpret.

"I'm not sure what you mean."

Toccara tilted her head as she assessed Michael. "Know someone who has that kind of capital?"

Rose's gaze moved back and forth between the two as they had some sort of silent conversation. After a moment, Michael nodded.

"I might, but I'll talk to Steven directly. Don't want my new boss to think I'm doing something underhanded."

Toccara's face broke into a smile. "I can't imagine anyone accusing you of that." She bit her lip as if she couldn't believe she'd just said that.

But Michael took it as encouragement. "Say, we're at karaoke. What do you think about singing a duet?"

She demurred. "I don't sing."

"Somehow, I doubt that." He raised his eyebrows. "But I'd love to see you prove me wrong."

"You're on."

They hopped up and rushed to the stage just as Lanie and Nate returned with two trays full of drinks. As they set the trays down, Lanie turned to Rose with a quizzical expression.

"What was that about?"

"Looks like those two turned this into their first date," Trudy said with a laugh.

"That was fast." Lanie grinned. "Maybe Steven won't have to worry about those DC law firms stealing Michael away after all." She took a sip of her drink. "What else did we miss?"

"Rose was describing her and Steven's financial situation." Trudy leaned forward. "But I might have a solution to your problem."

Rose frowned. "Oh?"

"What would you say to a fundraiser?"

Lanie's eyes lit up. "Yes! That's a great idea. We raised so much money for the school system after the one you hosted in January. I'm sure we can do the same now."

Heart in her throat, Rose raised her hand. "Wait, I don't want the whole town to know my business."

"Everyone's already heard about Steven's accident. I don't think anyone would be shocked to learn you're facing other struggles." Trudy shrugged. "Besides, after everything you've done for the town since you arrived, nobody would blink an eye at the idea of helping you and Steven have your dream wedding."

Rose bit her lip. It wasn't just about the money, though. Despite his reassurances, Steven still wasn't taking his health seriously. The last time Rose had seen him, the dark circles under his eyes had grown more prominent.

"Come on, Rose." Lanie bumped her shoulder. "You keep saying you want to reduce Steven's stress. Knowing the wedding is paid for would go a long way toward doing that."

"Don't pressure her," Nate said. When Rose glanced at him in surprise, he gave her a sympathetic smile. If anyone else could understand how it felt to be railroaded by a McAllister, it would be him.

"I'm not!" Lanie insisted. "I'm nudging her in the right direction."

Nate rolled his eyes at Rose, and she giggled. She appreciated having someone else on her side for once.

"Talk to Steven," Trudy said. "See what he thinks, and if it sounds like something you want to move forward with, let me know. I'd be happy to help with it."

"Me too," Lanie added.

Rose gave a noncommittal nod. It wouldn't hurt to at least discuss it with Steven. Though she hated the idea of charity, Trudy had a point. Both Rose and Steven had done a lot since coming to Cedar Haven. She had helped with several fundraisers, and Steven had done some pro bono work for townsfolk who couldn't afford legal assistance.

And maybe they could use some of the money raised to help Steven with his law practice. If he was willing to accept help with his business, then she could compromise and accept assistance with the wedding.

Chapter Fifteen

HOW WAS YOUR NIGHT out? Steven texted Rose when he woke the next morning. Last night had been the best sleep he'd had since his accident, and he felt stronger than he had in weeks. Though he'd pushed himself the day before at the office, he believed it'd done him some good to get out of the house and back to work. Maybe he could convince his doctor to let him go in for half days. Anything to stop being cooped up in the house day in and day out.

More fun than I expected. How are you?

He smiled, glad his sister had convinced Rose to go. She needed a night of fun after everything they'd been through recently. He was just sorry he couldn't join her.

After texting her that he was doing much better, he opened his laptop and began going through emails. Near the top of his inbox was a message from Mr. Willoughby. His heart sank as he read through it. His most lucrative client was only getting more demanding. Steven had drafted the motion for a pretrial conference and planned to file it with the court next week. Apparently, that wasn't soon enough for his client.

With a sigh, he crafted a reply, sprinkling in apologetic language while detailing the strategy he had outlined for the next steps in the divorce. Of all of his current caseload, Mr. Willoughby was by far the most important.

Between the contested divorce and his client's plans to sue his neighbors, Mr. Willoughby would rack up several billable hours for Steven's firm.

Steven had never planned to be a trial lawyer, and he expected both cases to settle out of court, but the amount of research and correspondence it required, not to mention taking witness depositions, was sure to help him build his practice into what he wanted it to be. But to do that, Steven needed to be at work. There was only so much he could assign to Michael. Besides, Mr. Willoughby wasn't the kind of client he could leave to a fresh-faced law graduate. Mr. Willoughby needed to be coddled, appeased. And Steven was the only one who could do that. Even Sandra had thrown up her hands the last time she'd had to deal with their most problematic client.

Once the email was crafted, Steven continued working on the case from home. He had access to his files through the VPN, and Rose would be working later that morning. The likelihood of him being interrupted was slim. Though he preferred to be in the office, he figured he could at least schedule depositions and conduct some research he had gotten behind on. Every little bit would help keep his client happy.

Just as he'd started getting into a groove, the front door to his house slammed open. He jumped, almost knocking his laptop over.

"Steven?" Lanie called. "The aides are here."

Since when does she come in without knocking? He pushed the blankets to the side to make it easier for the aides to help him out of bed.

His sister came tearing around the corner, her hair flying, the aides on her tail. For a moment, his heart stopped. Had something happened to Rose? But then he caught the fierce anger in her eyes.

"Lanie, what—"

"I just met with your wedding planner, and do you know what she told me?"

Steven blinked. *This is about the* wedding? "Look, I don't really have time—"

"You're going to make time if you still plan on getting married in August."

Rubbing a hand over his face, he glanced at the aides, who hovered at the back of the room, looking like they wanted to bolt. He gestured for them to come forward and perform the transfer. The sooner they completed the daily morning routine, the sooner they could leave. The fewer witnesses to the conversation he was about to have, the better.

To his relief, his sister seemed to realize her inappropriate behavior. She stepped to the side and tapped her foot while she waited.

Once they were alone, Steven headed to the kitchen. He needed some caffeine if he was going to get through the conversation.

"So, what's going on?"

Lanie removed a stack of papers from her book bag and slammed them on the table. "You're behind on several payments."

Trust Lanie to get worked up over nothing. "Oh, that. Don't worry. Rose and I have already discussed it, and we're handling it."

"With what money?" she demanded, hands on her hips. "I've seen the medical bills that have started pouring in. And have you forgotten that you granted me access to your firm's finances? You're not exactly swimming in dough here."

"I know, but Rose is paying the immediate deposits, and I believe Mr. Willoughby's next bill will pay the rest of what we owe."

She raised an eyebrow. "In time for the August payments?"

He swallowed. Leslie billed their clients at the end of the month, and the clients had fifteen days to pay. When he'd done his calculations, he hadn't accounted for that. It would be tight. Too tight.

He raised his eyes to meet his sister's. "How do you know all of this?"

"I met with Carissa this morning to discuss hiring her for our wedding. We weren't going to have a wedding planner, but she accosted Rose last night, and I thought I'd try to distract her, give you both some breathing room." She gestured to the pages. "But now I think what you two need is a financial advisor."

"It looks bad—"

"It more than looks that way, Steven," Lanie interrupted. "And Carissa said your vendors will cancel their contracts with no refunds if you don't pay them on time." She shook her head. "You should have postponed when you had the chance."

When he didn't respond, Lanie slid into the chair beside him. "What are you going to do?"

"I have no idea." And he didn't. The numbers staring back at him told a story, and if he didn't get them under control soon, that tale wouldn't have a happy ending.

They were quiet for a moment, though Steven could feel his sister's eyes on him. He shifted uncomfortably in his chair. It was bad enough that he had created the situation he was in, but that his little sister had witnessed his failure made it worse.

She sighed. "Look, last night, Trudy had an interesting idea you should consider. Why don't you, me, and Rose meet tomorrow? We can discuss what's going on and formulate a plan."

He nodded, though he had no idea how they would find their way out of that mess. She came over and laid her hand on his shoulder.

"Have faith," she said as if reading his mind. Then she left.

Once he was alone, he covered his face with his hands and groaned. Maybe Rose was right. Maybe putting off the wedding was their best bet. Only by that point, it might already be too late.

The next day, Steven's dad dropped him off at Bea's, where Rose, Lanie, Nate, and Trudy were waiting for him. Nate opened the door, and Rose pushed Steven inside with Lanie and Trudy following her. They found a table toward the back that could accommodate Steven's wheelchair.

"What are you thinking of having?" Lanie asked as she flipped through the menu.

Steven raised an eyebrow. "The same thing I always have—burger and fries." He glanced around at the rest of the table. Everyone was making small talk as they waited to order their food. "When are you going to tell me what's going on?"

"As soon as we order," Lanie whispered.

Shifting in his chair, Steven tried not to scowl. Somehow, it felt like everyone at the table knew what they were there to discuss except him. Even Rose appeared to be completely at ease despite the picture Lanie had painted of their financial situation.

When Bea came around to take their orders, his shoulders sagged in relief. The sooner Bea was done, the sooner he could figure out what on earth was going on.

"Good to see you out and about." Bea leaned down and ruffled Steven's hair. "I've been praying for you." She nodded to Rose and Lanie. "And your family. How are you feeling?"

"A little stronger every day. My cast is supposed to come off next week."

"Then you'll be walking again in no time," Bea said as she moved on to take the next person's order.

I wish. Though he'd attended his outpatient physical therapy appointments religiously, he wasn't seeing a lot of progress. But Dr. Bhati had assured him his spinal contusion was healing well and he'd likely start to regain some feeling in his legs soon.

After Bea had everyone's order, Lanie tapped a fork against her glass. "Let's get down to business, shall we?" She gestured to Trudy to begin.

"The other night at karaoke, I asked Rose to consider allowing us to host a fundraiser. At first, the idea was to help raise money for your wedding, but I think we can agree your financial situation has grown beyond that."

Warmth rushed to Steven's cheeks, and he stared at the table. He couldn't help being ashamed of their situation.

"The one thing everyone in town is asking is how they can help you as you heal." Trudy looked at Steven and smiled. "Even though it's only been open since last November, your law firm has already done a lot to help the town, and folks want to give back."

Steven glanced at Rose, expecting her to protest, but to his surprise, she appeared not only open to the idea but encouraging it. She turned toward him and gave him a smile before refocusing on Trudy.

"So, we're thinking of holding a fundraiser in late July. While it's for both of you, it would make sense to focus on Steven and his recovery." Trudy nodded at Steven. "The town is anxious to help you get back on your feet in whatever manner that requires."

"I don't know how comfortable I am with that," he said. "Won't people think I've squandered my money if I can't afford my own wedding?"

"Everyone knows you've been out of commission for a month while you healed, and you're not back to work one hundred percent," Trudy replied.

"People have asked me every day at the shop how they can help, and I haven't known what to tell them," Nate added. "So unless you want a bunch of questionable casseroles, you should consider the fundraiser."

Steven chuckled. The refrigerator at the law office already held a couple of casseroles and pies that people had dropped off when he was there. Thankfully, very few people had stopped by the house.

"So, how would we do this?" Rose asked, redirecting the conversation.

"While we're here, I plan to ask Bea if we can host it at the diner," Trudy said. "We should focus on raising funds to help Steven in a multitude of capacities. We can either set up various funding options for the wedding, the firm, or medical bills, or we can have everyone contribute to one big pot of money. The latter option provides more discretion on how the money is spent."

"And you aren't concerned people will refuse to help because they think we overspent on our wedding? I don't want this to look like some sort of cash grab."

Trudy cocked her head. "Why would anyone think that?" She glanced at Lanie before turning to Steven. "I believe everyone in town would agree the McAllisters have had more than their fair share of tragedy this year, between losing your mom and your accident."

"And let's be real," Nate said. "If you hadn't had your accident, you wouldn't *need* a fundraiser in the first place. Nobody thinks you and Rose spent beyond your means."

"Right, and even if some people do feel that way, no one is forcing them to contribute." Lanie shrugged. "It's a fundraiser, not a tax."

Their food arrived, and Steven was grateful for a chance to sit with his thoughts. The case they were making for the fundraiser was hard to argue against. But he wanted to hear how Rose felt. After all, she had insisted they pay for the wedding themselves. Would she really be okay with the town financing even a portion of it?

He leaned toward her. "What do you think about all this?"

"If you had asked me when Trudy first brought it up, I would have said 'absolutely not.'" She took a bite of her burger and tilted her head as she chewed, as if considering her next words. "I don't like to accept charity from people. But Trudy makes a lot of good points." Her eyes grew misty as she turned to him. "People love you, and they want to help. This seems like a good way to do that."

He nudged her. "They love you too. You nurse them back to health in some of their darker moments."

"True, but I'm not the prodigal son who returned after earning a law degree."

A laugh bubbled up in his throat. "I wouldn't go *that* far."

They finished the rest of the meal in silence, and Steven had to admit that the idea grew on him the more he thought about it. The fact that Rose was on board spoke volumes.

An idea formed in his head, but he kept it to himself. After all, there were no guarantees regarding how much money they would raise, and he wanted to make sure the funds went to their most pressing problems. But if there was a little left over, it wouldn't hurt to surprise his new bride.

"So, what do you think?" Lanie asked as Bea cleared their plates.

"Well, first things first." Steven gestured to Trudy.

Catching on immediately, Trudy waved Bea over to her side. "We have a proposition for you."

"Shoot," Bea said.

"How would you feel about us hosting a fundraiser in your diner later this month?"

"What's the fundraiser for?"

"Me," Steven said with an embarrassed smile.

Understanding dawned on Bea's face. "Nobody else deserves it more. Of course y'all can have it here. Just give me a date, and I'll be ready."

"How about July twenty-second?" Lanie suggested. "It's a little over two weeks away, which isn't a lot of time, but it's just over a month before the wedding."

Steven and Rose exchanged glances. Two weeks was no time at all to plan an event, but if they kept it simple, it might work.

"Let's do it," Rose said.

As the others set to work planning the event, Steven wrapped his arm around Rose, pulling her close. After everything they'd been through, he was ready for them to have a reprieve and some happiness.

Chapter Sixteen

LATER THAT AFTERNOON, ROSE headed into the hospital to start her shift. She'd barely set her things down at the nurses' station when Rebecca came running up. A feeling of déjà vu washed over her on seeing the panic in Rebecca's eyes.

"What's wrong?" Rose demanded. "Is it Steven?"

"No, it's Mr. Patrones. He was brought in a moment ago and is in ICU."

"Mr. Patrones? B-But he was just released the other day!"

Rebecca nodded, her face grim. "Apparently, he didn't heed Dr. Myers's advice to take it easy. According to the neighbor who called it in, he was on a ladder, cleaning his gutters, when he suddenly fell."

"Another heart attack?" Rose covered her mouth with her hand.

"Looks like it." Shaking her head, Rebecca sighed. "I'm sorry to be the bearer of bad news as soon as you started your shift, but I know you were fond of him."

"Thank you for letting me know," Rose whispered.

"I've asked the ICU nurses to keep me posted on his progress. I'll tell you if I hear anything more." Rebecca patted her arm and walked away, leaving Rose alone with her thoughts.

Sinking into a chair, Rose struggled to draw breath. *It's not the same.* Mr. Patrones was an elderly man who had no business being on a ladder at all but especially not right after a heart attack. In contrast, Steven was still confined to a wheelchair. And he was following the doctors' orders. *Mostly.*

Rose closed her eyes. And there it was, her worst fear rearing its ugly head at the news of Mr. Patrones. The truth was, even if he couldn't climb ladders or clean gutters, Steven was still at greater risk of a second heart attack. And his insistence on returning to work the moment he'd left the rehab facility further jeopardized his health.

Images of Steven lying on the floor of his house, cold and unresponsive, came unbidden to Rose's mind. She squeezed her eyes tight, trying to block the thoughts.

Get control of yourself. She forced herself to take deep breaths, trying to calm the erratic beating of her heart. Steven was fine. At the diner, he'd even looked healthier. The circles under his eyes had faded, and he seemed in better spirits.

Shaking off her morose concerns, she stood and wiped her eyes. She could check on Mr. Patrones later. It was time to start her shift.

She began making her rounds, changing fluids, dispensing medications, and catching up on her patients. As she finished up with a new patient, she rounded the corner and almost collided with a wheelchair. She blinked as she met the familiar hazel eyes of her fiancé.

Her heart jumped into her throat. "Steven? What are you doing here?"

He grabbed her hand and pulled her down for an awkward hug. "I had an appointment with Dr. Myers and Dr. Bhati this afternoon. Didn't I tell you?"

Just an appointment. That's all. But she allowed her eyes to rove over him to reassure herself nothing was amiss.

"Rose? What's wrong? You look like you've seen a ghost."

Forcing a smile, she shook her head. "Nothing. I don't recall hearing about your appointment, and seeing you here scared me for a moment. How'd it go with the doctors?"

"Everything's looking good. Dr. Bhati said the spinal contusion has healed enough to where we can increase my physical therapy to help me start walking again."

She frowned. "Is he sure you're ready for that? You don't want to overdo it."

Steven rolled his eyes. "We can trust the good doctor, but you're welcome to interrogate him yourself if it'll make you feel better."

Heat rushed to her face. "That's not what I meant." She swallowed around the lump in her throat. "I'm worried about you. That's all."

He sighed. "I'm sorry. I shouldn't have said that. It's just... I was excited to share the news with you, and I had hoped for a better reaction."

"No, it's my fault." At his questioning look, she continued, "A patient of mine who was discharged the other day is back in the ICU. He had another... heart attack." Her voice broke on the last word.

Steven's expression morphed into one of sympathy and concern. "Oh, Rose, that's awful." His eyes softened. "No wonder you were so frightened when you saw me."

"I certainly wasn't expecting it." She cleared her throat. "Anyway, where are you going for PT?"

"Dr. Bhati gave me a referral for an outpatient physical therapist closer to home. I don't have to go to the rehab center anymore." He held out a small piece of paper.

After scanning the information, she laughed. "Oh, Ronnie. You're in for a world of hurt."

It was his turn to frown. "Why do you say that?"

"Let's just say she believes in getting people back on their feet as quickly as possible." More laughter bubbled up in her throat, and she pressed her lips together to hold it in.

"I'm not sure I like the sound of that. But I'll do whatever I have to if it means you'll smile like that more often."

His words melted her heart, and for a moment, she could pretend all was right in their world. She slipped her arms around his neck and gave him a quick kiss.

"Are you going on break soon?" he asked.

"Unfortunately, no. I only arrived an hour ago."

His face fell. "Ah, okay. What does your schedule look like this week? Maybe we could have a date night."

"I'm off Tuesday and Wednesday."

"Let's plan for Wednesday. I've got a few deadlines on Tuesday."

And just like that, her earlier fears came rushing back, but she swallowed them. After all, he'd gone into the office only a couple of days that week. *And he has Michael now.*

But she still couldn't shake the nightmarish image of Steven on the floor of his house. Bending down, she kissed his forehead so he couldn't see her face. "Wednesday sounds great for dinner. We can figure out the details later. I've got to get back to work." Without waiting for a response, she spun on her heel and rushed away from him.

After her rounds were done, she headed to the cafeteria to grab a cup of coffee. When she returned to the nurses' station, Dr. Myers was waiting for her.

"How's it going?" he asked.

"Everything's great." It took effort, but she was pleased with the cheery tone she'd infused in her voice. "I hear you had an appointment with Steven today."

A wariness flashed in his eyes, but when he blinked it was gone. "I did. I was surprised you weren't there."

A knot formed in her stomach, but she ignored it. "He forgot to tell me, but my shift was starting anyway."

"Mm-hmm," he murmured, his forehead creasing. "Did you want me to tell you what we discussed? He's granted you access to his medical records."

The knot tightened, and she fought with herself. On the one hand, it would be smart for her to be kept informed. But on the other hand, it would be difficult for her to review his medical record with the clinical detachment she'd honed over the years in order to be a good nurse. Her reaction to the news of Mr. Patrones clearly demonstrated she couldn't be impartial when it came to Steven.

The concerned side won over her better judgment, and she nodded. At the very least, it would put her mind at ease to double-check that Steven hadn't left anything out in his vague report on the appointment.

At her nod, Dr. Myers produced a thick file and handed it to her. "He's looking much better, but I'm concerned with the level of stress in his life. I suggested that he consider doing some yoga or meditation classes to help calm him when he's not working."

Her head shot up. "You approved him to return to work full-time?"

A smile tugged at one corner of Dr. Myers's mouth, though he appeared to be trying to suppress it. "I appreciate the vote of confidence, but you know your fiancé. Would my approval really alter the course he thinks is best for himself?"

Pressing her lips into a thin line, Rose returned her attention to the file. *Pigheaded, stubborn man.* Of course, Dr. Myers was right. Steven had argued against most of the medical advice he'd been provided thus far. Sometimes, she wondered if Steven gave much credence to career paths other than his own. *After all, wouldn't he be offended if a client went against his sound legal advice?*

"Look, while I would prefer him to take things a little more slowly, he's doing well considering everything he went through." Dr. Myers put a hand on her shoulder, and she was too shocked by the gesture to flinch. "He's following the diet I prescribed, and as long as he keeps an eye on his stress level, I don't see any reason he can't return to work."

"Thank you," she said, relenting. After all, it wasn't Dr. Myers's fault Steven was being stubborn. Rose laid that character trait entirely at Max McAllister's feet. In the nature-versus-nurture argument, the trademark McAllister stubbornness could be traced to both genetics *and* learned behavior.

"Happy to help." Dr. Myers stepped back. "And if you have any concerns, you can always come to me." That time, he didn't bother to suppress his grin. "Especially if Steven waves them away without fully addressing them."

She found herself smiling back. He might not have known Steven well, but he clearly knew his type.

When Dr. Myers had gone, she pushed aside the files she had pulled to update, then she opened Steven's. As the doctor had said, Steven was progressing at a decent rate. Still, his attitude toward his health hadn't changed, and the similarities between him and Mr. Patrones haunted her. All she could do was continue to keep an eye on him and pray that luck was on their side.

Chapter Seventeen

"I'VE GOT THE PETERSON motion ready to go," Michael said as he entered Steven's office without knocking.

Ignoring his first instinct to chastise the newest employee, Steven gestured for him to take a seat. At that moment, the important thing wasn't manners, it was meeting deadlines.

Sure enough, the document was sitting in Steven's email. He clicked to download it and started skimming through. The arguments were sound, and the case law Michael had found seemed appropriate. Steven frowned. Michael's citations could use some work, but that was something Sandra, their resident Blue Book expert, could handle.

"How's the Harris pleading coming?" he asked.

Michael sighed. "Not great. I'm having a hard time coming up with relevant case law. I've found some persuasive cases in other jurisdictions but nothing that sets precedent here."

Steven looked up from his computer. "Have you asked Sandra for help?"

"I have, and she's not had much luck either."

"Hmm." Steven rubbed his chin. "What do the persuasive cases say?"

After fumbling through the stack of papers he held, Michael set a pile on Steven's desk. "That the hospital's medical negligence doesn't preclude the state's liability since Mrs. Harris fell in their building."

"And there's no Maryland case law backing that up?"

"I mean, there are other slip-and-fall cases, but the facts are distinguishable from our case. For instance, in one case Sandra found, the victim of the slip-and-fall had worn inappropriate footwear, and the court found them comparatively negligent. In another, the company admitted they had just mopped the floor but argued they had put up appropriate signage that the victim ignored."

"That's frustrating." Steven ran a hand through his hair. They were running out of time to file the pleading, but he held out hope of finding some obscure case that aligned closely enough to theirs to bolster their argument. "Keep looking. And double-check the cases you've found. Maybe there's something in there that can help us persuade the jury."

"No problem, boss." Michael stood and left the room.

Once he was alone, Steven put his head in his hands. Going up against a government agency was starting to feel like a fool's errand, but he wanted to get justice for his client. Mrs. Harris was a sweet, grandmotherly type who had tripped on a rug at a state building and fallen down a flight of stairs. As if that wasn't bad enough, the hospital had somehow missed a fracture on her left shoulder, which had caused her pain for days. His firm had sued the hospital as well on her behalf, but since the initial incident had occurred at the state building, he'd had no choice but to go after them too.

Just thinking over the situation caused his heart to beat erratically. Taking a few slow, deep breaths helped, but if Rose walked in at that moment, she would likely murder him on the spot. *With good reason.* He knew he needed to take it easy, but a lot was weighing on him. Once the Harris pleading and the Peterson motion were filed, he promised himself, he would take an afternoon off to rest.

Steven turned back to the will he'd been working on. Sometimes being a small-town attorney wasn't all it was cracked up to be. It required a lot more work than he'd realized. He would get familiar with one set of statutes and regulations, find case law to back up his arguments, then pivot to learn something completely new for a different client.

But he wouldn't trade it for the world because the end reward was worth the sacrifice. Once he'd built his practice, he and Rose would be set for a comfortable life. She might even be able to quit nursing if she wanted, though he would leave that choice to her. Either way, she and their future children would be well cared for.

"Knock, knock," Lanie said from his door. The scent of fast food wafted into his office. "I come bearing sustenance."

"You didn't have to do that." He moved some of the folders from his desk to make space. "I planned to order in."

"In a way, you did." Her hazel eyes danced with amusement. "And don't worry, my delivery fee is reasonable."

He lifted an eyebrow. "Why do I have a feeling you're about to ask me for a favor?"

"Because you know me so well." She smiled. "But first, you need to fuel up if you have any hope of making headway on that document you're writing."

The delicious scent of fries grew as he removed the food from the bag. But Lanie took the burger and fries from him, replacing them with a much less appetizing salad. She handed him a small soda before slipping into the chair opposite him.

He took a sip and grimaced. "Diet? Really?"

"You can't expect me to spoil your well-regimented diet all the time." Her lips pushed out in an unconvincing pout. "Rose would have my head."

As much as he hated to admit it, she had a point. If he was honest, he would rather eat rabbit food than try to figure out how to reduce his stress level at work. Still, he hated diet soda and much preferred water or lemonade.

"You need the caffeine," Lanie said, reading his mind. "I can't justify a coffee this late in the afternoon, but a soda is doable."

"Are you sticking around?"

She nodded. "I figured you could use some help with the research."

The tomato he'd taken a bite of turned to ash in his mouth. "I'm not sure you'll have more luck than Sandra or Michael. They've hit a dead end."

"Ah, ye of little faith."

He eyed her over his food. "What do you have in mind?"

Instead of responding, she gave him a mysterious smile as she popped a fry into her mouth. He hoped whatever she had up her sleeve would help him, though he doubted it would be enough.

After they finished their meal, Lanie gathered the wrappers and empty containers and tossed them into the bin. Since she didn't have an office, she set up her computer on the other side of Steven's desk. He considered telling her to go to the conference room but found her presence oddly comforting. It meant a lot that she was willing to devote her summer vacation to helping him.

"So, what's the favor?" he asked, figuring he'd better get that conversation over with or he would never be able to concentrate.

At first, she didn't respond, and he wondered whether she'd heard him. He was about to ask her again when she looked up from her computer.

"Nate and I are starting to work with vendors, and some of them have sent contracts. Between Mom's estate and helping here, I've taken a crash course in learning the law, but I'm still not quite up to speed on the legal lingo." She took a deep breath. "So I was hoping you'd take a look."

"Of course I'll review your contracts." He gestured to her computer. "You've been a huge help the last few weeks. It is, quite literally, the least I can do."

"Thanks," she said, visibly relaxing.

He cocked his head. "Why would you think I wouldn't do it?"

"It's not that I think you wouldn't. It's more I was afraid you couldn't." She waved a hand around his office. "With everything going on, I didn't want to add to your stress load."

He scoffed. "Of all the things that I'm juggling, contract review is probably the easiest to accomplish." Leaning back in his chair, he smirked. "Though it's probably the most boring aspect of law."

"Hopefully they won't put you to sleep." She started typing again on her computer. "I can bring the contracts over this evening, if that's okay."

"Sure, whenever you're ready. It shouldn't take me long to look over everything and share any concerns, but in my experience, wedding vendors have rather generic contracts just to cover their butts."

"That's good."

"So..." he began. "Does that mean you've picked a date?"

"We have." She kept her eyes on the screen, as if she thought that by not looking at him, he would drop the subject. Surely she knew him better than that.

"And?"

She sighed. "We're planning for November fourth."

He nodded then froze. "Wait…" It was like someone had kicked him in the stomach. "You're getting married on Mom's *birthday*?"

Her teeth worried her lower lip as she gave a stiff nod. "We want to get married in the fall, when there are still leaves on the trees. But October was too soon, and—"

"That's insane," he said, heat rising in his chest. Raking his fingers through his hair, he moved from behind his desk. "And you didn't think to discuss this with me before you made a decision?"

Her eyes widened. "I thought it might be nice to have another reason to celebrate that day."

For a moment, they stared at each other. He opened and closed his mouth as a million thoughts raced through his mind. Last year, he'd visited their mother's grave alone to mark the day. Lanie was in Seattle, finishing school, and Dad had refused to join him. Rose had come to see him after her shift. She'd asked him to wait for her before visiting the cemetery, but part of him had preferred to visit his mother alone.

It had been one of the hardest days since he'd lost her. As they approached July, another hard day was arriving soon—the first anniversary of her death. Lanie's timing in telling him the date she'd chosen couldn't have been worse.

"Find another day," he spat out through clenched teeth.

Her mouth fell open. "What?"

"Choose any day, any other day but that one." He pushed his chair around his desk and glared at her. "I will literally help you find a venue and vendors who can accommodate an October date, if you're insistent on having it fall themed, but choose a different day."

She stared at him. "Why are you being like this?"

He wheeled his chair back and forth, refusing to meet her eyes. "Do you have any idea what the last year was like for me? You were on the other side of the country, barely answering my calls, and Dad was too afraid of his own grief to even share the burden with me. The only one who was here for me that day was Rose, and she had to work for most of it."

"But don't you see?" She closed her laptop and stood. "This year will be different. And instead of being sad, we can celebrate, together."

"No." His tone was harsh, but he no longer cared.

Her eyes filled with tears, and before he could say anything, she grabbed her things and rushed from the room. The anger that had welled up in him dissipated.

"Wait, Lanie. You don't have to—"

But she didn't stop or turn to hear what he had to say. Instead, she ran through the lobby and out the front door, leaving Leslie staring after her.

A lump formed in his throat. He wanted to go after her, but he would never catch her in his chair. Besides, what would he say? He might have been harsh, but he believed she needed to hear it.

How could she think I'd be okay with the idea of making our mother's birthday into anything else? Doesn't she understand that there are two days that will always be dark for me, for both of us?

The one saving grace was that even November was probably too soon to plan a wedding. Maybe he could convince her to wait until next autumn. Their mother's birthday wouldn't fall on a weekend, and he could live with his sister getting married a day or two before it so long as the day itself remained sacred.

It took effort, but Steven pushed the scene with Lanie from his mind. He finished filling in the template for the will he was working on, adding the various items the client wished to bequeath. Mr. Rochester had quite the estate, and Steven couldn't help wondering why his client had left it all to chance for so long. The man had to be pushing eighty, and most of Steven's estate clients began the planning in their forties.

Perhaps Mr. Rochester thought he would be the exception to other humans and could beat death. Maybe he saw himself as some Dorian Gray character. *Though if that's the case, what caused him to finally take care of it now?* Steven didn't know, but he was glad for the business.

He saved his changes and closed the file. Mr. Rochester wasn't expecting an updated version for a few days, and Steven liked to let the draft marinate before he went in to edit and finalize it. But it probably wouldn't take many more iterations. During their meetings, Mr. Rochester had been very specific about what he wanted. His questionnaire response was the only one Steven had had to alter because it went over the maximum character count.

With a sigh, Steven stretched before making his way to Michael's office. That neither Michael nor Sandra had interrupted him that afternoon had caught him off guard. When he entered the lobby, he heard whispers coming from Sandra's room.

"Is everything all right in here?" he asked, not bothering to knock.

Sandra and Michael exchanged glances, and Steven crossed his arms. His gaze vacillated between the two.

"Lanie had a breakthrough in the research," Michael said.

Sandra shot Steven a look. Clearly, she was aware of his fight with his sister. He would deal with that later.

"That's good news," Steven replied, waiting for them to elaborate. "Isn't it?"

"It is." Michael turned the screen of Sandra's computer and pointed. "I mean, it's an old case, but we couldn't find anything that supersedes it."

Steven nodded. "More recent is always preferable, but I'll take what I can get. What are the facts?"

Michael summarized the case, and Steven smiled at how closely it resembled the Harris case. The incident at the center of the lawsuit had occurred at a government building. A coffee had spilled at a stand near a staircase. While the spill had been mopped up, the janitor failed to put up a sign. The victim had slipped on the wet spot and tumbled down the stairs.

"I had actually seen this case myself," Michael admitted. "But since the victim was an employee and not a member of the public, I thought it was distinguishable. However, the attorneys representing the plaintiff took multiple approaches to ensure victory. They went after workman's comp but also pointed out the danger to the public, including the testimony of a witness."

"What did the witness say that was so interesting?" Steven asked.

Sandra's eyes lit up. "It's not what they said but what happened to them."

He frowned, squinting at the screen. "I'm not sure I understand."

Sandra scrolled down and pointed. "The witness was almost a victim too. They slipped on the same area but managed to avoid a similar fate by grabbing onto the handrail before they tumbled."

"And the witness wasn't an employee," Michael added.

"Interesting." Steven studied the screen. "Send this to me. I'd like to take a closer look, but in the meantime, feel free to start plugging in the relevant facts to your pleading."

"Sure thing, boss." Michael gathered his papers and headed to his office, though he stopped at the door. "I'll get the pleading to you ASAP as well."

"Sounds good, thanks."

Once they were alone, Sandra leaned back in her chair with a frown. "I heard your argument with Lanie."

He bristled. "I don't want to discuss it."

"So you don't want me to tell you I agree with you?"

That caught his attention, and he raised his eyebrows. "You do?"

She sighed. "Your sister means well, but she's not thinking this through. It's like putting a Band-Aid on a bullet wound. She's trying to change the entire meaning of the day, but it's not going to cover the significance to all of you, herself included."

"Should I try to talk her out of it?"

She snorted. "Not if you're going to scream at her, no. But maybe allow someone with a softer hand, someone who has reached Lanie before when no one else could."

Steven scrunched up his face. "You mean Nate?"

Sandra stared at the ceiling in the way she always did when he was being especially obtuse. "I'm referring to Rose."

Right. "I'll talk to her, but she's got a lot on her mind right now."

"With the wedding?"

"And the fundraiser."

Sandra's eyebrows shot up. "A fundraiser? For what?"

Steven ran a hand through his hair and dropped his gaze. "Um, me? Well, and the wedding. I was supposed to help Rose pay off the final balances to our vendors, but after all the work I missed while I was in the hospital, my finances are dismal at best."

Sandra stood and crossed the room before laying a hand on his arm. "You should have told me. I'd do anything to help the two of you."

"I know," he mumbled, shifting away. "But it's embarrassing."

Her head tilted. "Because of the money?"

"I should be able to support us on my own, but failing that, I should at the very least be able to pay for a wedding."

"Hey." Sandra squatted so they were at eye level. "You've been through a lot. And I can only imagine how the medical bills are piling up. It's okay to ask for help." She smiled. "I planned to pay for my own wedding, but we ended up accepting some assistance from my family. They thought it was the least they could do since both my parents died."

Steven gave a weak smile. "Thanks, Sandra. That means a lot."

"So, this fundraiser..." She raised an eyebrow. "When is it?"

He shrugged. "July twenty-second. Lanie and Trudy are planning it. Er... Lanie was. I'm not sure if she'll do it now."

"She'll do it. And I'll help her."

"You don't have to—"

Sandra held up a hand. "I want to." Leaning against the wall, she peered out the door toward his office. "Did you finish the will?"

He nodded. "I want to go through it again before I send this version to Mr. Rochester, but I've included his latest additions."

"That man has more money than God."

Steven laughed. "Or at least, more money than he knows what to do with."

Her eyes took on a mischievous gleam. "Make sure you send him the latest version before the fundraiser."

His eyebrows pulled together. "Why?"

"Because he'll probably be a lot more eager to donate if you've finished the job he hired you to do."

Chapter Eighteen

"HE'S BEING UNREASONABLE," LANIE declared as she sank into the booth across from Rose at Bea's Diner. After shoving her bag into the corner of the bench, she began violently flipping through the jukebox by the wall.

"Who is?" Rose set down her menu and took in her future sister-in-law's uncharacteristically disheveled appearance. Her dirty-blond hair was pulled up into a messy bun, and her cheeks were blotchy, as if she'd been crying.

"Steven." Lanie said it like an expletive instead of a name. "I asked him if he would help me with vendor contracts for my wedding."

"He said no?" Rose couldn't help the incredulity in her voice. Though Steven had a lot going on, she couldn't imagine he wouldn't help his sister.

Waving a hand, Lanie shook her head. "No, he was fine with that. But he asked if we'd finally chosen a wedding date, and as soon as I told him the day we picked, he went ballistic."

That didn't sound like Steven at all. Rose put her hand on Lanie's to stop her frantic search for a song and to keep her from breaking the mini jukebox. With a sigh, Lanie sat back and crossed her arms.

"When's the big day?" Rose asked.

Lanie dropped her gaze and fidgeted with a string on her shirt. Her actions didn't make any sense to Rose. Lanie and Nate had discussed several dates, and Rose expected her to be excited to share the one they'd settled on. But Lanie seemed hesitant, almost guilty.

"Lanie?"

Finally, Lanie met Rose's gaze and squared her shoulders. "November fourth."

After racking her brain to determine why Steven would have objected to the date, a cold chill slid up Rose's spine. There was no way Lanie had chosen her mother's *birthday* to get married.

She was going to have to tread lightly. If Steven had already blown up at her, Lanie wasn't likely to take kindly to Rose tearing into her as well. But somehow, Rose had to make her see reason. Steven had been inconsolable last year on Melody's birthday, and Rose couldn't bear the thought of him forcing smiles and faking joy just to appease his sister.

"Why that day?" Perhaps if Rose asked enough questions, she could lead Lanie to understand not only why her brother had reacted negatively to her news but also why the date was a terrible idea.

"It used to be such a happy day for us, celebrating Mom. So I thought it would be a nice way to honor her memory and give another reason to celebrate the day instead of mourning her loss."

While Rose appreciated the sentiment, she wondered whether Lanie had thought the idea through. It wasn't easy to replace one memory with another. No matter how much she tried to paper over her grief with balloons and décor, the reality of who wasn't at the wedding would lurk in the shadows and pounce when Lanie expected to be happiest.

"How did you spend your mother's birthday last year?"

Lanie set her elbow on the table and, frowning, leaned her cheek against her hand. Then her face cleared as the memory seemed to finally come to her.

"I spent the day researching a specific area of my thesis." She bit her lip. "And trying to forget the significance of the day."

Rose nodded. "And do you think by throwing yourself into planning your wedding and celebrating with everyone you love, you'll be able to forget who *isn't* there to share in your joy?"

Lanie scowled. "I'm not trying to forget her. I thought it would be a better way to remember her."

"I believe your heart was in the right place," Rose said gently. "But have you considered Steven's point of view?"

"It's hard to get my head so far up my own backside."

Rose laughed. "Fair point." She cleared her throat. "I'm sorry Steven was hostile. He shouldn't have yelled at you."

"But?" Lanie raised an eyebrow.

"You can't get married on your mother's birthday." Rose blew out her breath. "At least, not if you want to maintain a good relationship with your brother."

"Maybe I don't," Lanie muttered.

"I don't believe that for a second."

"Fine." Lanie unrolled her silverware. "To be fair, Nate wasn't too keen on the idea either, but he was willing to go along with it if it made me happy."

"Smart man."

"But now I guess it's back to the drawing board."

"Do you have any other dates in mind?"

Lanie pursed her lips. "I thought about Christmas, but I'm not sure that will be received any better by Steven."

Tilting her head, Rose frowned. "Why would he object to Christmas?"

"I don't know. It's a family holiday, and it's kind of cliché."

The server came over and took their orders. Since it was late afternoon, neither of them wanted a full meal. Instead, they split a few appetizers.

Once they were alone again, Rose clasped her hands on the table. "If Nate is on board and you can plan it in time, Christmas is a great day for a wedding. And I'm sure Steven would agree." *At the very least, he'll be more amenable to Christmas than his late mother's birthday.*

Lanie's face broke into a smile. "I'll discuss it with Nate, but I appreciate your support."

"Anytime."

"Now"—Lanie removed a laptop from her bag—"we should probably discuss the fundraiser."

⁓ℓℓ⁓

The next evening, Rose stood outside The Muddy Oar, patiently waiting for Max to drop Steven off. Something about their new normal reminded her of being a freshman in high school. Steven's dad playing chauffeur necessitated a curfew they hadn't had previously. While she missed the freedoms they'd enjoyed before Steven's accident, she had to admit the changes made their time together all the more precious.

As Max maneuvered Steven's wheelchair through the parking lot, her fiancé gave an embarrassed wave. The restrictions were taking their toll on him.

"I'll be back in two hours to pick him up," Max said after pushing the wheelchair up on the sidewalk. "The aides will be coming to help him into bed around eight."

"She knows, Dad," Steven said, the irritability clear in his tone.

"Good luck," Max muttered under his breath as he brushed by Rose.

"I heard that," Steven grumbled.

Stifling a sigh, Rose grasped the wheelchair handles and steered Steven into the restaurant. The dining area was mostly empty, though it was rather early for dinner.

"Table for two, please," Rose told the host standing at the podium. He had dark hair and didn't look a day over sixteen.

With a nod, he led them to a table near the back corner. The host removed one of the chairs, and Rose angled the wheelchair into the empty spot. She took the seat across from Steven and accepted a menu.

"Your server will be with you shortly," the host said before returning to his post.

"How was work today?" Rose asked as she opened her menu.

"Not bad. Thanks to Michael, I'm at least meeting deadlines again. Though that may change in a couple of weeks."

"Why do you say that?"

Steven's eyebrows drew together. "He's taking the bar exam at the end of the month."

"But that's good, isn't it?" Rose asked. "He'll be able to do more when he passes."

"He won't have the results until October." Steven sighed. "That won't stop the offers from pouring in, though."

"He's committed to staying the summer, isn't he?"

Shaking his head, Steven set his menu aside. "That's what I advertised for, but we didn't sign any sort of employment contract. He's free to leave sooner if he finds something more permanent."

Then offer him something more permanent. Rose bit her tongue to keep from saying that out loud. They hadn't had a nice evening together in a while, and she didn't want to start a fight.

"Has he said anything about wanting to leave?"

"No, but that doesn't mean he won't."

Worrying her lower lip, Rose raised her menu to hide her face. He was starting to sound eerily like Mr. Patrones. It was making her uncomfortable.

"Anyway, how are things with you? I hear you had lunch with Lanie yesterday."

"Not really lunch, but we met at Bea's to discuss the fundraiser."

"Did she tell you she picked a wedding date?" he asked darkly.

Rose lowered her menu and met his gaze. "She did, and I successfully talked her out of it."

That perked him up. "You did? How'd you manage that?"

"For starters, I didn't blow up at her." She gave him a meaningful look.

"I know." He scrubbed a hand over his face. "I need to apologize to her. She caught me off guard. I mean, Mom's birthday? Really?"

"Although she was misguided, her heart was in the right place." Rose debated briefly whether to tell him the new date Lanie had proposed. Perhaps if she did, he would react better when Lanie told him herself. "She's considering Christmas now."

He rubbed his chin. "That's better, though a bit overdone." He groaned. "And so soon? Why is she in such a rush?"

Rose shrugged. "She and Nate lost so much time after what happened between them, I suppose they don't want to waste another minute."

"I guess." He didn't sound convinced. "Enough about my sister. How's work?"

"The board has scheduled a meeting on August first to discuss the head nurse position."

His eyes widened. "Oh? Do you think they'll offer it to you?"

"It's too soon to say, but Dr. Myers thinks it's likely."

"Wow, that would be quite the wedding present."

Her jaw clenched. *It's not a "present." I worked hard for this promotion.* Breathing in through her nose and out through her mouth, she shook her head. *Don't overreact. I'm sure he didn't mean it that way.*

She was saved from needing to respond by the arrival of the server. Steven gestured for her to go first.

"I'll have the Chicken Chesapeake with a salad," Rose said.

The server nodded and took her menu. "And for you, sir?"

"I'll have a New York strip."

He can't be serious. She stared at him, but he didn't meet her gaze. Her heart thumped in her chest as she willed the server to leave.

"What are you doing?"

Finally, he looked at her and smiled. "Having a lovely meal with my future wife."

"You know what I mean."

With an exasperated sigh, he gestured to the restaurant. "We're in a steakhouse, Rose. What did you think I was going to order?" He took a sip of water. "Besides, I haven't had any red meat since the accident. Dr. Myers said I had to *limit* how much I ate, but he didn't say I couldn't have any."

As much as she hated to admit it, he had a point. Still, it was risky. Especially since he was still in the wheelchair and had limited mobility. It would be better for his heart if he avoided certain foods until he could exercise regularly again.

Once more, they were treading toward dangerous territory. Rose decided to change the subject. "Lanie and I had a good conversation about the fundraiser, though she's going to run our ideas past Trudy before she makes any final decisions."

He leaned forward and took her hand. "I'm glad you're open to the idea. I know how much you hate relying on other people for help."

"It's not about me, it's about us. And we'd do the same for anyone else in Cedar Haven if the situation were reversed."

"Very true." He smiled and squeezed her hand. "Have I mentioned how excited I am to marry you?"

"Not lately," she teased, unable to stop the grin that spread over her face. The tension in her shoulders eased. She'd missed that, how easy things used to be between them.

"Well, I'd tell you my heart skips a beat every time I think about it, but I'd be afraid you'd haul me back to Dr. Myers for another round of testing."

Rose giggled, and a weight lifted as she fell into their familiar banter. "I'll have him do a full workup the day before our wedding just to be sure. Wouldn't want you to faint when you see my dress."

His eyes darkened. "I'm looking forward to seeing you in it... and out of it."

Warmth rushed to her cheeks. "Steven!"

Before he could respond, the server returned with their food. The sight of the steak made her feel like a bucket of cold water had been dumped over her, but she pushed her concerns away. She refused to let them overshadow the evening.

"So, how is physical therapy going now that your cast is off?"

Steven shrugged. "I wouldn't know. I haven't had a session without it yet." He cut a piece of steak and popped it into his mouth, closing his eyes. "Mm, this is delicious. Do you want a bite?"

And just like that, the cold water of reality washed over her again. "No, thank you." Her appetite had disappeared as she struggled to rein in the emotional rollercoaster she'd unwittingly stumbled on. "What do you mean you haven't had a session yet? You were cleared to begin more intensive therapy a few days ago."

"Things have been busy at the office, and I hadn't had time to make an appointment."

Don't make a scene. But the harder she tried to salvage their date, the worse she felt. Her feet ached from tiptoeing around the shattered glass of sore subjects for someone who refused to acknowledge that anything was broken.

He seemed to realize she'd stopped eating and set down his fork and knife. "Rose? What's wrong?"

"I'm worried you're still not taking your health seriously."

His worried expression gave way to a scowl. "I'm not having this argument again."

"It's not an argument," she protested. "It's genuine concern." Without thinking, she gestured to his wheelchair. "I thought you wanted to walk again as soon as you could."

His eyes flashed with anger. "Of *course* I want to walk again. Do you think I enjoy being stuck in this thing? That it's fun to have my dad chauffeur me to dates with my fiancée? To not know if I'm going to be able to walk with her down the aisle on our wedding day?"

She stared at him. "I don't care if you walk, roll, or crawl down the aisle, as long as we're together."

"Well, it matters to me." He waved his hand toward his back. "However, as I've yet to regain feeling in my legs, I can't imagine a few days is going to make any difference in my recovery."

Her clinical training clicked in. "It's about muscle memory—"

"I *know*!"

His raised voice caused something in Rose to snap. "Don't talk to me that way." She took a deep breath to try to calm herself. "Look, I'm sorry if it sounds like I'm nagging you. I *care* about you, and I want you to get better. I want *us* to get better." Tears welled in her eyes, and she furiously blinked them back.

That seemed to sober him. He bowed his head. "I know you do. I'm sorry."

She swallowed around the lump in her throat. *How did we get here?* It seemed only yesterday that their biggest problem was Steven's overworked schedule. In a moment, everything had changed.

With a sigh, he pushed away from the table and maneuvered his chair next to her. "I really am sorry. And I promise I'll try harder to follow the doctors' advice."

How many more times is he going to make that promise? But she didn't feel angry at his empty words. She felt hollow, like the fight had gone out of her.

"This isn't easy for me either. I may not be the one in the wheelchair, but that doesn't mean I'm not having a hard time with this too."

He nodded. "And I appreciate you sticking it out with me." A wry smile stole over his face. "Even when I'm being an insensitive jerk."

"Isn't that all the time?" she joked. While Steven laughed, the words had a ring of truth. Part of her wished she could chalk up his recent poor behavior to the accident, but the fact was, he'd been ignoring her pleas to take better care of himself for months.

After kissing her cheek, he made his way around the table and gestured to her food. "Let's eat before it gets cold."

Rose picked up her fork and knife and took a bite of her chicken, but the food, like her heart, had already cooled.

~*~

When Rose arrived at her condo, she didn't immediately go inside. Though the sun was low in the sky, it hadn't set, and the evening air hung heavy with warm humidity. Instead, she walked to the pond. She hadn't been by to check on the swans since the injured one had been transported to the wildlife rehab center. But as she neared the water's edge, only one swan remained.

The same man she had spoken to that first day with the swans was standing on the shoreline, watching the lone swan swimming in circles. When he heard her approach, he looked up with a grin.

"Coming back to check on them, are you?" He nodded. "My friend said the male is healing well and should be returned in the next few weeks." Inclining his head toward the female, he continued, "She'll be happy to have him home, I'm sure."

"Does she know he's still alive?" Rose asked.

"I imagine so," the man replied. "She's not gone into mourning."

That caught her off guard. She frowned. "What does a swan in mourning look like?"

"They often don't leave their nest, and I've seen females put their heads under their wings, almost as if they're covering their face while they cry."

I understand how she feels. "I hope she doesn't give up hope," Rose said, her heart going out to the swan. "It must get lonely with no other swans around."

"Oh, she's not alone. You can see her cygnets if you look closely." He pointed at a few small gray blobs in the water.

They were difficult to make out at that distance and with the muddy color of the pond. But when Rose squinted, she could discern three tiny fluffy feathered bodies gliding after the larger swan.

"Aw, they're adorable!"

"Best keep your distance, though. Swans are very protective of their young." He glanced at her. "If you want, I can give you a heads-up when the male is set to return."

Rose nodded. "I would like that very much. Thank you."

After waving goodbye, she headed to her condo, but her thoughts remained with the swans. She couldn't help seeing the parallel between her situation and theirs. Part of her envied the female swan's faith that her male companion was alive and well and would someday return. In contrast, Rose had multiple ways to reach Steven, but no matter how hard she tried, the two of them couldn't seem to connect.

Chapter Nineteen

A FEW DAYS LATER, Steven entered his office with renewed hope that he would soon be able to ditch his wheelchair. He had an appointment that afternoon for physical therapy, and he planned to ask when he might expect to graduate to a walker. Though his spine had healed considerably, he still wasn't able to do more than stand for short periods of time with most of his weight resting on his forearms and hands.

Focusing on his physical limitations was easier than letting his mind replay the conversation with Rose the night before. He wasn't being fair, but he also felt she wasn't either. Of course he understood she was going through this with him. Yet he wasn't sure she fully grasped the toll the accident and subsequent recovery had taken on him. Sometimes he procrastinated on scheduling his medical appointments so he could pretend, even for a moment, that everything was normal.

Pushing the thoughts from his mind, he opened his email, and a calendar notification popped up. Michael was out that morning to study for the bar exam. Steven's stomach flip-flopped. While he and Michael hadn't discussed what would happen if Michael passed the bar, Steven had seriously considered offering Michael a more permanent position. But once he passed the bar, he might not be interested in sticking around.

The results wouldn't be released until autumn. Hopefully, Steven had a couple of months to figure that out. He took comfort in knowing Michael had been instrumental in assisting with keeping the lights on.

A few hours later, the front door to the office opened, and pealing laughter filled the silence. Steven glanced at the time, rubbed his eyes, and stretched. Finally, he was through making the last edits to the will, and it was ready to sign. After maneuvering to his office door, he stood and leaned against the doorframe for balance.

"Sandra? That you?"

She came out of her office, and her eyes widened. "What are you doing, standing there like that? You're liable to fall!"

He shifted his back against the wall, though his legs were already shaking. "I've finished the will for Mr. Rochester. Can you set up an appointment?"

"After you sit your butt back in a chair." She rushed over and grabbed his arm before she helped ease him into the wheelchair.

"I can't wait for the day I'll walk again," he said with a sigh.

"You're making good progress, but you've got to be patient. Spine injuries don't heal overnight."

"I know." He leaned his head back against his chair and glared at the ceiling. "But it's frustrating. And I don't want to roll my way down the aisle on my wedding day. I want to stand on my own two feet, head held high." He shook his head. "It's supposed to be the best day of my life."

"I get it. Sometimes life happens in a way we don't expect or want it to. But you have to roll with the punches." Her lips twitched. "No pun intended."

He frowned, not finding her joke as amusing as she did. "Anyway, we're down a staff member today. Michael is at a study group to prepare for the bar."

"Oh, that's right!" Sandra exclaimed. "I'll keep my fingers and toes crossed for him, but I doubt he'll need it." She played with a piece of string on her shirt. "What are we going to do if he passes?"

Swallowing his concerns, he gave what he hoped was a nonchalant shrug. "It's still early summer. We have some time to figure it out."

"Assuming he doesn't find something sooner." Crossing her arms, Sandra released a long sigh. "He's been doing good work. I bet if you offered him something, he'd consider it."

"I can't compete with the DC law firms. He'd make three times what I could offer him."

"Maybe if you take the initiative and make an offer now, he won't consider going back. Or what if you made him a partner?" She sat in one of the chairs across from him. "He might be willing to give up the salary in exchange for an equal part of the firm."

His stomach hardened, but he fought to keep his expression neutral. "The firm isn't ready for that. I need more time to build up the clientele." What he didn't say was he needed to recoup what he had spent to start the business.

But Sandra read his mind anyway. "Look, you're in over your head, but—"

"The answer is no," Steven barked, and he immediately regretted it when Sandra's eyes widened.

"Suit yourself." Her tone had lost its friendliness, and she marched out of his office.

Great. First, he'd hurt Rose, and then he'd upset his best employee. If he wasn't careful, Sandra would be on Michael's heels as he ran out the door. And that would really put Steven in a bind.

⁂

Around lunchtime, Lanie popped her head in. "I'm here to take you to your physical therapy appointment."

Steven finished what he was typing and hit save before he glanced up and forced a smile. "Yay."

"I know you hate it, but it's good for you."

"Yeah, yeah." He pushed back from the desk and gestured to his chair. "I suppose if it'll get me out of this stupid thing, it's worth it." Without waiting for her response, he maneuvered his chair from behind his desk and out of his office.

"I talked to Rose," Lanie said as she pushed him through the front and headed for the van. "Sounds like you two had another argument because you aren't taking your health seriously."

"Don't start."

"I'm not." After locking his wheelchair into place in the van, she buckled him in. "I'm worried about you two. Maybe you should consider couples counseling or therapy."

"I'm already in enough therapy," he muttered.

Lanie snorted and shut the door. When she climbed into the driver's seat, she shot him a look in the rearview. For a moment, he couldn't breathe. She looked like their mother when she did that, and his heart ached. The first anniversary of her death was coming up fast, and he wasn't ready to face the reality that she had been gone a year.

He closed his eyes, willing his thoughts in another direction. Unfortunately, they turned to Rose. She hadn't said it, but the look in her eyes had told him she hadn't believed him when he'd promised to try harder to take care of himself. Their goodbye had been lukewarm at best, and though he had no real reason to doubt her, his gut told him something had changed between them.

With a sigh, Steven turned away from the window. "Sometimes I've wondered if Rose pushed to postpone the wedding not for my health but because she had an ulterior motive."

When his sister met his gaze in the rearview with a quizzical frown, he tried to think of a better way to word it. For once, the tightening in his chest had nothing to do with his heart attack and everything to do with his jumbled-up emotions.

"I knew after our first date Rose was the one for me. The only reason I waited to propose was because we both wanted to finish our degrees. And then we wanted to establish ourselves in our respective careers." He turned to the window as they passed Bea's Diner. "But I sort of blew that up when I got it in my head to move back here and open my own practice. Rose was doing well in Baltimore, and she'd received a job offer for a position in Boston."

"And now you're afraid she regrets that decision?"

A weight fell off his shoulders. "Yes, exactly. And my biggest fear, the one I can barely bear to think, let alone say out loud"—his voice lowered—"is that if we had put it off any longer, she'd wise up and leave me."

"Oh, Steven." Lanie shook her head as she turned off Main Street and headed toward the parking lot of a large building. "Rose loves you. She may not have promised 'for better or worse' yet, but she meant it all the same when she accepted your proposal."

"I wish I could believe that." When Lanie opened her mouth as if to protest, he hurried on. "Wait, let me finish." He took a deep breath. "Just... look at me. I'm not even thirty years old, and I can't walk, I—"

"But you've made progress in such a short amount of time!" After pulling up to the entrance of the building, she put the van in park then turned and looked at him. "You *will* walk again. You *will* have a beautiful, wonderful, *long* life with Rose."

Tears pricked behind his eyelids, and he blinked rapidly to keep them from falling. "Thanks, sis. That means a lot." He nodded at the clock on the dash. "We'd better go, or I'll be late for my torture appointment."

She laughed. "There's that sense of humor I know and love."

Lanie might have taken his statement as a joke, but Steven had meant it as anything but. No matter how much he tried to convince himself that physical therapy was necessary to reclaim his life and walk again, nothing would ease the sense of dread that grew within him the closer they got to the building. From everything he had heard, Ronnie, his physical therapist, sounded like a sadist. And he expected she would work him until tears literally poured down his cheeks before pushing him some more.

"Ah, my next victim," said a woman with spiky blue hair and a row of earrings climbing each ear. She rubbed her hands together. "I'm Ronnie, and you must be Steven."

Great first impression. Steven shot a pleading glance at Lanie, who shrugged helplessly. When he turned to look at Ronnie, she had a hand on her hip and a smirk on her face.

"Nothing like the smell of fresh fear to start a new session," Ronnie said with a laugh. She smiled at Lanie. "I'll take him from here."

"Good luck," Lanie whispered. After giving him a quick hug, she rushed out to the van. Steven watched her leave, wishing he could follow.

"Come on. It's just an hour." Ronnie steered him into the makeshift gym and over to a bed. "We're going to start you off with some transitions and go from there."

"Transitions?" Steven asked.

She moved in front of him. "You're going to move yourself from the chair to the bed and back again."

"But I'm barely able to stand!"

Instead of responding, she continued, "Watch me first. I'll show you how to support your weight on your arms until your legs are strong enough to hold you." She grabbed a chair and demonstrated using the bars by the bed to pull herself up, then she shuffled to the bed before extending one hand to the bedrail and hoisting herself onto it.

Steven raised an eyebrow. She made it look deceptively easy, but she had full control of her extremities.

With a grimace, Steven gripped the arms of his wheelchair and pushed himself to standing. He grasped the bar and held onto it for dear life as he tried to shuffle his feet. They moved incrementally toward the bed, but it took way more effort than he was expecting.

"That's it. Slow and steady."

He shot her a glare and took another precarious step forward. His leg shook with the effort as he dragged his opposite foot behind him. The weight of the boot on his leg served only to further slow his progress. After what felt like an eternity, he finally made his way to the edge of the bed. He grabbed the bedrail, turned his body, and lifted himself onto the bed with his arms.

"Good, though you need to pick up that back foot more, or else you're going to trip yourself."

"Tell that to my foot," Steven retorted. "It doesn't obey my commands."

She pursed her lips. "It doesn't hear them."

He scowled as he bent down and lifted his legs one by one onto the bed. Once he was securely in the middle, he lay down and stared at the ceiling, struggling to catch his breath.

"Now that you're here, I'm going to have you do some leg exercises."

Steven relaxed, but his sense of accomplishment was short-lived because Ronnie began a series of exercises that worked every muscle in his body. By the time they were done, he was panting.

It had been only fifteen minutes. He still had forty-five to go. *This is ridiculous. I've never been this out of shape in my life.*

"All right. Time to move back to the chair." Once again, Ronnie demonstrated how to transition from the bed to the chair.

His muscles screamed as he lifted himself off the bed and shuffled to the chair. But it took less time than it had to get on the bed, and when he eased into his chair, Ronnie smiled at him.

"Since you're doing so well, I thought you might like to have a bit of fun. What do you say?" Ronnie leaned against the bed.

What could possibly be fun about physical therapy? But he decided to humor her. "What do you have in mind?"

She wriggled her eyebrows. "What do you say we play a round of wheelchair basketball? It'll give you a chance to work your upper body without worrying about your legs."

He snorted. "You know, my grandfather used to be obsessed with me playing basketball because of my height."

She grinned. "But it wasn't for you?"

"I mean, I wasn't against it, but I wasn't really into it either. But I'll try anything at this point."

Her face fell, but she shook it off. "Not quite the spirit I was looking for, but I'll take it."

Without another word, she pushed him out of the room and down a hallway. They entered a gym that reminded him of middle school PE.

To Steven's surprise, the court was filled with other people in wheelchairs. "I thought this was going to be just you and me, one on one."

"What kind of challenge would that be?"

He swallowed, suddenly self-conscious, though he couldn't explain why. Every single person on that court except for the physical therapist was in the same situation as him. They might have arrived there because of different circumstances—Steven noted a few guys with missing limbs—but they would understand what he was going through. Then he realized the real reason Ronnie had brought him out there: to show him that he wasn't alone.

—— *ell* ——

A few days later, Lanie picked Steven up from yet another physical therapy appointment. His muscles ached but nowhere near as much as his heart. The day he'd been dreading had finally arrived, and his sister was taking him to the cemetery.

The weather matched his mood. Dark storm clouds gathered overhead, and he worried Lanie would abandon the plan. He prayed the rain would hold off. It wouldn't feel right not to visit Mom on the anniversary of the day they'd lost her.

As if his sister could read his mind, she increased her speed. If she was trying to outpace the storm, she was fighting a losing battle.

When they arrived, she quickly unfastened his chair from the van. Navigating what had once been a confusing mess of straps and buckles had become second nature since he'd started going to the office on an almost daily basis. After he was safely on the ground, he headed to the grave. It was important to him to show Mom his progress. He believed that even if she couldn't be physically present to witness it, she was watching him from heaven.

"Hey, Mom," he whispered as he stopped in front of the headstone.

Lanie's footsteps sounded quietly behind him, and she placed a hand on his shoulder.

The air had that familiar musky odor that foretold the coming rain. But it was tears that wet his eyes and slid down Steven's cheeks, not raindrops. He sniffled, trying to hold the wave of grief at bay, but when Lanie squeezed his shoulder, he lost all sense of control and let go.

"I miss her so much," he said, both to himself and to Lanie.

"I do too." His sister's voice was hoarse, and she cleared her throat. "But she'd be proud of you. Not just for the law firm but your perseverance, even with all that's happened."

"And to think"—he wiped his eyes—"I almost joined her."

"Don't say that," Lanie admonished, stepping around his chair and kneeling by the headstone. "I like to think she was there that night, protecting you. Keeping you safe so we wouldn't face another loss."

Despite the tears flowing down his face, Steven smiled. "That makes sense. She kept me alive but allowed me to get hurt enough to teach me a lesson."

Lanie raised an eyebrow. "I'm not sure you've learned it."

"I probably haven't," he admitted with a sad laugh.

A car door slammed in the distance, and Lanie stood to see who had arrived. Her mouth opened before she glanced at Steven.

"It's Dad," she said.

Steven shrugged. "I guess it's not surprising. He knew her longest."

When Dad caught sight of them, his steps faltered, then his mouth set in a grim line as he continued toward them. Steven noticed the bouquet of yellow daisies he held.

"Sorry to disturb," Dad mumbled as he moved by Lanie and laid the flowers against the cold stone. "I didn't realize you two were coming."

"Lanie promised we could make a stop after my PT appointment. I wanted to show Mom how much progress I've made."

Dad's dark eyes went a little misty, and he sniffled. "I'm sure she's glad to see it."

Lanie turned to the grave. "It's hard to believe it's been a year."

"Sometimes it feels like a lifetime," Dad whispered.

Whether his father meant since he'd lost Mom as his wife or since she'd died, Steven wasn't sure. But he was compelled to take Dad and Lanie's hands. After a moment, Lanie took Dad's other hand, and the three of them stood in silence.

"One of my last happy memories of Mom," Steven said a few minutes later, "was when she told me I needed to hurry up and propose to Rose because she wanted some grandbabies."

Dad chuckled. "She would have made an amazing grandma."

The words were like a dagger to Steven's heart. He'd had a wonderful relationship with his grandparents while he'd had them, and he'd hoped for the same for his children. Between Rose's parents living in South Korea and the loss of his mother, his kids wouldn't have the same experience. There was something about a grandmother's love that was irreplaceable.

Plop. A drop fell on Steven's head. He raised his face to the sky. The dark clouds were right on top of them, making it seem much later in the day. Thunder rumbled in the distance.

"We'd better get out of here, or we'll get soaked," Dad said, grabbing Steven's wheelchair handles.

"Wait," Steven protested. With effort, he shifted forward in his seat and placed a hand on Mom's headstone. "I love you and miss you."

Lanie laid her hand on top of his. "We all do."

Lightning flashed across the sky, and Steven jumped. "All right, Mom. We get the point."

Dad and Lanie laughed as they pushed him across the graveyard and toward the van. The raindrops increased the closer they got, then a full-out downpour started the moment Dad pushed Steven into the van.

"We'll stay here a moment until it lets up," Dad said. "No sense driving when you can't see five feet in front of your face."

It wasn't how Steven had planned to spend the anniversary of Mom's death, but somehow, it seemed fitting to be huddled in a van in the middle of a thunderstorm with the only family he had left.

Chapter Twenty

Rose stood outside Bea's Diner, trying to find the courage to open the door and walk inside. Looking in through the window, Rose guessed most of the town was in there. The diner was filled to the brim with bodies. And while they were all there because they cared for her and Steven and wanted to give them the wedding of their dreams, she couldn't quite bring herself to take that next step.

What if we don't raise any money because the town thinks we're spoiled kids who should have planned better for a financial crisis? The medical bills were one thing, but it felt wrong to accept money for the wedding. If the fundraiser didn't work, she had no idea how they would pay their vendors. Visions of appearing in small claims court and having her wages garnished danced before her eyes as she struggled to muster up the courage to enter the diner.

The door swung open, and Lanie stepped out. "Are you coming in?"

"Working on it," Rose said, trying and failing to smile.

"Hey." Lanie put a hand on her arm. "Everyone in there has come because they want to help in whatever way they can."

"I don't want them to think we're irresponsible."

Lanie shook her head. "Nobody thinks that." She pointed at the diner. "Everyone in there has faced a hardship at some point in their lives. They've been where you are now, and they survived because people helped them when they needed it." She slid her arm around Rose's shoulders. "In this community, we take care of our own. And that includes you."

Without another word, she led Rose to the door and opened it. As Rose entered the diner, the swath of smiling faces made the situation more bearable. Though she searched each face, she could find no trace of judgment or ridicule, only love and acceptance. She supposed Lanie was right. They'd all been in similar shoes at some point, and they'd survived life's ups and downs by rallying together.

"Rose," Toccara said. "It's good to see you." She kissed Rose's cheek and waved to the crowded room. "Quite a turnout, huh?"

Rose nodded. "Much bigger than I was expecting."

"Just shows how new you are to this town," Trudy replied, coming up behind her. "Where's your dashing fiancé?"

It took her a moment, but Rose located Steven near the breakfast bar. He was with his father, Michael, and Bea. They were laughing at something Bea said. Rose couldn't help comparing the carefree look on his face to the last time she'd seen him in the restaurant. His palpable joy brought a tightness to her chest.

"He's over there. If you'll excuse me."

When he saw her, his face lit up, and he grabbed her hands. It was as if their argument in the restaurant had never happened. He turned her around to face Max and Michael, and each gave her a nod.

"So, are we passing a hat, or how is this a fundraiser and not a party?" Michael asked.

Max rolled his eyes. "If you knew my daughter, you would know better. Nothing is ever that simple."

"It's multifaceted," Steven clarified. "Bea is donating some of the proceeds from sales, a couple of local organizations put together baskets that are up for auction, and there's a donation box for people who want to contribute something without making any purchases."

As if her ears were burning, Lanie stepped up to the counter and tapped a glass until the room quieted. She winked at Rose before hopping up onto a chair.

"First, I'd like to thank you all for coming. The best thing about Cedar Haven is the tight-knit community. When someone needs help, we don't hesitate to do what we can to lift them up, and that is never more evident than during one of our infamous fundraisers!"

A cheer went up through the room, and Lanie grinned. Nate came out of the kitchen, carrying several orders of fries. He broke into a smile at the sight of her before he turned to deliver the food.

"As you know, my family has had more than our fair share of tragedy this last year. After we lost Mom, I thought we might get a reprieve, but Steven gave us all a scare last month." Lanie's smile faltered, and Rose's eyes stung with unshed tears. Her future sister-in-law pressed on. "Thankfully, he's still with us, but unfortunately, it's caused a setback to the wedding with the medical bills piling up. But I refuse to let tragedy stop him from marrying the woman of his dreams." Pointing at the back of the room, she continued, "We've got several baskets up for auction, door prizes, and we'll be having a karaoke contest later. There's a minimal entry fee, but it's going to a good cause."

Turning toward the kitchen, she gestured Bea forward. "And our beloved Bea has offered to donate seventy percent of the proceeds from food and beverage sales."

The room exploded in applause, and Steven's hand tightened around Rose's. It felt a little surreal, seeing so many people there to support her and Steven.

"Without further ado, let's get this party started!" Lanie jumped off the chair to several hoots before disappearing to the back of the restaurant.

Steven signaled to Bea. "Can we get a couple of sodas?" He glanced at Rose, who nodded. "And maybe some food as well?"

"You've got it." Bea turned and headed to the kitchen to put in their order, and Steven maneuvered his wheelchair toward a small table.

"I'm surprised you found a free table with all these people," Rose said as she slid into a chair.

"Lanie reserved this for us," he replied, holding out his hand.

She placed hers into it and smiled. His sister really had thought of everything.

"How long is this supposed to last?"

He shrugged. "I don't know that there's a definite end to it. Sometime before Bea would normally close, I guess, but as long as people want to hang out and order, they'll keep going."

"Is someone keeping a tally of how much money is raised and who's donating what?" Rose bit her lip. "I'd like to send thank-you cards when this is over."

"I'm not sure, but maybe inviting them all to our big day will be thanks enough."

Her eyes widened as her stomach began to churn. "The whole town?"

He laughed. "Okay, maybe not everyone. Still, I'm sure there are other ways we can pay it forward."

The knot in her stomach eased, but she wondered how she would ever repay everyone for their kindness. Lanie's voice echoed in her head. *We take care of our own.* While that might be the case, she would feel unbalanced until she did something to show her gratitude.

Their food arrived, and she dove into her burger, surprised at how hungry she was. Truthfully, she hadn't eaten much that morning because she'd been a bundle of nerves leading up to the event.

But she was glad she'd come. She glanced up from her burger and smiled at Steven. He appeared in good spirits. The lines that creased his forehead when he was stressed had disappeared.

Maybe everything was going to be okay. Maybe *they* were going to be okay. While they still had a lot of things to work through, she had hope for the first time in a long time that things were going to work out.

Lanie popped up at their table with a smile. "We've only been here an hour, and we've already raised enough to pay off the catering bill."

Rose's mouth fell open. "What? Are you serious?"

With a nod, Lanie showed her the tally for the baskets. "People bid a lot higher than I'd expected on these."

"That's amazing!" Steven's eyes were wide. "I suspected we'd be able to at least offset some of the cost, but this..." He shook his head as if unable to finish his sentence.

Lanie beamed. "I'm hopeful the proceeds from food and beverage sales will give us enough to pay off what you owe for the wedding and start working on some of the outstanding medical bills."

"It would be nice not to start our new life together in debt," Steven said. "Thank you for doing this."

"It's not like I planned this alone." Someone called Lanie's name, and she smiled. "Duty calls."

When they were alone again, Rose shifted her chair closer to Steven. "How's physical therapy going?"

"Pretty well. I've been able to successfully perform most of the exercises my therapist has given me, and I practice them at home between sessions." He winked. "Though sometimes, it feels like it should be called physical torture instead of therapy."

She laughed. "How long do you think you'll have to go?"

"I'm not sure. Dr. Bhati has asked my therapist to send an update on my progress in a month, and we'll reassess after that."

At least he was listening to his doctors about something, but she kept that thought to herself. Despite her earlier reservations about the event, it was going well, and she didn't want to spoil it. Instead, she pushed her concerns about the future from her mind and tried to live in the present.

"What a success!" Lanie exclaimed as they left the diner. "We've got to wait to find out what Bea raised, but this wedding is practically paid for."

It had been a long day of shaking hands, fielding congratulations, and talking to friends and strangers alike. In some ways, it had felt like the engagement party they never got to have. They'd hoped to have one last summer, but when Melody took a turn for the worse, they postponed it. Then she'd died, and no one was up for a party after that.

The irony of how accommodating Rose had been during that time wasn't lost on her. Whereas when *she* had asked to postpone the wedding, she'd been railroaded. Steven would likely argue the circumstances were different, but were they? Instead of his mother, it was Steven whose health had taken a turn, and while he was on the mend, they still had a way to go.

Although they hadn't done much planning for their engagement party by the time Melody's health failed. So Rose supposed that in that respect, things were much different.

"Thank you for putting this together." Steven pulled his sister in for a hug. "You truly are the best sister ever."

Lanie laughed, patting her brother's back. "I expect my crown to have that engraved on it, but be sure to thank Trudy as well. She helped get the ball rolling." Once Steven released her, she rushed over to Rose. "How are you doing? Has this helped take some of the stress off you?"

Rose nodded. "It has, and Steven's right. We couldn't have done this without you."

"It was my pleasure." After linking their arms, Lanie pulled Rose away and lowered her voice. "And between you and me, there was a special box set up for people who wanted to donate to help Steven's law firm. It didn't raise much, but it might help offset some of the lost income from June. He can protest as much as he wants, but he doesn't realize how much people struggled to get legal advice before he set up shop."

"I won't tell him."

"Good." Lanie flashed a grin, but it fell as quickly as it had appeared. "Though I suppose I can't keep it from him for long. While I've been helping with bookkeeping, he'll eventually notice the extra funds."

"And he'd probably have to account for it come tax season."

Lanie pursed her lips. "True. I'll figure out a way to tell him. Maybe Michael will help me." She glanced over her shoulder and released Rose's arm. "You'd better go. He looks like he could use a nap."

Rose's brow furrowed as she assessed him. While his father buckled him into the van, he rested his head against the back of the wheelchair. Dark circles framed his eyes, and his skin was paler than normal.

As Max stepped away to allow her to say goodbye, she hesitated at the door to the van. Maybe she should ask Max to take him to the hospital and get a quick checkup. Dr. Myers was working, and he likely wouldn't mind.

Steven stirred and reached for her hand. "Will I see you at home?"

"You should get some sleep. You look exhausted." When he opened his mouth as if to protest, she hurried on. "And honestly, I'm pretty beat myself. But I'll stop by tomorrow after my shift is over."

"That sounds good," he replied with a sleepy smile.

Rose leaned in and gave him a quick peck on the cheek before heading to her car.

As she drove to her condo, she felt conflicted. On the one hand, the fundraiser had alleviated some of their financial concerns. But on the other, the exhaustion on Steven's face haunted her. Despite his promises, it looked like he still wasn't taking care of himself, and Rose was getting more than a little tired of sounding like a broken record when it came to his health. Her misgivings about the wedding had morphed into something more serious. She needed to talk to someone, to sort out her feelings, before it was too late.

Chapter Twenty-One

"Good game, man."

"Thanks for letting me play!" Steven fist-bumped Eric, one of his new friends.

"Anytime."

The rest of the guys left the court to hit the showers, but he stayed behind. He wanted to soak up as much of the moment as he could.

It had been a while since he'd had time to do anything remotely considered fun. Between work and the wedding, there weren't enough hours in the day to finish everything he needed to and enjoy some of his favorite hobbies. For months, he'd promised himself that after he and Lanie finalized their mother's estate, things would change. Then he'd pushed it until after the wedding. And even at that moment, he found himself thinking it would all come together once he'd gotten the law firm off the ground.

Maybe Rose was right. Maybe he was working himself into an early grave. But he didn't know any other way to be. Most small businesses failed within their first year, and he had less than six months to prove that statistic wrong.

Something had to give, and if it wasn't the firm or the wedding, what was it? What ball could he drop or hand off to someone else until he improved?

He didn't have an answer. While Michael had been instrumental in bringing his law practice back from the brink, there was only so much the law clerk could do until he passed the bar. And Steven already felt bad enough about the wedding plans that he'd forced onto Rose's shoulders. He was glad they'd raised enough money to alleviate the financial fears.

His earlier fears rekindled at the thought of Rose. If he lost momentum, if he couldn't keep up with their plans, she might second-guess her decision to marry him. He didn't want to lose her the way his dad had lost his mom.

Images of his parents' fights flooded his brain, and he squeezed his eyes shut to block them out. But they persisted. His father never could live up to his mother's expectations, and Steven's worst fear was repeating that history. He'd tried his hardest to learn from their mistakes. And yet he feared he was headed for the same fate, assuming he and Rose ever made it down the aisle.

"Hey, hot shot, you plan on baking all afternoon?"

He turned to find Ronnie standing by the door, one hand on her hip, the other shielding her eyes from the sun. Only then did he realize how hot the day had gotten.

"Just enjoying the fresh air," he lied as he came over. "I don't get out much."

Her eyebrow rose as she glanced at his ghost-pale legs and arms. "You don't say? You're practically translucent."

"Ha ha," he retorted, but his tone lacked its usual biting sarcasm.

Ronnie noticed. "Something wrong?"

"Lot on my mind is all." He took one last look at the basketball court before he went through the door she was holding open. "Can I do this again sometime?"

"Absolutely!" She grinned. "I thought this would be good for you."

"It was," he said. They were halfway to the waiting room when Steven stopped. "Be honest with me. Will I be able to walk again by my wedding?"

Ronnie gave him a quizzical look. "What brought this on?"

Though she seemed genuinely curious about his change in demeanor, Steven couldn't help feeling like she was avoiding his question. Instead of responding, he stared at her and waited.

"Uh, I mean, it's early yet. Your body is still recovering from your accident, and sometimes it can take up to six months for it to—"

He held up his hand. "I've heard this song and dance before. But you've worked with patients who've been through what I've been through, right? What was their experience? Were they further along in their progress than I am by this time after their injury?"

"Steven, you can't judge your progress by someone else. Spinal contusions are a tricky business, and everyone heals differently. I've had patients who could walk just fine for the most part but would have random bouts of numbness in one or both legs. And then I've had patients who never regained the feeling in their legs."

He winced. That wasn't what he wanted to hear.

"But that's clearly not you," she hurried on, gesturing to his legs. "Your cast is off, and you're already improving in your transitions. Every session, you not only get a little stronger, but I can tell you're gaining more control over your muscles. I imagine you'll regain feeling in your legs before your wedding, but I can't guarantee you'll have total motor control by then."

That was something, at least. With a sigh, he rolled his chair forward. "I'm frustrated. Every day, I feel a little more like my old self. But I'm still in this blasted chair."

"Give yourself some grace and some credit." Her eyes swept over him. "I have absolute faith you won't be in the wheelchair much longer." His face must have betrayed his doubt because she huffed in exasperation. "I understand it doesn't seem that way to you, but as you said, I've been doing this awhile. I've worked with people from all walks of life and with myriad illnesses. Take my word for it."

Before he could respond, the door to the waiting room opened, and Lanie rushed out. The frown on her face faded to a smile of relief when she saw him.

"There you are! I got here a half hour ago, and no one knew where you were." She threw her arms around his neck.

He awkwardly patted her back with one hand while the other stopped the wheelchair from running over her foot. "Sorry for worrying you, but Ronnie banished me outside for my PT."

Lanie straightened and raised her eyebrows. "Oh?"

"Your brother decided to finally pursue the basketball dreams your grandfather laid out for him."

"Figures you'd wait until your height didn't give you an advantage to try to make old Pop-Pop proud," Lanie said with a laugh.

"I'm not sure how proud he would have been," Steven grumbled. "Those guys wiped the court with me."

"But you had fun, right?" Ronnie asked.

He gave a grudging nod. "Yeah, I had fun."

Lanie put a hand over her heart. "I didn't know you knew that word!"

"Oh, hardy har har," Steven retorted. "Come on. Let's get out of here before she finds something new to torture me with."

"See you in a few days!" Ronnie wiggled her fingers in a silly wave before turning to find her next victim.

"So, you had fun, huh?" Lanie pressed.

"Don't make it into a thing." He pushed the chair up to his sister's car.

"I'm not doing anything of the sort!" She tucked a lock of hair behind her ear as she opened the car door. "It's nice to hear that you enjoyed yourself for a change. With everything that's been going on, you deserve to blow off a little steam."

Ronnie was right about one thing. His improvement with performing transfers had made the van unnecessary, and his father had canceled the rental contract. Riding shotgun was a vast improvement to being strapped into the back of the van. With Lanie's help, he pulled himself into the car then busied himself with settling into his seat and buckling in so he had an excuse not to respond. But Lanie wasn't one to give up easily.

"Did you play with anyone I know?"

"I don't think so."

She drummed her fingers on the steering wheel, a clear sign she was getting annoyed with his evasiveness. And really, what was his goal here? She'd asked because she cared, not because she was trying to hold something over his head.

"To be honest, I told Ronnie I'd like to do it again. I can't remember the last time I had such a fun afternoon."

"That's awesome!" The genuine joy in her voice touched his heart.

"And I've been thinking," he continued, unable to resist the excitement in her tone, "maybe Rose is right."

"Uh, what?" Lanie glanced at him out of the corner of her eye. "Could you say that again? She'll kill me if I don't get a recording."

He ignored her antics. "Just that I need to take better care of myself and find a better balance in my life."

"Rose isn't the only one who's been saying that."

It took effort not to roll his eyes. "Yeah, yeah. But the problem is the timing. There's so much going on right now."

"Maybe that's the point," she said.

"What do you mean?"

Her lips twisted to the side as if she was debating how to answer his question. "Health issues often show up when our body is trying to tell us to slow down. If it waited until we weren't stressed, it would kind of defeat the purpose, right?" She glanced at him. "I know you're worried about the firm and the wedding, but it's not as catastrophic as it once was. I've been looking over your financial situation—"

"Again?"

She flipped her hair over her shoulder. "You're the one who gave me access to your accounts."

That was true, though he'd been reluctant to do so. Still, it had freed up some of his time to allow her to take a look at things while he focused on the stuff no one else could do.

"Anyway," she continued when he didn't respond, "Sandra has booked you a few new clients that I don't think she's discussed with you."

"Like who?"

"Our old neighbor Cassandra wants to have a will drawn up," Lanie said.

He stared at her. "Really? I didn't know she had anyone to leave anything to."

"I don't know the specifics." She shrugged. "But she's lived in that house all our lives. I imagine it's paid off by now and is probably worth a small fortune."

"Who else?"

"Nate's parents want wills as well. His father had that heart attack not long after Mom died." Her lips quirked up. "Though I suppose it's more

Nate's mom who will be dragging his dad in. And Bea is thinking of taking on a partner for the diner."

"Wow, I thought she was going to sell it."

"So did we all, but she's not ready to give up. She seems to be hoping one of her nephews will be interested in it when they're older."

A moment later, they pulled into the parking lot of the law firm. Steven unbuckled his seat belt and waited while Lanie pulled his wheelchair from the trunk and came around to his side.

"I hope what I told you alleviates some of your stress."

"It does and it doesn't." Steven accepted her hand and shuffled out of the car and into the chair.

Her brow furrowed. "Why do you say that?"

He sighed. *How can I explain this in a way that doesn't sound like I'm ungrateful to her, Sandra, or the town?*

"New clients only help the practice if I'm capable of doing the work for which they hired me. If I can't, they'll move on, and I'll be right back where I started." He patted his legs. "And I barely have enough time now to keep up with my *current* workload thanks to all of my various medical appointments."

"But that won't last forever," Lanie countered as she pushed him into the office.

"No, but the timing is still awful. If this had happened when I was more established, it wouldn't be stressing me out as much."

She snorted. "Oh, please. You'd be stressed no matter when it happened."

He opened his mouth to protest but thought better of it. "Be that as it may, I need to find a better balance between my health and my work. Preferably one that doesn't cause me to go bankrupt or my business to go under."

After pushing him into his office, she stooped and gave him a hug. "I have faith you'll figure it out, and we're here for whatever you need."

Once he was alone, Steven opened the spreadsheet they used to track new clients. Sure enough, Sandra had booked several new ones. She'd set up meetings with them for the following week on both of their calendars.

Shaking his head, he couldn't help but smile. If his law firm survived, Sandra deserved a raise.

Chapter Twenty-Two

Rose found herself dragging her feet to her appointment with Carissa to discuss the rehearsal dinner. Time kept flying by, and she couldn't catch her breath.

As she walked through the lobby toward Carissa's office, the sound of raised voices caught her attention. After tiptoeing to the corner, she peered into the room. Max and Carissa sat opposite each other, clearly in the middle of a heated argument.

"You're being unreasonable," Carissa said, flipping her salt-and-pepper hair over her shoulder. "Rose's parents have already paid for the rehearsal dinner. We're just deciding on a location."

Rose sucked in a breath. *My parents sent Carissa money?* They shouldn't have done that. Between her grandparents moving into long-term care and her parents' struggle with employment, the last thing they needed to be worried about was her wedding. *Looks like I have a phone call to make after this is over.*

"It's not unreasonable to want to follow tradition." Max crossed his arms.

Carissa rolled her eyes. "As I told you before, they contacted me privately to pay for the rehearsal dinner because they can't attend or pay for the wedding. It's their wedding gift to their daughter and is important to them.

If you want to contribute, I have a binder full of other outstanding items right h—"

"And as *I* told *you*, what is the difference if the money they sent is used toward one of those outstanding items?" He gave a stiff shrug that Rose suspected was meant to be nonchalant. But as she had never known him to be an easygoing kind of guy, it failed in execution.

"If it doesn't matter where their money goes, why does it matter where *your* money goes?"

"Because I'm here. I'm attending the wedding, and I insist on paying for the rehearsal dinner. I want to have a say in where it's held."

Rose had heard enough. The wedding was becoming way more trouble than it was worth. She walked into the room, making sure her heels clicked loudly on the floor to mark each step. Both Max and Carissa turned toward her.

"Rose!" Carissa rushed over, the angry flush on her face dissipating. "I'm glad you're here."

"I hope I'm not interrupting anything," Rose said, keeping her tone neutral. She raised her eyebrows at her future father-in-law, and he shrugged, clearly not at all perturbed at being caught midargument.

"Not at all." Carissa grabbed her arm and pulled her over to the table, where a number of menus were set up. "I've chosen several options for the rehearsal dinner. We need to book one of them soon."

Before Rose could respond, Max angled himself between her and Carissa. "I brought a few menus as well."

Carissa's hands curled into fists. If he saw the death glare she gave him, he didn't let on.

"A little less upscale, perhaps, but much more in line with what the people of Cedar Haven are used to."

"Quaint," Carissa said, her voice deceptively sweet. "But since the guests aren't limited to locals, we should plan for a variety of tastes."

"You mean the dinner my parents have apparently paid for, which you conveniently never mentioned?" Rose asked, narrowing her eyes at Carissa. To the wedding planner's credit, she had the decency to look guilty.

"They wanted it to be a surprise." Carissa's eyebrows pulled together. "They planned to tell you after the wedding. Your mother feels terrible that they're going to miss it."

So do I. With a sigh, Rose sank into the chair that Max pulled out for her and began sifting through the mountain of menus. But her heart wasn't in it anymore. She wished Steven was there, both to act as referee and to help her sort through her complicated emotions.

Like he's helped me talk through my feelings the last few weeks. Heat built in her belly before shooting through her. There she was, tying up loose ends for a wedding she was beginning to wonder if she even wanted anymore. The cracks she'd ignored in their relationship had grown too big to overlook.

Before she could change her mind, she pushed back from the table and stood. "Carissa, I need to talk to you." When Max made a move to go with them, she held up a hand. "Alone."

"If this is about the rehearsal dinner, I should—"

"It's not," Rose said. At his hurt expression, she softened her tone. "I won't make any decisions about that without you, I promise."

Max's eyebrows lowered in suspicion, but something in her face must have told him not to argue. After giving a quick nod, he settled back in his chair and pointedly picked up a menu from a local establishment.

Rose headed outside with Carissa on her heels. The air was stifling, and the blinding heat made her second-guess whether that was the time or place for the conversation, but she needed advice, and she wasn't sure where else to turn.

"So." Carissa leaned against the building. "What's up?"

"What would happen if we canceled the wedding?" Rose asked in a rush, afraid if she didn't ask right then, she would never again find the nerve.

Carissa's eyes widened. "You can't be serious." When Rose didn't immediately respond, she touched her arm. "Rose? What's going on? Is it cold feet or...?"

"I wish it was cold feet." It had taken all of her energy to force the question out. Her back slid down the brick wall of the building until she landed on the sidewalk. Wrapping her arms around her knees, she shook her head. "I don't know if I can go through with it."

After a moment of hesitation, Carissa knelt in front of her. "Talk to me. What's going on?"

Rose wasn't sure where to begin. "It feels like everything that could go wrong has gone wrong."

"The accident was bad," Carissa said. "But Steven's recovering, and I suspect he'll be back on his feet in no time."

"But that's just it." Rose raised her head. "He's so focused on getting back to normal, he isn't taking care of himself like he needs to."

"How do you mean?"

"He had a *heart attack*." For once, the words didn't get stuck in her throat. "He could have died. But he's more focused on his spine and the ability to walk, which I get. It's easier to see the broken parts of ourselves when they're on the outside. It's harder to comprehend when something is wrong inside."

Carissa was quiet. "That sounds like you're talking about more than just his heart."

"I suppose I am." Wiping the tears from her eyes, Rose bit her lip. "I'm sorry. I don't mean to burden you with this. But I don't have anyone else to talk to."

"Hey, don't apologize. You're not the first bride who has had second thoughts." Carissa pursed her lips. "Though you are the first to stump me."

Rose groaned. "That's not what I needed to hear."

"I know." Carissa stood up and brushed off her pantsuit. "Have you tried discussing this with him?"

"Several times. He either blows me off or gives me empty platitudes about how he's 'trying.'" Her throat constricted. "It makes me feel like he sees me as a pest instead of someone who genuinely cares about his well-being."

A throbbing in her head became more pronounced the more she stewed over how Steven had treated her concerns. He'd vacillated between blowing them off and snapping at her for pushing him.

Carissa held out her hand. "Come on. It's doing you no good to sit and stew in that anger. Let's go for a walk."

"But what about Max?"

"He'll probably still be poring over his menus when we get back."

They walked through the parking lot and crossed the street. Then Carissa led the way to a small park with a few trails.

"We won't go far," Carissa said. "But it's cooler beneath the trees, and sometimes, being in nature helps me process my thoughts."

As they walked deeper into the woods, the tightness in Rose's chest loosened. But she had no idea what she was going to do. No matter how much she might try to deny it, canceling the wedding would send a message. And it might also spell the end of her relationship.

"Have you ever been married?" Rose asked suddenly.

The question appeared to catch Carissa off guard, as she stumbled. Regaining her balance, she turned to Rose with a wary expression.

"I was up until five years ago."

"What happened?"

To Rose's horror, tears welled up in Carissa's eyes. "He died."

"Oh my, I'm sorry." Rose shook her head. "I shouldn't have asked."

"No, it's okay." Carissa sniffled and dashed a hand across her face. "I understand why you did." After taking a deep breath, she continued, "Chuck and I had a wonderful marriage, but it wasn't easy. Those last few years, he was sick, and I truly learned the meaning of those vows about 'in sickness and health.'"

"Did you regret it?" Rose couldn't help asking.

But Carissa's face broke into a sad smile. "Not for a moment. I treasure every second we got to spend together." She frowned. "It's not the same as your situation, though. Before Chuck got sick, we had a life together. To face such a challenge so soon in your relationship is a hard pill to swallow. I'm not sure how I would have felt if Chuck had gotten sick before our wedding."

Rose took a shuddering breath. "I know that anyone's health can fail at any time, and I'm not thinking of abandoning Steven because of what happened to him."

Carissa stepped forward and put a hand on Rose's shoulder. "That never crossed my mind."

"But I'm not sure I could bear it if he passed soon after our wedding."

They walked awhile in silence. Rose grappled with the choice in front of her. The idea of canceling the wedding and risking her relationship broke her heart, but the bleak vision of a future with a husband who wouldn't listen to her broke her soul.

When they reached the end of the trail, Rose was surprised to realize they'd completed a circle and were back in the park. Unfortunately, she was no closer to making a decision.

"Rose," Carissa said, breaking the silence. "Can you imagine a life for yourself without Steven?"

Closing her eyes, Rose tried to picture what that might look like. All she could see was the past and the different decisions she might have made. If she had never met Steven, she would have taken the job in Boston. She'd be working at a busy hospital in the heart of a thriving city. But whether she'd be happier in that other life, she couldn't say.

"I'm not sure."

"Give yourself some time to think on it."

They headed to Carissa's office. Once they were across the street, Carissa stopped Rose.

"As far as canceling the wedding, it's likely too late for most of your vendors to rebook the date. That means you'll lose all of the money you've paid thus far, and you'd have to start over from scratch if you decide to reschedule in the future." Carissa crossed her arms. "So I highly suggest you be sure of whatever decision you make before you take action."

Rose nodded. Nothing Carissa said had come as a surprise. "Thank you for listening."

"Do you still love him?"

The question was blunt and caught Rose by surprise. She nodded, not trusting herself to speak.

Carissa's face softened. "That's worth more than you may realize." She pressed her lips together. "But unless you plan to tell your soon-to-be father-in-law that you're no longer marrying his son, I suggest we go back inside and fake it." A rueful smile pulled at her lips. "Though I wouldn't mind taking him down a few pegs."

Laughter bubbled up Rose's throat. "He's not so bad, once you get to know him."

"I've always taken that saying to be a nicer way of telling people 'he's a jerk, but you'll get used to it.'"

"That's probably more accurate." Rose chuckled.

"What's so funny?" Max asked when they reentered the office, his bushy eyebrows pulled down over his dark eyes.

"Nothing," they said at the same time. Rose bit her lip to keep from laughing again. "Why don't you show me the places you had in mind for the rehearsal dinner?" She hoped to keep him from asking additional questions.

His face brightened, though his jaw was tight, probably with suspicion. But he nodded and handed her a stack of menus, all local places. Carissa's tastes couldn't be further from Max's, and they would be hard-pressed to find common ground, but Rose found herself drawn to the local options. It would be easier for Steven, especially if they went through with the wedding they'd already planned. At the same time, those sites were such a vast contrast to the location of the wedding reception, it would almost seem like they were planning two completely different events.

Perhaps that wasn't a bad thing. It would incorporate different aspects of their lives—and their relationship.

As if he could sense her wavering, Max stepped closer. "All of these places have wheelchair access. I checked."

Whether he meant it as a comfort or simply as a fact, she didn't know, but the words weighed heavy on her chest. Those were things she hadn't had to consider mere months ago. How privileged she had been to never have to think about the sort of access a person with a disability might need.

An image of the male swan with its leg wrapped in a splint popped into her mind. If only she could tap into the faith of his mate, she might be able to find the strength to save her relationship.

Chapter Twenty-Three

STEVEN STAYED LATER THAN he intended at work. Lanie had been right about the influx of new clients. Whether it was because the community needed a local firm or because they knew he was in dire straits, he appreciated that they were bringing him business. And Sandra's detailed notes from the initial client interviews she'd done made him think the new wills and estates wouldn't be terribly taxing. Most of them were simple and could be handled without a lot of extra research or effort.

A knock sounded at his door, and he glanced up and did a double take. "Michael? What are you still doing here?"

"I need to talk to you." Michael stared at the floor, fidgeting with his hands.

"Sure." Steven's stomach dropped. Something about Michael's demeanor told Steven it wasn't going to be good news. "Have a seat." After waiting for what seemed like ages, Steven cleared his throat. "So, um, what can I help you with?"

Finally, Michael lifted his head. His brown eyes were wary. "I got a call today from a law firm in DC."

"Oh?" Steven's palms began to sweat. "What did they want?"

"To offer me a job."

It felt like Steven's throat was closing. He attempted to clear it, but it did no good. *Is this it, then? Am I back to square one with my law practice?* Michael had just begun to get into the swing of things. Steven couldn't imagine starting over with someone new, not to mention how much time and energy interviews would take.

"And what did you say?"

"I-I told them I would give them an answer by the end of the week." Michael ran a hand through his hair. "But I don't want to leave here if I can help it."

"Is there anything I can do to convince you to stay?"

"In my interview, Lanie mentioned I might be able to be brought on full-time. And I've heard you might be looking for a partner..."

Steven shook his head. "I'm not ready for that yet."

Michael nodded. "I figured. It's just, well, the DC law firm has a clear partner track, which is rare. And they have openings in areas of law I'm interested in, like environmental and small business."

"It sounds like you've decided," Steven said as his heart pounded. The news was quite literally the last thing he needed right then. Shadows swam before his eyes, and he put his head on his desk. He was vaguely aware of Michael calling his name, then everything went dark.

The next thing Steven knew, a hand was violently shaking him. As he opened his eyes, it took him a moment to realize what had happened and why he was on the floor.

"Steven! Can you hear me?" His sister's hazel eyes, filled with worry, swam into his vision.

"Yes," he croaked. He tried to sit up, but she pushed him back down.

"Don't move. You might have had another heart attack. I've called 911, and they're on their way."

Another *heart attack?* No, it couldn't be. He swallowed and pressed his hand to his chest. It didn't hurt, but that might not mean anything.

"Why are you here?" he asked.

"I was on my way to pick you up when Michael called me." She closed her eyes as if trying to shake the memory of what she'd seen from her mind. "We both called to you, but you were shaking, and then you fell on the floor." Her eyes opened, and she grabbed his hand. "I've never been so scared."

Before he could respond, someone banged on the front door. Lanie squeezed his hand again before hurrying away to let the paramedics in.

He lay there staring at the ceiling and listened as his sister quietly explained the situation. A moment later, a grim face appeared above him.

"Mr. McAllister, can you hear me?"

Steven nodded and made to sit up, but a firm hand grasped his shoulder and held him down. "Don't move, sir, until we assess you."

A small light shone in one of his eyes, and he grimaced but made an effort not to flinch. It felt different that time. While he didn't remember falling to the floor, he was pretty sure he hadn't been unconscious for nearly as long as before.

The man who'd been examining him asked a series of rapid-fire questions. It took a lot of effort to keep up, but Steven did. When the man was finished, he stepped back and held out his hand, which Steven accepted.

"It looks like he might have fainted or had a seizure, but it doesn't appear to be another heart attack." The man turned to Lanie. "Still, we should get him to the hospital so they can run some tests to rule out anything more serious."

Steven squeezed his eyes shut and tried not to dwell on how much the incident would set him back. All those new clients Sandra had found weren't going to make a lick of difference if he couldn't perform the work for which they'd hired him.

"Sir? Are you still with me?"

Apparently, shutting one's eyes and grimacing wasn't the best choice of facial expressions after a possible seizure. Steven opened his eyes and faked a smile to put everyone in the room at ease. But inside, he was a mess.

***

After Steven arrived at the hospital, Dr. Myers had him admitted and started a series of tests, by the end of which Steven felt like a human pincushion. He winced as the orderlies rolled him into his room and bumped into the doorframe. When they left, he took a deep breath and tried to relax, but he struggled to turn his brain off.

A knock at the door startled him, and he braced for yet another test. Rose stood in the doorway—or "clung to it" would be more accurate. Her brown eyes were wide and wary, and she stared at him as if waiting for permission to enter.

"Rose." For once, his voice didn't sound like a croaking frog's.

"Lanie called me," she replied, and the coolness in her tone caught him off guard.

"I'm sorry we're meeting like this again," Steven said in a poor attempt at a joke. "They think I had a seizure and—"

She held up a hand. "I know. I spoke with Dr. Myers."

"But I'm okay," he hurried on. "I mean, at least it wasn't another heart attack."

That was the wrong thing to say. Her mouth twisted before it set in a grim line. She stepped into the room but only so far that she could lean back against the wall next to the door. She crossed her arms.

"Rose? What's wrong?"

Her eyes flashed, and he shrank against his pillow. *Maybe that wasn't the best choice of words, but why is she mad at me?* It wasn't like he *wanted* to be back at the hospital.

"'What's wrong?'" Her voice was incredulous. "Are you kidding?"

"I mean, this looks bad, but—"

"No, Steven, it doesn't just *look* bad. It *is* bad." The rage simmered off her like steam from a pot that threatened to boil over. "I told you. I *warned* you." Her eyes narrowed with barely repressed rage. "I said if you didn't take care of yourself, you would end up back in the hospital." She gestured wildly. "And I was right."

"But it's not as bad as last time," he protested, though it sounded stupid and pathetic even before the words left his mouth.

"So? Does it matter what brought you here?"

"Dr. Myers said it's common to have seizures after a heart attack."

"And did he also tell you excess stress can induce seizures?"

"Not in so many words." Dr. Myers had told him he needed to take it easy, multiple times, but doctors always said things like that. Besides, being a doctor was one of the most stressful jobs there was. *If they can't take their own advice, how can they expect their patients to?*

Of course, Steven said none of those things out loud. One look at the murderous expression on Rose's face convinced him to tread lightly.

"I'm sorry," he said instead, though he imagined that to her, that phrase sounded repetitive and empty. "You were right. I should have taken more time for my health."

She sighed. "At least that's something, though it doesn't change anything."

The muscles along his spine spasmed as he sat up straighter. Something about her tone and the way she had dropped her gaze to the floor told him that whatever she meant by that statement couldn't be good.

"What's that supposed to mean?"

Before she could respond, Dr. Myers came in.

"I suppose it's good that you're here, since it means I only have to say this once."

Chapter Twenty-Four

Rose braced herself against the doorway. Whatever Dr. Myers had to say wouldn't surprise her, but it would add to the pain she was about to deliver, both to Steven and herself. Part of her wished the doctor had been delayed. Then she could have done what she came to do and escaped without hearing about Steven's condition. But the other part, the part that had questioned over and over whether she was making the right decision, needed to know Steven was going to be okay.

Dr. Myers moved beside Steven. "You were lucky. It wasn't a heart attack or a seizure but convulsive syncope. Which basically means you fainted due to loss of blood or oxygen to your brain. It can often look like a seizure."

Steven sagged against his pillow, and his lips turned up in a tentative smile. "That's a relief." When Dr. Myers crossed his arms, Steven's mouth tightened. "Isn't it?"

"This was yet another warning sign that your heart is under too much stress. Syncope episodes are common following a cardiac arrest, but it's a bad sign. It means you aren't healing as well as you should be." Dr. Myers took a deep breath. "Stress can be one of the worst things for someone with heart disease. Your body is already in a vulnerable place, and it's trying to heal. But if you don't provide it that time and space to heal itself, you won't survive the next heart attack."

The way he said it, with authority and conviction, seemed to finally break through to Steven. It was no longer a question of whether he would have another heart attack but when and how severe. A hole opened in Rose's chest, and she pressed a hand to it as if it was a gunshot wound and she was trying to stanch the bleeding. But the bleeding was internal and emotional, and there was no way to stop that outpouring of pain.

"I understand." Steven's voice was strained. It sounded so broken and childlike. Rose almost went to his side to comfort him, but she stopped herself.

"I hope you do." The note of doubt in Dr. Myers's voice was unmistakable. Rose peered over his shoulder at Steven, and her breath bottled up in her chest. Maybe he was finally comprehending the seriousness of his situation. She squashed that feeling of hope before it could spread. Even if he did see reason, it was too little, too late.

"We'll be keeping you here for observation for a few days, then we'll discharge you." Dr. Myers glanced at Rose before continuing. "I'm willing to send you home instead of back to the inpatient rehab facility but only if you follow my instructions to the letter."

"I will," Steven mumbled. He shot a mournful look at Rose. "I promise."

Her resolve faltered, especially when Dr. Myers patted her hand on his way out. But once they were alone again, she straightened her shoulders and marched to Steven's bed.

"I'm sorry," he said again, taking her hand. "I should have listened to you. But I promise I've learned my lesson, and I will take better care of myself. What happened was Michael told me he'd been offered a position in DC. He asked me about a full-time position or a partnership, but I told him I wasn't ready for that. When I realized how much finding a new law clerk would set me back, I panicked." He sighed. "But clearly I need more help. I'm going to talk to Michael and see if I can convince him to stay, but I'll also start putting out feelers for a new law clerk so I can get them in before he leaves. It's going to work out. I promise."

Tears pricked her eyes, and she blinked them back. How long had she wished he would take that action? How long had she prayed he would take his health seriously? And he finally had. *Too little, too late* repeated over and over again in her head, like a scratched CD.

"I'm glad you plan to take better care of yourself." She was proud that her voice shook only a little.

"I don't want to be a burden to you." He lifted her hand to kiss it, but the contact would be too much.

She pulled away and stepped back. The hurt in his eyes pierced her heart, but she couldn't back down. The heart attack had been a warning sign, not only for his health but also for where their future was headed. She needed to rip off the Band-Aid and allow her pain to bleed out so she could start over.

Sucking in air for strength, she lifted her left hand and slid the engagement ring off her finger. Steven's eyes widened and flickered back and forth between the ring she held out and her face. It took effort, but she managed to arrange her features into a neutral expression despite the category-five emotional hurricane building inside her.

"Rose." His voice was hoarse and strangled. "Don't do this."

"I'm sorry, but I can't do this anymore." She was amazed at how calm she sounded.

Tears filled his eyes. "Why?"

"I begged you, repeatedly, to take it easy, slow down, take better care of your health." A lump formed in her throat, and she could barely speak. "But you wouldn't listen to me. You blew off my concerns as if they were nothing."

"I'm listening now."

That was probably the worst thing he could have said. Her hands shook as she tried and failed to gain control of her anger. "*Now?* Now that you're back in the hospital?" She gestured to the machines he was hooked up to. "And I suppose you're also finally listening to what your body has been trying to tell you, too, right?" The pounding in her ears increased in rhythm. "But you wouldn't listen to *me*. I may not be a doctor, but I'm not an idiot either. I knew what your workload was doing to you and how stressed you were after your accident. I tried to reason with you. I tried to convince you that you were making a mistake, but you wouldn't *listen*."

Her carefully put-together demeanor cracked. "So, now *I'm* done listening to your excuses."

"We can postpone the wedding, if that's what you want! We can reschedule it for next summer or for however long you wish." He reached for her, but she moved farther away. "But don't do this. Don't throw away everything we have because I made a mistake."

"A mistake?" She stared at him. *Is that all he thinks this is?* "A mistake is when you mess up the numbers in a budget or forget an important date. Ignoring your health and brushing off the advice of medical professionals isn't a mistake. It's a choice." He opened his mouth as if to respond, but she didn't give him the chance. "I didn't come here to convince you that it's over but to *tell* you it's over." Tears stung her eyes, but she blinked them back. "I love you too much to sit by and watch you kill yourself."

"Rose, please—"

The pain in his voice might have made her falter at one time, but the more he fought her, the more resolved she became. No matter how much she loved him, she had chosen the right path—for both of them.

"No." For once, she didn't try to temper the finality of the word with excuses or platitudes. It might have been only one word, but it was a complete sentence.

"Please, Rose." His eyes searched her face. "I love you, and I promise, I'll do everything the doctors tell me to do."

"I hope you do." And she meant it. "I hope you listen to Dr. Myers, to all of your doctors, and follow their advice." Her voice cracked because the alternative was something she couldn't bear to consider. If breaking both their hearts was the only way to get him to understand the gravity of the situation, so be it. At least she could walk away knowing she'd done everything she could to save him. But it was time to save herself.

Her emotions bubbled up inside, and it was only a matter of time before they spilled over. She had to leave before he saw her break down. He would only take it as a sign that he needed to push harder.

With a small smile, she grasped his hand one last time and gave it a squeeze before turning and bolting from the room. She ran past Lanie and Max on her way out, but she didn't stop to speak to them. They would find out everything soon enough.

———ℯℓℓ———

"Are you sure this is what you want?" Rose's mother asked.

Rose nodded then remembered she wasn't on video chat. "Yes, Mother, I'm sure."

She hadn't wanted to FaceTime her parents, afraid they would see right through her facade, even on the other side of the world. After she'd gotten home, she'd spent a good hour sobbing into her pillow. When her tears ran out, she forced herself out of bed and washed her face.

Her mother sighed on the other end of the line, and Rose braced herself. "Aren't you being a bit rash?"

She bristled. "I've been asking him for months, even before the accident, to slow down and take it easy. I thought the heart attack would be a wakeup call, but it wasn't." *Calm down.* Getting in an argument with her mother wasn't going to help things. "And now, he's passing out from stress, and I don't know what else to do. I've tried to reason with him. I've tried nagging, begging." She swallowed around the lump in her throat. "He dismissed my concerns or made empty promises. I started to wonder, what kind of future can I have with someone who so easily disregards my feelings? What if that bleeds into other areas of our relationship? What will happen when we have children?" She took a deep breath. "I love him. I do. But sometimes love just isn't enough."

The line was silent, and she held her breath as she waited for Mom to respond, though she supposed it didn't matter whether her mother agreed with her or not. She'd made her choice.

"It's better this way," she continued when her mother didn't respond. "Can you imagine how much worse it would be if we had gone through with the wedding? Now, we can both move on, and maybe I'll go back to Baltimore."

Her mother tsked, and Rose rolled her eyes. That was the other positive point for Steven. Her parents had never liked the idea of her working in a hospital in Baltimore. They hated the city and worried about the things she would witness while working there. She hadn't had the heart to tell them it didn't really matter where she worked, gruesome sights were pretty much universal. In Cedar Haven, she might not have seen gunshot wounds, but she'd seen some tractor accidents that were far bloodier.

"Maybe you can come home to Korea," her mother said.

Rose cringed. The possibility that her mother would mention a return to the home country had crossed her mind, but she'd hoped it wouldn't be during that conversation.

"I'll think about it." Though they both knew that was a lie. "Anyway, it's getting late, and I'm working the early shift tomorrow."

They said their goodbyes, and Rose collapsed onto her couch. The one saving grace in the whole awful situation was that she hadn't moved in with Steven yet. She didn't want to imagine how awkward it would have been to try to find a new place to live when he was released.

She had just flipped on the TV when there was a knock at the door. She debated pretending not to be home. There were only so many people who would have stopped by her house at that time of night.

"Rose? It's Lanie." A pause. "I know you're in there."

With a sigh, she stood and opened the door. Lanie leaned against the wall outside the condo, her eyebrows pulling together. She held up a brown bag.

"Thought you could use some wine."

Rose rocked back on her heels, not sure how to react. Without waiting for a response, Lanie pushed past her and set the bag on the counter before removing two wineglasses from the cabinet.

"You planning to stand there all night, or are you going to join me?" Lanie asked.

Bewildered, Rose shut the door and went into the kitchen. Lanie poured two large glasses of wine and handed one to Rose.

"What are you doing here?"

"Bringing you wine." Lanie shrugged. "And I figured you might want some company."

"So you're not here to convince me to reconsider?"

"Would you listen to me if I was?"

Rose shook her head.

"Then I'm not." Lanie carried her wine into the living room before sinking onto the sofa.

Unsure of what else to do, Rose followed and sat on the other side, keeping some distance between them. As close as Rose had gotten to Lanie recently, she was Steven's sister, and Rose suspected that was where her loyalties lay.

She waited to see if Lanie would start the conversation, but her future sister-in-law... Scratch that, her *former* future... No, that didn't quite work either. While she debated how to define their new connection, Lanie leaned back and gazed out the window. Her face was serene, and she seemed perfectly content to sip her wine and sit in silence.

But Rose was like a firecracker left too close to a bonfire. One small spark, and she would explode. She shifted in her seat, hoping the movement would break Lanie's reverie and force her to speak. When that didn't work, she heaved a sigh to break the silence.

"Something wrong?" Lanie asked before taking yet another unbothered sip of wine.

Rose couldn't put her finger on why, but the nonchalant attitude grated on her nerves more than if Lanie had stormed in demanding answers. The former Rose could have understood, because breaking up with Steven had been like pulling the pin in a grenade. Just because she left before it detonated didn't mean she expected to escape unscathed.

"Why are you really here?" Despite her best attempts at trying to keep her temper in check, the question came out much more harshly than she'd intended.

Lanie blinked. "I told you already. I wanted to be here in case you needed to talk."

"Even if I did need someone to talk to, you wouldn't be my first choice."

To her surprise, Lanie's expression became pained. "Ouch."

"I'm sorry." Rose pursed her lips. "Actually, no, I'm not. Look, I don't mean to be rude, but you're Steven's sister. You may have your differences, but he's your family, and I don't expect you'll understand my reasons for doing what I did."

Lanie leaned forward and set her glass on the table. "Really? You don't think I feel like my brother has brought this on himself?" She lifted her hand and began ticking things off on her fingers. "He left the rehab facility early against medical advice, went back to work sooner than was recommended, worked himself to the bone despite everyone in his life telling him to take it easy, then has the audacity to fight with you about your very reasonable request to postpone the wedding."

Rose opened her mouth to speak but couldn't find the words. Apparently taking satisfaction in Rose's obvious shock, Lanie sat back on the couch with a triumphant smile.

"He may be my brother, but he's being a real knucklehead. I'm hoping the breakup will be the wake-up call he needs."

"But it won't change my mind," Rose insisted.

"Good." Lanie raised her glass and clinked Rose's. "It serves him right."

Is she serious? Her brother was laid up in the hospital as they spoke, but Lanie didn't seem the least bit fazed by that fact. Or by the reality of what Rose had done.

"Though I appreciate your support, I wonder if it's a bit misplaced."

"How so?"

Rose squirmed in her seat. "I mean, he *is* your brother, and he *is* in the hospital."

"As a result of his own actions."

"But don't you feel even the slightest bit sorry for him?"

Lanie raised an eyebrow. "Do you?"

Is this some weird version of reverse psychology? Does Lanie think by acting as if she doesn't care about her brother, she'll get to the heart of how much I do care?

"I'm not completely heartless—"

"It's not heartless to call someone out on their actions." Lanie shook her head. "Am I worried about Steven? Of course. But does that mean I don't think he's reaping what he's sown? Absolutely not."

Rose's mouth fell open in shock while Lanie went on sipping her wine as if she hadn't confirmed everything Rose had been feeling for weeks. And Rose had to admit that for once, she didn't feel quite so alone.

"Look, I love my brother. But he can't get out of this one with empty promises. If he wants to live to see his business thrive, he's going to have to make some changes. If he wants a chance to grovel at your feet and beg you to reconsider, which I have no doubt he plans to do, he'll have to prove he's going to do what needs to be done to get better." Lanie gave her signature one-shoulder shrug. "He gambled with his health and the love of his life, and he lost."

"Don't you hate me, though?" Rose pressed. "For kicking him while he's down?"

Lanie snorted. "Are you kidding? I'm surprised you didn't do it sooner."

Frowning, Rose stared at her hands. As much as she appreciated Lanie's support, something didn't sit right with her. While yes, Steven should have paid more attention to his health, she didn't love the idea of him sitting alone in a hospital room.

"That means a lot to me," she said. "But I do worry about him."

Lanie's face softened. "I know you do, and I do too." She laid her hand on Rose's. "And I worry about you."

"Me?" Rose stared at her. "I'm perfectly fine."

"Are you?" Lanie tilted her head. "You broke up with the man you planned to marry." She sniffed. "I wasn't engaged to James, and I still struggled after we broke up."

Tears pricked behind Rose's eyes, but she refused to let them fall. She didn't want to cry, not with Lanie there. She wanted to wait until she was alone, when she could have a full-on wallow fest. Thank goodness she'd had the forethought to stock up on ice cream. The best comfort for a broken heart was a pint of Ben and Jerry's.

But Lanie's probing eyes wreaked havoc on her resolve. Rose cleared her throat. "Okay, maybe I'm not *fine* at the moment." Squaring her shoulders, she lifted her glass and downed the rest of her wine. "But I will be." Her gaze fell on the wedding binder teetering on the edge of the coffee table. "Though while you're here, maybe you can help me. I don't want to bother Carissa, and I should get a start on calling the wedding vendors."

When she moved to pick up the binder, Lanie put a hand on her arm. Rose shot her a questioning look, but Lanie shook her head.

"Not tonight." Lanie stood and retrieved the bottle of wine before pouring them each another large glass. "Tonight, we wallow and let the dust settle."

"But—"

"Trust me, Rose. You'll thank me tomorrow."

Chapter Twenty-Five

STEVEN OPENED HIS EYES the next morning, hoping it had all been a dream, but the incessant beeping of the heart monitor betrayed the truth. Not only was he back in the hospital, but he was also single. The ring he had searched for over several months, determined to find the perfect one, mocked him from his bedside table.

If he were honest, he could admit he should have seen that coming. And as if losing Rose wasn't bad enough, his stupidity might have cost him his firm as well.

"Ah, good, you're awake." Dr. Myers popped his head into the room.

I wish I wasn't. The thought came out of nowhere and caught him off guard. Thank goodness he had a filter. Otherwise, he would likely be put on some seventy-two-hour hold. And that was quite literally the last thing he needed.

"I wanted to talk to you about discharge."

That got his attention. "Already? Aren't you keeping me here for observation?"

"Oh, we are," Dr. Myers said. "But I also told you I would discharge you home."

"And you're not planning on doing that anymore?" Steven read between the lines of what the doctor wasn't saying.

Dr. Myers sighed. "If you really want to go home, we can certainly make that happen, assuming everything looks good." For a moment, the good doctor appeared at war with himself, which only amped up Steven's irritation.

"Just spit it out, Doc."

"You won't want to hear this, but you were making significant progress in the inpatient rehab facility." His eyes narrowed as he leveled a stern gaze at Steven. "You should consider going back."

The no was on the tip of Steven's tongue when Rose's face flashed before his eyes. A weight as heavy as an elephant settled on his chest. He would do anything to see her again, anything to convince her to give him another chance.

"You have a better chance of healing and getting back to your life if you spend a few more weeks working through an intensive therapy program," Dr. Myers continued when Steven didn't respond. "I've spoken with the medical team there, and—"

"Okay," Steven whispered as he squeezed his eyes shut.

"They said they can get you Wi-Fi—Wait, did you say yes?"

Opening his eyes, Steven nodded. "I'll do it."

"Well... great!" Dr. Myers's face broke into a broad smile. "That went better than I'd expected." He turned as if to go then glanced over his shoulder. "And just so you know, the facility is making special accommodations to allow you to work from there. You'll still need to focus most of your energy on getting better, but I don't want you to stress about your business. Just... try to find a balance, all right?"

"I will," Steven promised, and the conviction in his words took him by surprise.

◦ₑₗₑ◦

True to his word, Dr. Myers kept Steven for observation for a few more days, and they were the most boring days of Steven's life. Only his father and a few friends came to visit. He hadn't expected Rose, though he couldn't quite quash the small piece of hope in his heart. After all, she worked at the hospital, so it wouldn't have been difficult for her to swing by.

But the visitor he missed even worse than Rose was Lanie. It wasn't like his sister to avoid him, especially since she'd arrived right after he'd collapsed. He'd thought she would come by every day, but he hadn't seen her since the breakup. To say he was hurt was an understatement. *Doesn't she understand that blood is thicker than water?* Sure, she and Rose were friends, but he was in the hospital. *Shouldn't my needs take precedence?*

Deep down, he could admit, at least to himself, that he understood why she hadn't come. She must have been so angry with him for screwing up the best relationship he could have ever hoped to have. Maybe she was helping Rose cancel the wedding. His throat burned, but he swallowed the pain. Perhaps Lanie believed he deserved it.

"Are you ready to bust out of this place?" His dad entered the room with an uncharacteristic smile on his normally grumpy face.

"More than ready," Steven said. The nurses had allowed him to briefly wander the grounds, but it had been a while since his last outdoor adventure.

"The doc says they'll spring you in an hour or so."

He'd been throwing himself a pity party for long enough. The transition to the rehab facility sounded like just the distraction he needed.

"Have you heard from Lanie?" Steven asked, trying to sound casual.

His father gave him a strange look. "I mean, we keep different hours, but she does still live with me."

So much for trying to sound nonchalant. "I, uh, figured she spent most of her time at Nate's."

"She's been spending several hours at your law firm this week." His father raised an eyebrow. "Hasn't she checked in with you?"

Steven shook his head. Sandra had called and texted a few times, which he appreciated. It helped break the monotony of the hospital stay. But his messages to Lanie had gone unanswered.

"Well, she's meeting us at the rehab center this afternoon, so you'll see her then."

The fact that his father sounded unbothered by Lanie's absence alleviated some of Steven's concern, but the churning in his stomach wasn't likely to subside until he saw his sister.

"I saw Rose yesterday," Dad continued, and there was an edge to his voice.

"Oh?" Steven took deep breaths to calm his racing heart.

"Ran into her on my way here. Seems she's keeping busy with extra shifts at the hospital."

A million questions bubbled on his lips, but he didn't know how to ask them without sounding as desperate as he was. Instead, he nodded and stared straight ahead, trying to look like he didn't care.

Dad ran a hand through his salt-and-pepper hair. "She looked good."

Steven opened his mouth, but nothing came out. What was he supposed to say? That he was happy she was doing well while he wasted away in a hospital bed? That he wished she'd come see him?

"Anyway..." His father shifted his weight to his other foot and dropped his gaze.

Steven took some comfort in the knowledge that their conversation was as awkward for his dad as it was for him.

"Just thought you'd want to know."

"Why?" Steven blurted out without thinking, and he immediately regretted it.

"Look, things aren't good between you two, but I think it's temporary—"

The thin hold he had on his emotions broke. "Temporary? Oh, okay. So she just temporarily broke my heart. That makes everything better. Thanks, Dad."

"Don't be like that."

"Like what?" And all the pain he had pent up inside since Rose left him erupted like a raging river breaching a dam. "What good does it do me to hear Rose is moving on? That she's doing great while I'm lying here, day after day, with little to distract me."

"You're about to be discharged," Dad protested, though the fact that he wouldn't meet Steven's gaze betrayed how weak those words sounded.

"To an inpatient rehab for who knows how long." When Dad opened his mouth again, Steven held up a hand. "And before you tell me it's good for me, I know. I get that it's what I need, but it doesn't mean I'm happy about it." He stared at his hands, clenching them into fists as he fought to push his anger and pain back down his gut, where it belonged. "I was this close to having everything I ever wanted, and now I may lose it all. So forgive me if I'm having some trouble processing it."

Before Dad could respond, a familiar blond head appeared around the doorframe. "Everything okay in here?"

The joy Steven felt at seeing his sister was tempered by the memory that she hadn't been by sooner. He forced a smile, determined not to let her know how much her absence had hurt. The last thing he needed to do was alienate his entire family in one day.

"Lanie!" Dad said with faux excitement. Steven suspected his father was more grateful for the interruption than he was happy that Lanie had arrived. "I didn't expect to see you here."

"I finished helping Sandra with a major project at the law office. I was able to slip away earlier than expected." She slipped past Dad and wrapped an arm around Steven. "How're you holding up?"

Spiteful words sprang to mind, but he held his tongue. It began to ache with the effort. "Looking forward to getting out of here."

"I'll bet." Her arm tightened around him, and she lowered her voice. "Listen, I'm sorry for not stopping by sooner, but I needed to take care of a few things."

Why is she whispering? "Yeah, Dad said you were working at the firm. I appreciate it."

"Well, yes, I've been at the firm." She glanced at Dad, but he had wandered over to the window and was staring pointedly out at the parking lot. "But I've also been with Rose."

A flash of hot rage shot down his spine as he pulled away. "Seriously? You've been comforting her? Need I remind you *she* broke up with *me?*"

To his surprise, his sister rolled her eyes. "Oh, get over yourself. Don't act like you had no part in her decision. Besides, you should thank me. I was doing damage control."

"What is that supposed to mean?"

"I convinced her not to cancel the wedding."

You did what?

Even Dad spun away from the window, betraying the fact that he'd been listening to their every word. Steven gritted his teeth as he tried to process what she'd said.

"Why would you do that?" he demanded. "She might still be able to get some of the money back if she cancels now."

Lanie stared at him as if he was the one being obtuse. "As long as there's a wedding, you won't lose any money."

Maybe Lanie had lost her mind. "Um, how is there going to be a wedding when Rose broke up with me?"

She lifted her eyes to the ceiling. "Do I have to spell everything out for you?" Shaking her head, she sat on the bed and took his hand. "Rose didn't want to break up with you. She still loves you, but she doesn't trust you to actually follow through on your promises, and she's scared she's going to lose you soon after the wedding."

Pulling his hand back, he scowled at her, but she ignored him.

"Correct me if I'm wrong, but this latest health episode seems to have been the wake-up call you needed."

Steven nodded, not quite sure where she was going.

"Better late than never," she said under her breath.

"Can we cut the shaming and get to the point?"

"If you can prove you're taking things seriously this time *and* that you're doing it for yourself, for your health..." She took a deep breath. "I have reason to believe Rose will give you a second chance and the wedding can move forward as planned."

"But it's barely a month away at this point," their father piped up. "And we don't know how long Steven will be in rehab."

"The doctor said if I follow the advice of my therapists, I could be out in a couple of weeks."

"Perfect." Lanie searched his face. "I assume you'd still like to be able to walk at the wedding as well?" At his nod, she smiled. "Great. And what about the first dance?"

Chapter Twenty-Six

"ARE YOU GOING TO visit Steven before he leaves?"

Rose started at the sound of the voice and spun around. Dr. Myers leaned against the doorframe of the nurses' station, one eyebrow raised.

"I doubt he wants to see me." She turned back to her paperwork to hide her face. How she had any tears left at that point was beyond her.

"You'd be surprised." He snatched the patient file from the desk, which forced her to face him again.

After making a few attempts to reclaim her file, she crossed her arms and glowered at him. "Why do you care? Weren't you the one who warned me away from becoming his caretaker? How did you put it?" She tapped her chin. "'Don't become the next Melissa.'"

To her immense satisfaction, he shifted uncomfortably. "That was a different situation."

Her mouth dropped open. "Are you serious?"

For a moment, he wouldn't meet her eyes, but when he finally did, his expression was grave. "I am." He ruffled his hair. "Look, this is going to sound like a line, but Steven has finally seen the light. I expected him to argue against returning to the rehab facility, but he willingly agreed. And he—"

She shoved past him, not wanting to hear another word. Without a backward glance, she raced off to do her rounds. *So what if they aren't due for another hour, and who cares if he has my files?* She would improvise.

But she had barely reached her first patient's room when he caught up to her. "Rose, stop."

"No," she said, and they both blinked at her sharp tone. She'd never spoken to him like that before. Clearing her throat, she tried again. "I understand that as Steven's doctor, you want to reduce his stress level, and I'm sorry if my actions have made your job more difficult." Her eyes burned with unshed tears, and she lowered her head to hide them. "But you can't expect me to go see him. What good would it do either of us? It'd cause more pain, and he doesn't need that right now."

He placed a gentle hand on her shoulder. "What he needs is to be surrounded by people who care about him." Her face must have betrayed her feelings, because he released her and raised his hands in surrender. "I'm not saying get back together with him. Just... talk to him. It'll be less awkward to do it here than at the rehab facility."

Before she could respond, he turned and walked away. With a frustrated sigh, she went back to the nurses' station where he'd left her files and got back to work. But his words needled her.

Isn't it bad enough that I let Lanie convince me to hold off on contacting the wedding vendors? When she'd left the hospital the day of the breakup, she'd been determined to take the necessary steps to cancel everything so that there was no turning back. However, all of her resolve had gone out the window after a night of wallowing with Lanie. She should have started making calls as soon as she'd made her decision, regardless of what Lanie said.

Perhaps it was the way Lanie had approached the situation. Rose had expected her to say she might change her mind or that she should consider giving Steven a second chance. But instead, she'd suggested they repurpose the wedding and maybe throw another type of party. A part of Rose wondered whether Lanie hoped to repurpose the wedding for herself. She and Nate had been having a tough time finding a venue that would accommodate a Christmas wedding since it was less than six months away.

With a sigh, Rose shook her head. No, repurposing the wedding would be out of character for Lanie. Then again, weddings made people do crazy things.

Like end relationships. She closed her eyes. *Has it been only a few days since that fateful conversation with Steven?* It felt like weeks ago, but that was probably because she'd picked up so many extra shifts at the hospital. In some ways, it was counterintuitive to want to spend more time where Steven was, but she hadn't actually seen him. The hospital policy forbidding staff from treating family members had gone from a thorn in her side to a godsend in the span of a couple of months.

Dr. Myers's words replayed in her head. Maybe she should visit Steven, if for nothing else than to check on him. Perhaps even bolster her resolve that she'd made the right choice.

She argued with herself for the rest of her shift. By the time she'd finally worked up the nerve to head to his room, it was empty. He was already gone.

The next day, Rose stepped off the elevator onto her floor, ready to start another shift. But as she approached the nurses' station, her belly fluttered at the sight of a crowd gathered around the desk, their backs to her.

"What's going on?" she asked.

Everyone turned at the sound of her voice and yelled, "Congratulations!"

Some of the nurses held balloons, one had a card, and Rebecca stood in the center of them all with a two-tiered cake. Rose stared, bewildered about what on earth was going on.

"Dr. Myers is going to kill me for planning this," Rebecca said as she set the cake down and walked over to Rose. "But I wanted to share the good news." Her eyes lit up. "You've got the head nurse position."

"What?" Rose could hardly believe her ears. "But... Why? How?" Questions raced through her mind as she digested the news. "Nobody called me."

"Consider this your offer." Rebecca handed her a stack of pages. "It's all detailed in here." At Rose's silence, she frowned. "I'm sorry. Did I overstep? I thought after everything you've been through, it would be nice to receive news with a bit of fanfare."

Rose shook her head. "No, this is wonderful." She raised her eyes to look at the rest of the nurses. "Thank you so much."

"The board would like to meet with you at ten this morning to formally make the offer and discuss any questions you have." With a smile, Rebecca began cutting the cake. "In the meantime, let's celebrate your achievement."

Forcing a smile in return, Rose began skimming the documents Rebecca had given her. A few weeks ago, she would have been ecstatic. The bump in pay alone would have been a welcome addition to the start of her new life with Steven.

But that was then. Since their breakup, Rose had been leaning toward going back to Baltimore or trying to find a position at that hospital in Boston. She'd never dreamed she would stay in Cedar Haven. It was Steven's hometown, and she didn't belong there if she wasn't with him.

"I realize it's a bit early for cake," Rebecca continued. "But I wanted us to have a chance to eat it before things get hectic."

"It's never too early for chocolate." Rose accepted her piece and took a bite. Her heart panged at the realization that it was red velvet, the same flavor she and Steven had chosen for their wedding cake.

Her appetite disappeared, and she set the cake down. "Excuse me."

Without waiting for a response, she rushed to the bathroom. She ran into a stall and emptied the contents of her stomach.

A knock sounded at the stall door. "Rose? Are you all right?"

Say yes. "No." She couldn't bring herself to fake joy for one more moment.

"Talk to me," Rebecca pleaded. "Tell me what's going on."

"I can't take the job," Rose said dully. After hauling herself off the bathroom floor, she flushed the toilet and left the stall. Avoiding Rebecca's gaze, she washed her hands at the sink and rinsed out her mouth.

"What do you mean you can't take it?"

"I'm leaving."

Rebecca touched her arm. "Where are you going?"

The contact almost pushed Rose over the edge, and she stepped back. She needed to keep control of her emotions, or she would never get through her shift.

"I don't know yet. But I can't stay here. Not now. Not with St—" Her voice caught in her throat, and she buried her face in her hands.

Rebecca sighed. "I shouldn't have sprung this on you. I was excited to share the news and hoped it would lift your spirits." She wrapped an arm around Rose's shoulders. "Please don't go. I know things with you and Steven are raw, but leaving isn't the answer. You're needed here. And you're valued."

When Rose didn't respond, Rebecca continued, "At least talk to the board before you decide anything."

Though she wanted to protest, Rose didn't have the energy. "Fine. But I'm not making any promises."

"Keeping an open mind is all I ask."

Chapter Twenty-Seven

IT HAD BEEN A week since Steven entered the rehab facility. Though he hated being cooped up, he appreciated having some distance from his real life. He hoped it might eventually ease the pain of his broken heart.

"Knock, knock," a voice called from his door. When he turned, Lanie stood in the doorway with two cups of coffee.

"I can't have caffeine right now."

She shrugged. "It's decaf."

"Thanks, I think." By that point, he'd gotten used to not having coffee. The facility didn't offer decaf, and tea didn't do it for him.

"Any word from Rose?" Lanie asked.

Steven raised an eyebrow. She knew perfectly well he hadn't heard from Rose since that fateful day at the hospital. He'd long since given up on hoping she would stop by.

"Have you seen her?" he countered.

"Here and there." Lanie dropped her gaze. "She was offered the head nurse position at the hospital."

That wasn't surprising, though it pained him to hear it secondhand. "I'm proud of her."

"Though she's not sure she's going to take it."

Steven frowned as he sipped his coffee. "Why wouldn't she?"

Instead of answering, Lanie stood and walked to the window. "You have a nice view from here."

"Lanie," Steven said. "What's going on?"

With a sigh, Lanie turned to him. "She brought up moving back to Baltimore."

Pain radiated in his throat as he struggled to swallow the news. If she was leaving, that meant things were well and truly over between them.

They needed to change the subject, or he was going to lose it. He'd kept it together pretty well thus far and didn't want to fall apart in front of his sister.

"Are you going by the office today?"

The question appeared to catch Lanie off guard. "Yeah, I promised Michael I'd help him with some filing. Why?"

"Could you ask Michael to visit?" Steven asked. He might have lost Rose, but he still had hope of saving his practice.

His sister's eyebrows shot up. "Uh-oh. Is he in trouble?"

He rolled his eyes. "Of course not. He's been there over a month now, and I want to check in with him."

"And try to determine whether he plans to accept the offer from the DC law firm?" Lanie teased.

Am I that transparent? "That may be part of it."

"For what it's worth, he seems happy to me. They may have offered him more money and a career track, but if you consider bringing him on as, like, a junior partner, he might stick around."

Steven gave a noncommittal nod. Ever since his conversation with Michael, he'd been reconsidering his stance on expanding his business to include a partner. Michael had not only far surpassed his expectations, he'd also shown Steven that he didn't have to do everything alone. While he still had misgivings about sharing his business, if he had to bring on a partner, Michael would be an ideal candidate once he passed the bar.

A knock at the door caused them to start. His physical therapist leaned against the frame and offered a tight smile to Lanie.

"Sorry to interrupt, but it's time for you to head to the gym."

"Ah, my daily torture appointment," Steven quipped. "Lanie, this is Ursula, my least favorite member of my rehab team."

"I guess that's my cue," Lanie said as she stood. Leaning over, she wrapped her arms around his shoulders and gave him an awkward squeeze. "I'll be back tomorrow."

"I'll hold you to that."

When she was gone, the therapist stepped over to his bed. "Want to walk or ride to the gym?"

Steven peered out the door. "Is there anyone else here to see me?"

After glancing up and down the hallway, Ursula shook her head. "Your secret is safe."

"Good." Steven grinned and swung his legs over the bed. With Ursula's assistance, he stood and grabbed his cane.

~ ele ~

The next day, Steven was pleased when Michael entered his room, a stack of folders in his arms. He set the folders on the bed and pulled up a chair.

"I brought everything I've been working on for the past week," Michael said as he shuffled the folders into some semblance of order.

Steven waved a hand. "I actually didn't invite you here to go over your workload."

"Oh, sorry. I just assumed..."

"It's no bother. And we should discuss it at some point, but I wanted to finish our last conversation."

Michael shifted uncomfortably. "We can wait until you're out of rehab. Even if I accept the offer, I plan to give a good deal of notice."

"I appreciate that, but it's best if we discuss it now." Steven cleared his throat. The conversation was harder on him than he'd expected it to be. Swallowing his pride and going back to inpatient rehab was one thing, but handing over a substantial share of his business was another thing entirely. "I've given a lot of thought to what you said, and I'd like to discuss what you imagine a track to partnership would look like."

"Well, it would be much different than the typical track at an established firm. But..." Michael scratched his head.

"Yes?" Steven prompted.

"I'd like to be an equal partner, and with that in mind, I'd like to buy into the business."

Of all the things Steven had expected him to say, that was not one of them. "What do you mean?"

"I mean that in addition to sharing the workload, I'd like to invest in the firm." At Steven's frown, Michael hurried on. "My grandparents created a trust fund for me when I was a baby. I planned to use it to open my own firm one day, but this seems like a better opportunity. There's clearly a need in town, and you're a known entity to the people here. So I wouldn't be starting from scratch."

A plethora of emotions shot through Steven. While he'd once feared an established attorney would want to buy his firm or merge it with their own, he'd never considered that someone might own the business equally with him. *And why would I?* Most law school graduates were drowning in student debt. They couldn't afford to invest in an established firm. After all, he'd barely managed to scrounge together the funds to open his own firm.

"So, what do you think?" Michael asked when Steven didn't respond.

The excitement building inside Steven was tempered only by the fear that Michael wouldn't want to be stuck in a small town. "Would that be enough to entice you to stay, though? I can't promise we'll make anywhere near what you would even as an associate in a larger firm."

"I'm not hurting for money," Michael said with a sheepish grin. "And I have other reasons for wanting to stick around."

"Such as?"

The blush that bloomed over Michael's cheeks confused Steven for a moment, then it clicked.

"Ah, this is about a woman, isn't it?"

"I may have gone out with Toccara a few times," Michael admitted.

Steven laughed and raised his hand. "Say no more."

"There is one thing you should know, though." With a sigh, Michael leaned forward. "My father wants me to make a name for myself, and he's one of the main reasons I received the offer that I did."

"I see," Steven said. "It sounds like you have a lot to consider."

Michael nodded. "But I promise to give you an answer soon."

"There's no rush. You'd have to pass the bar before we could make anything official, but I'd love to have you come on board as an equal partner."

"Believe me, if it were up to me, I'd much prefer working in a small-town firm where I might make a difference over slaving away in the big city for corporate cronies who don't even know my name."

Steven laughed. "They're not all bad." His experience was centered in Baltimore, but he didn't miss the hustle. He nodded at the folders. "In the meantime, why don't you bring me up to speed on where you are with things."

Michael seemed eager to change the subject and launched into a detailed presentation on all he'd been working on. While they spoke, a question nagged at Steven. If Michael turned him down, what was plan B?

Chapter Twenty-Eight

WHAT AM I DOING here? Rose asked herself for the millionth time as she parked outside of the rehab facility and looked at herself in the rearview mirror.

While she could blame it on the need to discuss canceling vendors or even asking for Steven's assistance in alerting his side of the family, the truth was Max had asked her to come. He'd called the night before to check on her and had ended the conversation with a simple request that Rose find it in her heart to visit Steven.

"I'm not asking you to forgive him or to take him back," Max had said. "Only to see for yourself how far he's come."

And so she had. She just hadn't quite mustered up the courage to get out of the car and walk into the building.

"No matter what he says," she told her reflection, "it doesn't change anything."

The doubt in her eyes did nothing to help her resolve. She debated putting the car back in gear and hightailing it out of there, but she'd come that far. She might as well see it through.

Steeling herself for an unhappy reunion, she forced her body from the car and dragged her feet to the rehab entrance. It took more effort than she cared to admit to open the door and step inside.

The receptionist's face lit up when she saw Rose. "He'll be thrilled you're here!"

Did Max tell the whole place I was coming? Ugh, what they must think of her, deserting her fiancé in his condition. She shook her head. *You're over-reacting.* The more likely explanation was that the woman had recognized her from her visits when Steven was there before.

She followed the receptionist down the hall. When they reached Steven's room, she moved aside to let Rose pass.

But her feet were frozen to the floor. Her heart pounded in her ears. She'd made a terrible mistake in going there.

Just as she turned to leave, a familiar voice rang out. "Rose? Is that you?"

"Go on," the receptionist urged. "He's been expecting you."

With a sigh, Rose shuffled into the room and closed the door behind her. She held onto the doorknob longer than necessary as she warred with a fight-or-flight reaction. Finally, she peeled her hand away and slowly turned to face him.

She didn't know what she expected to see, but the sight of him sitting up in bed with a smile wasn't it. Part of her wondered if she had dreamed the whole breakup.

"It's good to see you," he said with a slight edge to his voice. It was all the confirmation she needed that the meeting was awkward and uncomfortable for both of them.

"You too." Her feet glided toward him of their own accord, like a magnetic force was pulling them together. *Or a moth to a destructive flame.*

If she wasn't careful, she was going to get burned... again. He didn't give her a chance to react before he reached for her hand as if it were the most natural thing in the world.

Warning bells went off in her head as the warmth that spread up her arm was too much, and she pulled away. There was no missing the disappointment in his eyes.

She cleared her throat. "How've you been?"

"Better, actually." He patted the space beside him, but she shook her head. Things were different between them, and she needed to maintain physical distance if she had any hope of preserving her sanity.

"That's good."

"Yeah," he continued as if he couldn't bear the awkward silence any more than she could. "Dr. Myers is supposed to come by today and talk to my doctors here." A wry smile pulled on his lips. "I might be released by the end of the week."

She blinked. "That soon?"

His face fell. "I'm not sure I'd call it 'soon' after being stuck here for a couple of weeks, but I've improved immensely." His hazel eyes flicked to hers before he returned to pointedly staring at a loose thread on his blanket. "So I'll be leaving with full support from my medical team."

"This time," she said without thinking.

He pressed his lips together. "Yes, this time."

His chest rose and fell as he took a deep breath, and she braced herself for a subject change.

"How are the wedding cancellations going?"

Warmth crept up her neck and into her cheeks, and she bowed her head to hide it. Ever since the night Lanie had stopped by, she'd avoided anything wedding related. Carissa had been blowing up Rose's phone, likely having heard the wedding was off through the town's gossip mill. But she didn't want him to know about her hesitation. It might give him the wrong idea. *Should I lie and say I've already canceled everything?*

"I'm sorry I can't help with that," Steven said, his voice sincere enough to make her look at him. "And I'm sorry that it's... necessary."

So he didn't know. *Good.* It was better that way. No need to get his hopes up that she had changed her mind.

A heaviness settled in her body. On the one hand, she was relieved he seemed to have accepted her decision. It would make their visit more pleasant if she didn't have to worry about defending her choice. But on the other hand, a part of her felt cheated. After all they'd been through, he wasn't even going to fight for her.

I'm not some damsel in distress. I don't need *a man to want to be with me.*

While the truth of those words reverberated through her, a tiny voice inside questioned whether her disappointment was about needing him to fight or *wishing* he wanted her enough to do so.

"Rose?" he prompted. "Are you still with me?"

"Uh, yes, sorry," she stammered. "I have a few things to take care of, but I've almost canceled everything." The lie almost caught in her throat, but she forced it out.

"That's news to me," a voice said from behind her. When she turned, her stomach dropped to the floor as she saw Lanie leaning against the doorframe.

Rose shot Lanie a pleading look. "I haven't had an opportunity to tell you."

"And it's probably going to be news to the catering staff at The Muddy Oar," Lanie continued, her tone cool. "They asked me to request that you call them the next time I see you. Seems they've been having a time getting in touch with you."

Rose's mouth went dry. Her gaze vacillated between Steven and Lanie as she thought fast. Things had been going so well, but if he found out she hadn't canceled their wedding, it might give him false hope.

"They're next on my list." *Play along,* Rose silently begged Lanie.

Steven's face fell the slightest bit, confirming to Rose that he'd held some hope they could mend things. But his sister's eyes glinted with suspicion.

"I see." Though from her tone, it sounded like Lanie didn't believe her at all. "Anyway, I stopped by to drop off some homemade cookies." She pushed past Rose and set them on Steven's bedside table before kissing his forehead.

"Thanks, sis," Steven said with a stiff smile. "Would you mind giving us a minute?"

Before Lanie could respond, Rose said, "No, that's okay. I need to go anyway." She spun on her heel and practically ran to the door.

She didn't stop moving until she was in the parking lot, the blinding sun blazing down on her head. But she would take the humidity. Anything was less stifling than being in that room.

"Rose, wait!"

Despite every bone in her body telling her not to, Rose turned and faced Lanie. "Why did you do that? Why would you give him false hope?"

"Is it false?" Lanie cocked her head. "In spite of your insistence to Steven, you haven't canceled anything, have you? Instead, you've been dodging calls from both your vendors and Carissa."

There was no point in denying it. If Lanie had spoken to Carissa, then she knew everything.

When Rose didn't respond, Lanie took a deep breath. "I won't pretend to know why. But I can't help hoping that once you hear what I have to say, you'll definitively decide not to cancel the wedding and give him another chance."

Not likely. Rose crossed her arms with a frown but didn't interrupt.

"You know Steven entered rehab of his own accord. But what you don't know is he also offered the partnership to Michael."

Black dots swam before Rose's eyes, and she grabbed onto her car to steady herself. "He what?"

"Now don't get too excited." Lanie hurried on. "Michael received a job offer in DC, and he has to pass the bar before he can accept either opportunity."

While Lanie continued talking, Rose barely heard her. Not only had Steven gone into rehab, but he'd also chosen to find a partner. Something told her if Michael didn't work out, Steven would find someone else. He was listening and learning like she'd always hoped he would.

Is it enough, though? She couldn't ignore that it had taken her breaking up with him and calling off the wedding to finally get to that point. *If I give him another chance, how far will I have to go the next time he refuses to listen to me?*

"This latest incident shook him," Lanie was saying when Rose tuned back in. "I mean, don't get me wrong, losing you was also a wake-up call." She gave a weak smile. "But the reality that his health issues might actually kill him was ultimately the kick in the pants he needed."

"I'm glad something did." Rose tried to keep her tone neutral. She needed time to consider her next move—and whether she could trust Steven again. "And I appreciate you telling me."

"But it doesn't change anything?" Lanie's face fell.

"I need more time," Rose said.

With a reluctant nod, Lanie threw her arms around Rose and pulled her into a tight hug. "I understand." She stepped back and gave a sad smile. "I'd say if you need to talk, I'm here, but I'm not sure I can play the unbiased third party."

"Nor would I ask you to," Rose said.

They hugged once more, and Lanie moved aside and let Rose into her car. She waved goodbye before heading back into the building.

As Rose left the parking lot, her mind raced. Steven had made many strides in fixing things, and the fact that he hadn't told her all of them meant he wasn't doing it for her. Or at least, he wasn't doing it *only* for her. *And that has to mean something, right?* But whether it was enough for her to give him another chance, she didn't know.

Chapter Twenty-Nine

"I'm here to spring you!" Lanie rushed into Steven's room with a huge smile on her face.

"What do you mean? I thought I wasn't leaving until the end of the week."

"Call it time off for good behavior." Dr. Myers grinned as he strode into the room, followed by Dr. Bhati. "Or more accurately, early release for massive improvements." He flipped through Steven's chart. "Your therapists think you can continue on an outpatient basis."

The room was silent as if everyone was waiting for his reaction. He expected to feel excited, but that wasn't the emotion churning away in his stomach. There were too many what-ifs. *What if I relapse? What if I have another heart attack?*

Lanie frowned and took his hand. "What's wrong?"

The old Steven would have brushed her off and insisted he was fine, just in shock. But between his health scares and losing Rose, something had changed within him. He no longer wanted to push people away and pretend he was fine.

"I'm scared."

Dr. Myers's face softened. "That's normal after what you've been through, but I promise you, we wouldn't discharge you if I didn't have the utmost confidence in your continued recovery."

That was something, especially since last time, he'd left rehab against medical advice. The fact that he had the full support of his medical team helped calm his anxiety. But one other thing nagged at him.

"Do you think I'll be able to walk on my own, without a cane?"

Dr. Bhati frowned. "Your physical therapist believes so…"

Steven could hear the hesitation in his voice. "But?"

"But we're not sure when."

"I suppose it doesn't matter anyway," he grumbled. Since the wedding was already canceled, there was no deadline for him to be able to walk again anymore. That was the other reason he wasn't in a hurry to leave. He had no one to rush home to.

"Don't be like that." Lanie squeezed his hand. "You've got to stay positive."

He forced a smile for her benefit, but by the expression on her face, it wasn't very convincing.

"Anyway," Dr. Myers said, clearly trying to keep them on topic, "I've got some discharge paperwork here for you with instructions." His face turned stern. "But just because we're letting you go home doesn't mean you can jump right back into your life. You still need to take it easy and avoid overexerting yourself."

"Understood," Steven said. The last thing he or his business needed was another stint in the hospital—or worse.

"I brought you some clothes." Lanie handed him a bag and hooked her thumb over her shoulder. "I'll wait outside while you change."

"And I'll see you next week for a follow-up appointment," Dr. Bhati said.

They all left the room, giving him some much-needed privacy. He stared at the bag in his hand, trying to ignore the anxiety clawing up his chest. *Am I ready for this? Can I really keep from stressing out once I'm back in my old life? Will the changes I've made stick?*

A part of him wished it had been Rose instead of Lanie who had shown up. He wanted to talk to her again, show her all he'd done to get better.

Maybe she would come by once she heard he was home. He crossed his fingers as he dressed.

Less than a half hour later, Steven and Lanie drove away from the facility. It was the first time he'd been in a car in weeks. Despite his misgivings about leaving, he couldn't wait to be home. The rehab bed wasn't comfortable, and while he didn't consider himself an introvert, there was something to being able to shut out the world and enjoy some alone time.

"Welcome home," Lanie said as she pulled into his driveway.

Two cars were parked to one side, and he held his breath as he searched the yard for his visitors. But his ribs tightened when he realized the cars belonged to his father and Michael.

Dad came to the passenger side and opened his door. "How does it feel to be free?"

Steven laughed. "It's not like I was in prison, Dad."

His dad harrumphed. "Might as well have been."

Even though it was pointless, Steven allowed his eyes to sweep over the yard one more time in case he'd missed Rose hiding somewhere. Dad didn't miss the look.

"I'm sorry she's not here, son."

With a nod, Steven grabbed his cane and walked to his front door. On the bright side, he was alive, he was home, and he was no longer confined to a wheelchair.

"We'll bring your stuff in and unpack it," Lanie called from behind.

Michael held the door open. "Welcome home, boss."

Once Steven was inside, he headed to the dining room, where a nice spread of all his favorite lunch fixings had been laid out on the table—ham, turkey, an assortment of cheeses, and spicy mayonnaise. His stomach was churning too much to be hungry, but he decided to humor his family. The last thing he needed was for them to report to Dr. Myers that he wasn't eating.

"Would you like something to drink?" Michael asked, coming into the room behind him.

He nodded and slid into a chair, leaning his cane against the table. A moment later, Lanie appeared and moved it to the corner. He frowned at her, but she rolled her eyes.

"I'll bring it back when you're ready to get up," she said, waving her hand before disappearing with Dad to Steven's bedroom.

He wanted to follow her and not just because he was particular about how his clothes were put away. But he couldn't find the energy to do so.

Michael stared at him expectantly. *Oh, right, he asked if I wanted a drink.* "Water, please."

When Michael left to go to the kitchen, Steven leaned forward and rested his head in his hands. Though he had no reason to do so, he couldn't help hoping Rose would be there to greet him. But he had only himself to blame for the crushing disappointment he felt.

Michael returned with the glass and set it in front of Steven. "So, are you glad to be home?"

"I am," Steven said. "How are things at the office?"

"They're going well," Michael continued when Steven didn't say anything more. "Even Mr. Willoughby seems to be appeased."

Steven snorted. "I wonder how long that will last."

Michael chuckled. "His divorce date is scheduled for September. I give it a month."

Finally, Steven couldn't stand the small talk anymore. "Why aren't you at the office today?"

Michael stared at his hands. "I wanted to tell you I made my decision."

Swallowing his fears, Steven nodded. "And?"

Michael squared his shoulders. "I discussed your offer with my father. At first, he had some misgivings, but when I showed him the good work you're doing, he agreed it would be a good investment for me and a way to make a name for myself."

Steven stared at him, dumbstruck. "Wait, so you're..."

"Accepting your offer to come on as an equal partner?" Michael beamed. "Absolutely."

Once Steven had recovered from his shock, he stood and stuck his hand out. "That's the best news I've heard all day. Welcome aboard, partner!"

Chapter Thirty

When Rose answered a knock at her door, the last person she expected was the bald man from the pond. He tipped his ball cap in greeting.

"Hello there. How can I help you?" she asked.

"I promised I would tell you when the male swan was being rereleased into the pond. My friend is dropping him off in ten minutes if you want to come see."

"Oh!" She'd almost forgotten about the swans. "Of course. Thank you for remembering."

They walked down to the pond, where a large truck had pulled up. The men who had captured the swan were lowering the tailgate, and the bald man went to help them lift the cage from the back of the truck.

After they opened the cage, the bald man reached in and lifted the swan, whose body was secured in a bag. He carefully unstrapped the bag from around the swan, and once the swan's wings were free, it dashed into the water to join its mate. The female swan immediately swam over.

"They're so happy to be reunited," Rose breathed, awed by the scene in front of her.

"Just wait," the bald man whispered with a grin. "The show's about to start."

At first, Rose didn't understand what he meant, but as she watched, the swans bent their necks toward each other as if they were bowing. They started moving their heads in a synchronous motion. Circling each other, they raised their wings and pressed their foreheads together in an intricate ballet.

"They're dancing!" Rose exclaimed in delight.

"That, they are. It's part of their mating ritual. Some say it helps them to rebuild the bond to dance together like this, especially after time apart." The bald man wiped his eyes. "It's one of the most beautiful things I've ever seen."

Rose couldn't think of a response worthy of what she was witnessing. The swans continued their coordinated movements, coming together in the sweetest reunion she had ever seen.

"She never lost faith," Rose whispered, more to herself than the stranger who had brought her there.

"That's true love," the man agreed.

Her heart broke anew. *Why can't Steven and I have what these swans do? Why do humans have to complicate things?* The female swan trusted that her mate would recover from his injury and return to her, and her reward was the swan version of a loving embrace.

But life—well, her life anyway—wasn't like that. Swans didn't have day jobs that kept them from their families. They didn't have a million distractions that prevented them from truly connecting. And Rose couldn't help feeling that swans got the better deal.

As she continued to watch, the swans placed their foreheads together and formed a heart shape with their necks. It was the perfect symbol of their devotion, and her heart longed to have a love like that again.

Ping. Rose removed her phone from her pocket and read the text message from Lanie. It contained only two words: *Steven's home.*

The fact Steven hadn't texted was a message in and of itself. It told her he wasn't going to push her to visit, that he was giving her all the space she could possibly want.

Maybe he truly has changed. The thought gave her stomach a flutter, the first real feeling of hope she'd had in a while.

Turning her attention back to the swans, the knot that had formed in Rose's belly the moment she'd heard of Steven's heart attack loosened, and everything suddenly became clearer. She understood why the female swan had held onto hope her mate would return. She knew what she wanted to do, but she needed to talk to Steven first.

～ℓℓ～

When Steven answered Rose's knock, she wasn't expecting him to stand before her on his own two feet with a cane for support. It took every ounce of control she had not to rush into his arms. He looked much improved from the last time she'd seen him.

"May I come in?" she asked.

Without saying a word, Steven nodded and stepped to the side. Rose took a deep breath and entered the home they'd planned to share. Part of her questioned her decision to speak to him there instead of somewhere less meaningful, but she didn't want to risk having the whole town hear their business.

He led her to the couch and sat stiffly on one side. Her heart in her throat, she sat opposite him. They stared at each other as Rose tried to decide where to begin.

"Not that I'm not happy to see you," Steven said, breaking the silence, "but why are you here?"

Speak from the heart. "Your sister said something the other day as I was leaving the rehab facility, and I wondered if it was true."

Steven's hands clenched into fists. "And what was that?"

She chewed her lip before responding. "That you offered the partnership to Michael."

"Oh." His shoulders visibly relaxed. "Yeah, I did."

"Why didn't you tell me?" she asked in a rush.

He shrugged. "I didn't think you'd care."

With one eyebrow raised, she leaned forward. "I practically begged you to take on a partner. Why on earth wouldn't I care that you finally did so?"

Dropping his gaze, he fidgeted in his seat. "I guess I was worried you'd question my motives."

Though it hurt to hear, she understood. "I suppose I deserve that."

"No." His eyes widened. "You were right. I wasn't taking care of myself, and I'm sorry it took losing you to realize it."

"Well, losing me and going back in the hospital," she joked, though her voice shook.

"Yeah, that too." He gave her a tentative smile. "But I'm better now. I've been making great progress in therapy, and I'm happy to report Michael has accepted my offer."

It was as if a huge weight had lifted off Rose's shoulders. "He did? When?"

"This afternoon. He's coming back over tomorrow so we can finalize the details."

"Oh, Steven, that's wonderful news. I'm happy for you."

"And I hear that the hospital offered you the head nurse position," Steven said. "Congratulations."

She ducked her head. "Oh, um, thanks. I haven't actually accepted it yet." She squared her shoulders and looked him in the eye. "But I intend to tell them when I go in for my next shift, and then I'll start the position mid-September."

"That's good to hear. They're lucky to have you." The smile on his face faltered, and he cleared his throat. "Anyway, now that I'm home, I'm happy to help with any remaining wedding cancelations. I'm sorry you were on your own with that for so long."

Warmth spread across her cheeks. "Um, about that."

He cocked his head with a frown. "What's wrong?"

"Look, I want to say I'm sorry for how I reacted when you went into the hospital this last time." She closed her eyes as she recalled how terrified she was when she got the call that he was being admitted again. "I was hurt and scared. You weren't taking care of yourself, and I couldn't bear to watch you dig your own grave."

He grabbed her hand and squeezed it. "I'm sorry, Rose."

She took a shaky breath. "I just... You're so stubborn." She rolled her eyes. "Your whole family is, and I feared you'd never see reason. But when Lanie informed me of everything you'd been doing..." Her eyes met his, and everything clicked into place. "The fact that you didn't use it to try to win me back when I came to see you showed me how much you'd changed."

"I swear to you, I have." He tightened his grip on her hand. "And I promise I will do anything if you would consider giving me another chance."

"That's the thing. I realized recently how much I miss you."

The smile on his face took her breath away. "I've missed you too. So very much."

"And I've not been fair to you," she continued, dropping her gaze.

His eyebrows pulled together. "You have that backward."

If the situation had been less serious, she might have laughed. "No, I mean it." She cupped his cheek. "You were so hopeful when Lanie called my bluff about canceling the wedding, and I should have decided right then and there if I was going to actually go through with it or not."

"You needed time," Steven said. "And if you still need time, I understand. There's no rush. We can cancel or postpone it until we're ready. We don't have to—"

She held up a hand. "You see? You're bending over backward to make sure I'm okay, but what about your needs?"

He swallowed, and his eyes went a bit misty. "What I need is you. And I don't want to risk losing you by making you go through something you aren't ready for."

Her heart melted. "What I'm trying to say is, I want us to try again, and I'm not going to run away at the first sign of trouble." She bowed her head. "But I understand if you don't trust me because of what I did."

His eyebrows shot up. "Of course I trust you, but I also put you through a lot. So I understand if you're not sure of me."

"But I am sure of you," she said. After a moment's hesitation, she took his hand and pressed it to her heart. "I only broke up with you because I thought I could protect my heart from the pain of losing you if I did it on my own terms. But I was wrong. I know now what a mistake that was because you're the one for me." Her eyes filled with tears. "You're my swan."

"What?" he asked, a quizzical expression on his face.

"Never mind," she said with a watery laugh. "Just know I love you."

"Wait." His eyes widened. "Does this mean—"

She nodded. "Let's make this official."

The joy on his face left her speechless. She wrapped her arms around his neck and pressed her lips to his.

"Rose," he murmured into her hair as they parted. "My Rose."

And they were the sweetest words she had ever heard.

Epilogue

"I can't believe I'm getting married today," Rose said as she sat beside Lanie at the salon.

"And to think, it almost didn't happen." Lanie reached over and grabbed Rose's hand. "But I'm glad you and Steven worked things out. I'm excited to have a sister."

Rose smiled. Her heart was so full that her eyes kept filling up with tears. That was proving to be a problem for the woman working on her hair and makeup. Ellie, Bea's granddaughter, groaned in frustration.

"If you keep crying, you're going to ruin my masterpiece," she complained.

"I'm sorry." Rose blinked rapidly, which only made the situation worse. "This is just such a happy day."

"Better put on some waterproof mascara, El, if you have any hope of that face making it to the picture portion of today," Lanie teased.

Ellie rolled her eyes. "I'm not sure that'll be enough with Ms. Waterworks over here."

"Excuse me, that's *Mrs.* Waterworks," Rose quipped.

"You're not a Mrs. yet, and at this rate, it may never happen." Lanie pursed her lips at Rose in the mirror.

"Fine, fine." It took effort, but Rose managed to control her emotions. When they were both finished, Lanie helped Rose into her dress, a simple white ball gown with off-the-shoulder straps and a sweetheart neckline. Once they were dressed, Ellie had them pose by the window and snapped a few pictures.

"Now at least I'll have evidence of my skill in the event she cries it all off later."

Before Rose could respond, a knock sounded at the door. It was Dr. Myers, dressed to the nines in a tuxedo. He smiled at both women then raised an eyebrow at Rose.

"You ready?"

She nodded and handed Lanie her bouquet. Since her father couldn't be there, she'd asked Dr. Myers to give her away. She'd wanted to ask Max, but when Steven had asked him to be his best man, it didn't seem appropriate.

Lanie gave her arm a squeeze before she left to begin the wedding procession. The moment they were alone, Dr. Myers turned to her.

"I'm glad you decided to go through with it."

"You don't think I'm making a mistake? After what you went through with your ex, I mean."

He shook his head. "If Steven had continued the path he was on, then I would have worried for your welfare. But he's truly gained a new perspective these past few weeks. I have no doubt he'll continue to work at finding a better balance in his life and make his health more of a priority."

She smiled, as she felt exactly the same way. When he stuck out his elbow, she grabbed her bouquet and linked her arm through his. She took a deep breath, and they headed outside.

The church sat on top of a hill, overlooking the river. Closing her eyes, Rose lifted her face to the warmth of the late-August sun. The air was sticky with summer humidity, but when she opened her eyes, there were hints of the coming change in season. Some of the leaves on the tops of the trees had already begun to transition from the bright green of summer to the rich red of autumn. She was glad she and Steven had a weeklong cruise to look forward to, as she wasn't ready to bid goodbye to her favorite season just yet.

They reached the steps outside of the church, and Dr. Myers stopped. "This is where I leave you."

Rose frowned. "What? You have to walk me down the aisle."

With a sly smile, he put his hand on her shoulder and spun her around. There, standing directly behind her, were her parents.

Her heart leapt into her throat. "What? How?" She couldn't form a coherent sentence.

"Steven used some of the money from the fundraiser to buy the plane tickets before you broke things off," Mom explained as she embraced Rose. "When you called and said the wedding was off, I tried to cancel, but he wouldn't hear of it."

More tears welled up in Rose's eyes, and she prayed Ellie's mascara would hold. "I can't believe you're here."

Dr. Myers stepped to her side. "I assume my services are no longer needed. I'll go find a seat inside."

"Thank you," Rose said. "For everything."

With a nod, he climbed the stairs into the church, leaving Rose alone with her parents. Her father held out his arm.

"May I do the honors?"

"You both can," Rose said, taking his arm and grabbing her mother's as well. Together, they climbed the stairs to where Lanie was waiting.

Lanie gave Rose a thumbs-up before she and Max entered the church. As the door swung closed, Rose caught a glimpse of Steven standing at the front, waiting for her. He stood tall and proud and, if she wasn't mistaken, without his cane.

"Is he...?" Before she could finish the question, the door opened again, and the sound of the wedding march filled the room. It was her turn to walk down the aisle. Her heart hammered in her chest as she moved, her eyes never leaving Steven's. It took effort not to run straight into his arms, into her future.

When they reached the front of the church, her parents placed her hand in Steven's before kissing her cheeks and finding their seats. And then, it was as if everyone else disappeared when she looked up into Steven's face. She barely heard the preacher welcoming the crowd and paid only enough attention to what he was saying to know when to say "I do."

Before she knew it, the preacher said, "I now pronounce you husband and wife. You may kiss your bride."

Steven's eyes shone with unshed tears as he wrapped his arms around her waist and dipped her in a kiss. Cheers and whoops could be heard from the crowd, but Rose barely heard them. In spite of the trials they had faced, in spite of almost losing him twice, they had finally done it. And he was hers. Forever.

When he finally released her, breathless and grinning, he turned her to their gathered loved ones and raised their joined hands in triumph. Rose giggled at the silliness of the action. Soon, she found herself jostled away into the arms of her family, both old and new alike.

The first faces she saw were those of her parents, and she pulled them into a hug. Their presence had made the day so much more wonderful.

Lanie embraced her next, and the warmth and joy exuding from her now sister-in-law touched Rose. But she should have known nothing could break their bond. She and Lanie were soul sisters through and through.

Then she threw her arms around Max. Her father-in-law's hug was stilted and awkward, and he shifted away too soon.

"Welcome to the family."

"Thanks," she said with a wry smile. "So, now that your two children are paired up, don't you think it's your turn?"

Lanie laughed. "The day my dad remarries is the day hell freezes over."

Crossing his arms, he shook his head. "I gave marriage the old college try. It's the bachelor life for me."

"Pity for the rest of us," Carissa said as she reached them, a clipboard in hand. "Not to break up this celebration, but we've got a schedule to keep."

Max rolled his eyes. "Not everything has to be planned out to the second."

"Just because you live life by the seat of your pants doesn't mean the rest of us have to," Carissa retorted. Then she wrapped an arm around Rose's shoulders and led her over to Steven.

Rose grasped his arm and gently pulled him away from his friends. "We've got to go get photos taken."

Her parents and Lanie and Max met up with them outside. Rose wondered whether they shouldn't have skipped formal shots and stuck with candid photos. Neither of them had a very large family, and there were only so many ways to position their small group.

After posing for several photos, Rose was ready to eat. The photographer told their families to head into the reception hall while he finished up with a few shots of just Rose and Steven.

As soon as they were released to join the festivities, they quickly made their way to the reception for their grand entrance. Rose danced from foot to foot, anxious to get inside and enjoy a well-earned meal.

"And now, ladies and gentlemen, put your hands together for the new Mr. and Mrs. McAllister!"

Their friends and family clapped as Rose and Steven made their grand entrance. Her vision for the wedding was inspired by *A Midsummer Night's Dream*. Tea lights hung in small globes from the rafters. Scalloped glass vases filled with white and pink roses and rich green leaves sat in the center of each table. Wreaths of hydrangeas and ivy adorned each window and twinkled with hidden fairy lights. The beauty of the room momentarily took Rose's breath away.

She headed straight for their table, hoping to scarf down some food. But before she got to her seat, Steven grabbed her hand and pulled her to a stop just as the DJ called them back to the dance floor.

"What's going on?" she hissed, following Steven. "We agreed no formal dances." It hadn't seemed right at the time because her parents hadn't planned to attend and Steven's mother was gone.

Instead of responding, Steven smiled. Though he still had a slight limp, she'd been amazed at how steady he was on his feet.

"Are you sure?" Her eyes strayed to his legs, and she worried he would tire if he pushed himself too much.

"I am," he said, drawing her in close and taking her hand. "I've been practicing."

"You have?"

"Lanie and I started before the accident." His lips twitched. "She didn't want me to make a fool of myself for our first dance." He shrugged. "And once I'd made enough progress in PT, Dr. Bhati thought it would be good for improving my dexterity and coordination."

Taylor Swift's *This Love* began to play, and Steven led Rose in a simple waltz. She stared into his eyes, overwhelmed at the realization of how hard he'd had to work to make the moment happen.

"Oh my goodness. I can't believe you did this for me." Tears spilled over her cheeks, and she knew Ellie would kill her if she saw her.

He twirled her before enveloping her in his arms again. "I wanted to make today as special as I could, to show you how much you mean to me."

She rested her head on his shoulder and sighed. "It's just like the swans."

"I'm not sure I follow."

Lifting her head, she placed a hand on his cheek. "Swans mate for life. And when they are separated due to an illness, they perform this beautiful dance together to rekindle their bond."

"I never knew that," he said with a smile.

"I only learned it recently." She tightened her arms around him.

As the last notes of the song played, Steven twirled her once more before lifting her hand to his lips. Their friends and family cheered, and Rose felt on top of the world.

"I know you're hungry," he murmured into her ear. "But how would you feel about taking our dinner down to the river? There's a picnic table by the pier, and we could have a few minutes to ourselves."

A moment alone, just the two of them, was exactly what Rose needed. She grabbed her plate and followed him, slipping out the back door unnoticed.

The sun hung lower in the sky, and the breeze coming off the river held the promise of autumn. They sat on opposite sides of the picnic table near the pier and enjoyed their meal. Just as they were ready to leave, a fluttering of white feathers caught Rose's eye. There in the middle of the river was a pair of swans. Their long white necks formed a heart as they pressed their foreheads together before lifting their wings and circling each other.

"You see," Rose said, pointing. "They're dancing!"

Steven stood and pulled her into his arms again, swaying them back and forth. "And so are we."

~*~

Enjoyed this story? You can make a difference! Honest reviews of my books help bring them to the attention of other readers.

Please consider leaving a review (it can be as long or as short as you like) on the book's Goodreads page. You can jump right to the page with the QR code below.

Can't get enough of The Love Birds series? Check out *When Cardinals Appear* to read Lanie's story or read on to learn about the final book in the trilogy!

Coming Fall 2024
When Doves Lament

Neither expected to fall in love again. But together they might just discover that the love of their lives came later.

Max McAllister swore off love before the ink was even dry on his divorce papers. Between his attempts to salvage the strained relationship with his daughter and rekindling his passion for woodworking, he doesn't have time for the drama that romance brings.

Carissa Owens has finally found her footing again after losing her husband five years ago. Her wedding planning business is thriving and she has her sights set on expanding to corporate events—if she can secure a meeting with a lucrative new client.

But when Max's daughter hires Carissa to plan her wedding, he insists on being involved in every aspect of the process, ruffling Carissa's feathers. As they spend more time together, an unexpected attraction sprouts wings.

That is, until Max reveals a surprise for his daughter that puts Carissa's professional reputation at risk. Can they find a way to dovetail their plans or is their budding romance about to have a crash landing?

Preorder When Doves Lament now!

Sneak Peek of When Doves Lament

AFTER PAYING THE BILL, Max led her outside and they walked along the streets until the came to the beach. The water of the Patuxent River lapped gently against the shoreline as the sun sank low on the horizon.

"We always seem to end up near water on our dates," Carissa said, taking his hand and entwining their fingers.

"It's hard to find a place in Maryland that doesn't have access to water. We're kind of surrounded by it."

"Touche."

"But that sounds like a fun challenge. I'll have to find a place away from the water for our next date."

She raised an eyebrow. "Who said anything about another date?"

"I did," he said with conviction. "Besides, the cat's out of the bag. Lanie knows, and she's okay with it." He brought their joined hands to his lips and kissed her knuckles. "You're stuck with me now."

Her responding laugh warmed his heart. "You're quite sure of yourself."

"I know what I want." Wrapping an arm around her waist, he bent to kiss her.

"And what's that?" she murmured against his lips.

"You."

He kept the kiss short, not wanting to cause another public scene. But it was difficult to let her go. As they continued walking along the small beach, his heart was full for the first time since he'd lost Melody.

"I've never been here at night," Carissa said. They stopped at the edge of the beach and watched the sun slowly descend into the water. "Chuck didn't like being so far from home in the evening."

Normally, Max might be put off with how much she talked about her late husband, but since losing Melody, he understood. It wasn't the same as someone who was still in love with their ex. Death gave a finality that nothing could overcome, and grief was a testament to the strength of love.

"I prefer it." A chilly breeze made her shiver and Max wrapped an arm around her. "But we should probably get going. It's a long drive back."

"Just one more minute," she said, leaning into him. "I'm not ready for this night to end."

"Me either."

Time seemed to stop, even as the sky changed from orange to pink and then a deep purple. Her scent wafted over him with the breeze, and he closed his eyes, savoring the moment.

"Have you ever thought about getting married again?" she asked softly, her voice barely a whisper.

That wasn't a question he was expecting, and he spoke without thinking. "No."

She stiffened in his arms. He grimaced. Clearly, that was the wrong answer. It might have been the truth, at least, up until recently. But even since things between them had changed, he'd never thought once about marrying again. For one thing, it felt too soon. And for another, he'd been a bachelor for so long, he wasn't sure how he'd feel about having a wife again.

"Never?" she asked, turning to look at him.

"Uh, I mean, I never really expected to date again either, so I haven't given much thought to marriage." Ugh, he wasn't making much sense. "I guess I haven't had much of a reason to think about marrying again, if that makes sense."

Though she nodded and smiled, there was a hint of disappointment in her eyes. "I get it."

"What about you? Have you thought of remarrying?"

She sighed. "At first, I didn't. I couldn't imagine ever finding what I had with Chuck again, and anything else would just be a poor substitute." She gestured toward the street and he nodded, taking her hand and leading her back up the beach. "But after a few years, I started thinking it might be nice. I've still got a lot of life to live, God willing. And I'd like to share it with someone."

Wanting to share your life with someone doesn't have to mean marriage. But he didn't say that out loud. A comment like that would likely ruin what had otherwise been a pleasant evening.

"It's not something I'm looking to rush into," she continued when he hadn't responded. "Right now, I want to focus on my business."

"That makes sense, and it's where your focus should be."

She frowned, but didn't contradict him. They walked the rest of the way in silence, but it wasn't as comfortable as before.

When they arrived back to his truck, he opened her door. She searched his face for a moment before climbing in. As he drove her home, he tried to think of a way to salvage the night, but he kept coming up empty.

Finally, she broke the silence. "I'm sorry if I spooked you with the marriage talk."

"Not spooked," he corrected quickly. "Just caught off guard." He glanced at her before turning his attention back to the road. "I'm not necessarily against getting remarried. It's just not something I've had occasion to think about since I haven't dated anyone in over ten years, until you."

"I understand." She rested a hand on his knee. "I shouldn't have brought it up."

"No, I'm glad you did." He squeezed her hand briefly before returning his to the steering wheel. "If we're going to keep seeing each other, I think it's important that we are both honest about what we want now, and in the future." He cleared his throat. "And it's okay if that changes, as long as we talk about it."

They kissed good night when he dropped her off at home, and then he spent the drive back to his place mulling over their conversation. Marriage wasn't something he'd ever thought he'd consider again. His first one had ended poorly, even if he and Melody had reconciled before she died. The idea of trying again with someone new was completely foreign to him. But then again, he'd also thought he'd sworn off dating. A rueful smile played on his face. *And look how that turned out.*

Coming Autumn 2024

Also By Katie Eagan Schenck

A Home for Christmas
A Marine has just one wish this Christmas: a home.
Available at all major retailers.

The Love Birds trilogy
When Cardinals Appear, When Swans Dance, and *When Doves Lament*
Available at all major retailers.

About the Author

Katie Eagan Schenck writes sweet romance and women's fiction that warms the heart and gives all the feels. She has an MFA in creative writing from Queens University of Charlotte and her debut novel, A Home for Christmas, was released in October of 2022. When she's not writing she's either drafting regulations for the federal government, baking delicious treats, or binging Hallmark movies. She lives in Maryland with her husband, daughter, and their three cats.

Connect with Katie through her website at https://keschenckauthor.com or social media below.

Facebook: keschenck; Instagram: keschenckauthor

Twitter/X: faery_whisper; TikTok: @keschenckauthor

Acknowledgements

As ALWAYS, I WANT to start by thanking my mother, who encouraged me to pursue my dream of writing from the tender age of eight. I want to thank my husband and daughter, who have provided me with so much love and support throughout the whole process. My deepest thanks to my father and step-mother, who have supported me for the past several years through all the ups and downs of my life. A huge debt of gratitude to my sister and sister-in-law who have helped spread the word about my books! And a shout out to my brother and his partner, who played tourguide on a much needed vacation last summer after I finally finished the first draft of this book.

I'd be remiss not to thank Rashida and Angela McRae at Red Adept Editing for their assistance with making this story shine! I also want to thank Kathleen Sweeney and the amazing staff at Book Brush for the beautiful cover.

Finally, thanks to all my friends who have offered feedback on my writing over the years, especially those of you who were unfortunate enough to read my angsty teenage poetry. They say it takes a village to raise a child, and I think it takes at least that, and so much more, to raise a writer.